WARLORD BORN

WARLORD BORN

THE GREAT INSURRECTION™ BOOK ONE

DAVID BEERS

MICHAEL ANDERLE

DISRUPTIVE IMAGINATION

Copyright © 2021 LMBPN Publishing
Cover Art by Jake @ J Caleb Design
http://jcalebdesign.com / jcalebdesign@gmail.com
Cover copyright © LMBPN Publishing
A Michael Anderle Production

LMBPN Publishing
PMB 196, 2540 South Maryland Pkwy
Las Vegas, NV 89109

First US edition 2021
eBook ISBN: 978-1-64971-295-0
Print ISBN: 978-1-64971-296-7

THE WARLORD BORN TEAM

Thanks to our Beta Readers

Mary Morris, Kelly O'Donnell, James Caplan, Rachel Beckford , John Ashmore, Billie Leigh Kellar

Thanks to our JIT Readers

Dave Hicks
Peter Manis
Jackey Hankard-Brodie
Chrisa Changala
Angel LaVey
Jeff Eaton
Diane L. Smith
Jeff Goode
Paul Westman

Editor

SkyHunter Editing Team

DEDICATION

For my brother, Danny.

— David

*To Family, Friends and
Those Who Love
to Read.
May We All Enjoy Grace
to Live the Life We Are
Called.*

— Michael

My name isn't important. It has been and will continue to be spoken, but it truly doesn't matter much to this history. I follow, and there is no shame in that for me or any of the legions that do the same.

The only important thing about me is *who* I follow.

I stand next to a man who some call a devil, a demon. Others remember him as "Odin" or "Alistair Kane." Some whisper "Prometheus" when they speak about him, saying he is a god who brings fire to humanity, while others only talk about how the Greek myth was doomed, as this man is.

Perhaps it's all true, or perhaps none of it is. That isn't why I write this, to decide one way or another.

I don't know how this story ends. Neither does he. I only know that he won't quit, which means I will go to whichever destiny he races toward as well. Victory or failure, I will follow him.

Whatever name history records, however it records his deeds, I will live or die with him.

He is my friend, the greatest I've ever had. Perhaps he isn't the greatest of us all, but he is the one who leads, and while this isn't *his* story, it is he who will bring it home.

Welcome to the Great Insurrection.

CHAPTER ONE

"The Titans are the best of us. Pure of heart. Pure of body. They and they alone protect the Commonwealth from humanity's worst instincts."

–Aurelius de Finita, First Imperial Ascendant

Alistair Kane stood in the back of the elevator, his Mech-Pulse primed to maximum power. Ares stood at his right, shoulder to shoulder, and two rookies in front of them. Alistair didn't know their names, and he didn't like that. Ares hadn't mentioned the two newcomers since the operation began, then saying only, "These are who Control sent."

He didn't know the last time he'd performed an operation without knowing the details of every man or woman within his purview, but it certainly hadn't occurred during his time as Primus.

They know, he thought as the elevator moved up another floor. *They know, and this is the end.*

Alistair's MechSuit covered his entire body, practically a metal exoskeleton that turned even the slightest of his movements into a powerful force that could break concrete. It allowed four men to ride to the five hundredth floor of a skyscraper without fearing that they'd soon be fighting upwards of one hundred combatants.

Alistair's left hand held the MechPulse while his right dropped and lightly touched his Whip. It was attached to his MechSuit, one of his oldest friends. He shouldn't need the weapon for this operation, but no Titan would enter an operation without it.

They know, his mind whispered again. *Control knows.*

But that would mean Ares knows, and there isn't any way they'd send him. He wouldn't hurt you, not in this life or the next.

Alistair didn't turn his head to look at his protégé, just kept staring forward. They had about one hundred more floors to climb. By now, the Subversives would know something was wrong. The building had been completely shut down, their windows were no longer working, and attempts to fly vehicles to the top floor were being denied.

Most likely the Subversives could see the elevator rising, at least digitally. Those on the top floor were probably preparing for the arrival of the Titans; Alistair always wondered what that felt like, knowing fate had decided your time to die was here, and you could do nothing about it. For Alistair and his Titans, there were less dangerous ways to go about putting these Subversives down. They could have simply used the MechSuits' jets to fly to the correct level, but that didn't fit the purpose.

Control—indeed, the Commonwealth as a whole—

wanted the Subversives to understand they had no hope. Once they were found, the entire building they occupied quit obeying their commands and would only obey Control's. Thus, the elevator's slow creep upward. Moving toward fate.

The MechSuits were climate-controlled. Alistair kept his at a crisp sixty-five degrees regardless of his body temperature, yet he felt a drop of sweat run down his brow. *You're scared,* he thought. *And not of the Subversives. You're scared they know, and if they do, then fate has come for you, hasn't it?*

"Activate HUDs," Ares commanded from Alistair's right. He meant the Heads Up Displays that formed outside the MechSuit's helmet, overlaying augmented reality onto whatever the Titan looked at. "Odin, you ready?"

Odin was Alistair's callsign, and "Ares" was what the man next to him answered to.

"Locked in," Alistair responded as the elevator rolled to a smooth stop. "Control," he said into the comm that linked back to the digital bay, "open doors."

Overhead, there was a soft ding and the doors opened, splitting down the middle. The two Titans in front moved out, their MechPulses sweeping the area. Alistair and Ares stepped out next, Alistair's pulse at eye level, his fears from before gone. He had turned into his callsign, the name by which he was known as from one side of the world to the other, from Earth to the very farthest reaches of the Commonwealth, the ice-planet Pluto. Alistair Kane was Odin, the modern-day God of War and Justice.

The HUD overlaying his vision showed heat traces where the Subversives were scattering, running behind doors and down hallways, doing anything to stay away from the Titans. From fate.

Alistair glanced to his right, noting that Ares was too close to him. At the same moment, he saw the elevator door had closed behind him. Both of those things were against protocol. Alistair didn't know if Ares realized he'd noticed, so he turned his pulse toward a door showing a Subversive's traces.

"There's no need," Ares said from behind. His voice was masked now; in case anything was being recorded, it would be impossible to tell who'd been inside the suit. "There's no one here, Odin. Just us."

Alistair didn't turn around. He didn't need to. The room made sense now. His HUD couldn't see through this type of construction material, meaning he couldn't actually *see* the Subversives, only their traces—and those had been placed here before the Titans began their trip up in the elevator.

The other two Titans came back from their false chase. They'd only been awaiting Ares' signal.

Alistair lowered his pulse so the barrel faced the ground.

One of the strangers spoke. "Careful, Odin. Don't think about grabbing that Whip."

Ares' voice was like iron. "You're not here to talk, so don't do it again."

Alistair knew why the stranger had spoken. He was scared. He knew of Odin, and he knew how much death Odin could cause if he unleashed the Whip that was two inches from his fingers. Alistair dropped his head to the right so that he could half-see his partner. "You're going to kill me?"

"Is that supposed to strike a chord with me?" his partner asked. "I'm not going to kill you, Odin. You killed yourself when you listened to the Subversives."

Alistair's eyes found the new Titans. Were they really Titans, or just people wearing SUITs to help finish the job? Control probably didn't think Odin was capable of what he'd done in the past, so they believed Ares could take him out by himself. Those two were most likely here to reinforce for Odin that he had no chance of survival.

The newcomers stood twelve feet from him. A pulse hit from here would evaporate a human, but Alistair would survive inside the MechSuit. It would be damaged, without a doubt, but he'd live.

"What do you think the Subversives told me, Ares?" he asked, his body as still as a sphinx's.

His partner laughed, the sound distorted and evil. "I don't have to think. I know exactly what was said because I watched it. Did you really think that blocker would work? Or that we didn't know you *let* them go?" He shook his head. "I will say it was a nice acting job, Odin, making it look like three Subversives could take you and your Whip down."

"You're sure of that?" Alistair said. "You're willing to bet my life on the fact that I let them go? That I was acting?"

Ares didn't lower his weapon an inch. "Our Institutes are based on *your* skill sets. *Your* style of fighting and tactics. Where do you think I learned how to be a Titan? Simple Subversives can't put you down. If they could, they'd have killed you."

Alistair's eyes were still on the newcomers, though his helmet kept them from knowing. "Did you listen to what they said? Did you do any checking?"

Ares shook his head. "No. I tracked them down and killed them yesterday. Any doubt I might have had about your complicity in their escape died with them."

"What now?" Alistair asked. "What are your orders?"

Another laugh from the person Alistair considered his second-closest friend. A cruel laugh. One without mercy, without even a semblance of love. "You know what happens. You've done it to others who gave up the Code. There's no need to rehash it here, is there?"

"I suppose not," Alistair whispered. He *had* done it to others for the exact reason they would now do it to him: because he had given up the Code. They would kill him here and either have a fake public execution or most likely say the great Odin had been slain by the AllMother's Subversives. Put it on her head to stir up more hatred. "And my wife?"

"I'll make sure she's taken care of. She won't know of your betrayal." It was the first sign of any humanity from Ares. "No more questions. Die like a Titan. I expect nothing less, despite your fall."

Alistair checked his breath and his heart rate. His HUD displayed them both: seventy-seven beats per minute, respiration normal. Even now, his body wouldn't panic. It was part of what made the two newcomers fear him. In situations when the body should break, his remained calm. "Do Titans die, Ares? Or do we fall?"

"In your case," his friend answered, "both."

Alistair didn't think. His suit could handle one pulse

shot, but not three at once. He dropped to a knee, let his pulse fall to the ground, and put his right hand on the Whip. A shot passed overhead, and the wall on his left disintegrated. The two newcomers were pumping their pulses for a reload, but it was too late for them. Perhaps they knew it, perhaps they didn't.

It was all the same to Odin.

He grabbed the Whip's hilt, and the genetic codes traveled to it as he pulled it free. No other hand, no other person could operate it, and as it read its master, the weapon flowed from the hilt. Red light flooded into three whip-like strands. It would be a beautiful thing to watch under other circumstances, but Odin had no time just now.

He lunged forward as Ares' pulse disintegrated the wall he'd been standing in front of. The newcomers tried to raise their weapons, but he slashed his Whip at them, and the red lasers sliced through the first man, cutting him in two. Odin spun around his remains to reach the second Titan. Ares' blast struck the second man head-on, damaging his suit.

Odin raised his Whip, and it responded to him without hesitation. The three individual strands coiled around one another as they wrapped three times around the newcomer's neck. The suit sizzled and started melting, but Odin didn't allow the strand to tighten further.

Ares fired again, the MechPulse shattering the second newcomer's suit's knee joints. His suit wouldn't function any longer, at least as far as walking went. "STOP!" the stranger. He'd probably pissed himself.

Odin stayed directly behind his hostage. Showing even

an inch of his suit would put him at risk. Ares wielded the pulse like a surgeon. "You going to kill him to get to me?"

The MechSuit was too large to shrug in, so Ares raised a hand in an equivalent gesture. "That's up to you. You're not surviving this, and however many people need to die to make that happen is on you." Ares nodded at the body that lay in two pieces on the floor.

Odin whispered to the man in front of him, "I'm going to step back. If you don't move with me, your head is going to come right off your body. Nod if you understand."

The newcomer nodded, causing the Whip to melt a bit more of his metal suit. Odin took a step back, and the soldier followed. His knees didn't bend, but his hip joints allowed him to shuffle awkwardly.

Ares laughed. "Where do you think you're going? You going to fly out the window? Try to get home to your wife and protect your house? You know there is no hiding from the Commonwealth. You think your wife hasn't already been detained? Do you think she's at your house, Odin?" He shook his head. "All the pieces were in play long before you got into that elevator. Give it up. There is no valor in stupidity. Die like the Titan you were, the one you'll be remembered as."

Odin took another step. His HUD showed him the distance to the window behind him. This leap wouldn't be easy, and regardless of what the newcomer had done, he didn't deserve to die right now. Odin didn't *want* to kill him, which added another layer of complexity to the maneuver. He hadn't thought about what came next, not truly—there hadn't been time. All he knew was he wanted to get to Luna, and from there, they could decide what to do. He wasn't going to listen to anything else Ares had to say.

Odin gripped the Whip tighter. "If Luna isn't at home, Ares, it's you I'm coming for next."

His left foot pushed off the ground while his right launched into the newcomer's back. The Whip unfurled from the man's neck, and Odin threw himself toward the window. He turned in the air, commanding the three strands of his Whip to uncoil. They began circling in a saw-like fashion. Odin heard and then felt the pulse shot from behind, part hitting the hostage and the other part slamming into him.

The Whip touched the window, and the three strands cut a circular hole just before Odin's helmet slammed into it. He felt another blast from the pulse and his left boot's shield went down. His HUD showed it as red, but he wasn't *inside* the building any longer. Odin started his fall from the five hundredth floor, and he could see the entire world below him. The edges of his right boot blasted fire as the jet activated.

He knew going up would be impossible with only one jet, so he let himself fall. The force of the blast sent him swerving to the left and launched him at an extra thirty kilometers per hour. Odin tilted his head back to the window and saw Ares look out. He wasn't aiming the pulse since he realized one of Odin's feet had been damaged.

He could simply let the Titan fall to his death.

Odin's HUD showed time until impact, and there wasn't any way he could slow down before he splattered all over the ground below. He looked over his shoulder and saw that Ares had him in his line of fire, obviously having decided not to risk any more mishaps.

Odin twisted his foot to the left and gripped his Whip. It connected instantaneously with him, and he had it spin its strands once more. The blast missed him by inches, though its wake threw him off-course. The Whip tried to adjust but wasn't quick enough, carving only a short way into the wall before Alistair's suit smashed through it.

He slid on his back as concrete, metal, and brick scattered before him. People screamed since the floor hadn't been emptied before the Titans' arrival. He laid on the ground staring at the ceiling for a few moments, and his Whip retracted into its handle, waiting for his next command.

He pulled up his current location on the HUD. He'd dropped three hundred floors, and by now, Control would know where he was. There wasn't any way out of this, but he had to get to Luna.

He rose to his feet as people rushed toward the doors and elevators. None were working, at least not in their favor. He scanned the crowd quickly, his HUD identifying everyone and showing no threats. Odin looked over his shoulder to see the hole in the wall, wind flinging loose papers around.

That was the only way out—two hundred floors down with a damaged MechSuit.

Think, he told himself. Could he carve his way out of here? The Whip was strong, but multiple uses to cut steel would wear it out, possibly even break it, and that could *not* be risked. He knew reinforcements were coming. The elevators were moving, and he could hear quadcopters in the distance. Control hadn't thought it would take this much to kill him, but they were prepared all the same.

He knew how they were following him: the MechSuit. They'd be able to find him as long as he wore it, but could he survive without it?

There wasn't any real choice.

"Fold off," he said into the helmet, and the suit collapsed into itself. Helmet went to neck, neck to shoulder, and so on until it had all compacted except for his damaged left boot. He used the Whip delicately and cut himself loose, then he stood up in standard armor, flexible black fabric that wouldn't hold up to a tenth of a pulse blast.

To his right, he saw a man cowering behind his desk. He hadn't run. Odin turned to him. "Give me your clothes. Now."

The man froze for a second, not understanding. Odin raised the Whip and lashed with all three strands, blackening the floor beneath him. "Your clothes!"

Odin didn't want to hurt these people. He didn't want to even scare them, but fear was his most potent weapon right now if he wanted to find his wife. Ares would have said anything upstairs to keep him from fighting back, but Odin didn't believe one word of it at that moment.

The cowering man stripped quickly, knowing from the armor and Whip who stood in front of him, or if not who, then *what*—a Titan.

Odin wished he had his HUD, but that was in his discarded MechSuit. The man had stripped to his skivvies, and Odin quickly dressed in the discarded clothes. Modern day business attire. It would give him only seconds, but that was all he would need.

He looked at the people huddling against walls, in corners, and under desks. "I'm not going to hurt any of you. Men are coming right now, and *they* will if you get in their way. Do *not* get in their way. When they get here, they're going to ask where I am. Don't answer." Odin knew that if any of these people lied to the Titans when they arrived, there'd be severe punishment. "All you need to do is look out the hole in the wall. Nothing else."

These people were fearful, but they also understood that Titans were on the side of justice. They most likely thought the men hunting him were Subversives, so they would listen to what he told them. It would only be later that they'd realize they'd been duped, but he wouldn't care at that point. Odin pocketed his Whip, now silenced, and shoved the undressed man beneath his desk. He followed, leaving the damaged boot where he'd once been.

Seconds ticked by. Odin could smell the man's urine. He placed his hand on the stranger's shoulder, at the same time keeping his eyes on the still-closed elevators. "You're safe. Nothing's going to happen to you. Just stay right here."

The man sniffled and nodded, his relief palpable. Odin moved his hand back to his pocket, gripping the silent Whip. This was taking them too long. They should have already been here.

The whine of the quadcopter grew louder outside. Odin thought he heard a second as well.

They won't let me leave, he thought.

The elevators opened. Odin recognized the first three Titans: Thor, Freya, and Mars. Ares walked out last, his red MechSuit the color of blood—the only one of its kind.

"Where is he?" Ares asked the cowering room full of people. He didn't need to specify who he was talking about, given the massive hole in the wall and the wind rushing through it.

Odin watched as everyone slowly turned as he'd instructed. Ares nodded. "Go," he told the other three Titans.

Damn it, Odin thought. He didn't want Ares behind him under any circumstances. He watched as the Titans moved across the room, their boots thumping heavily on the floor. Odin quietly pulled the Whip from his pocket, the hilt glowing red as it activated.

The man next to Odin stared at it with a slack jaw. Whips were known throughout society but rarely seen. Usually, if you saw one and *weren't* a Titan, death was imminent.

The Titans went past the desk and peered out the hole.

"I don't see—" one started to say. Odin moved before they finished.

He leapt from behind the desk, the Whip's three strands falling out of the handle. They crackled with energy, which gave away his location, but the Titans were too slow. Thor moved first, turning his head over his shoulder, his own Whip spilling out. Odin brought his down across the Titan's right arm, cutting it off in three different sections, the final one above the elbow. Blood spilled on the floor as screams ripped from the man.

Mars was in the middle, and he formed his Whip into a solid sword. It slashed across Odin's, trying to pin it to the ground.

Odin's Whip wrapped around Mars' sword and he

yanked. The Titan was pulled forward, but Odin couldn't attack him with his body--he'd break his hand or foot on the suit.

Freya swung from his left, aiming for his midsection. He ducked, and the Whip sizzled over his head. Mars had jumped back quickly to avoid Freya's Whip. He now grabbed Odin by the throat with his left hand and thrust him into the air as he stepped in Thor's blood.

Ares remained at the elevator. "That's enough, Odin. There's nowhere to go."

The MechSuit's hand was impossibly strong, and it slowly strangled him as he hung in the air. Odin relaxed his Whip, letting Mars go. The young Titan should have cut the older one's Whip arm off at that point, but he didn't. He wanted to make a show, maybe for Ares, maybe for himself, to prove that though he was young, he'd been the one to capture Odin. He brought his Whip, still in the sword form, up to an inch from Odin's eye. "Some Titan," he mocked.

Odin's vision was blackening at the corners, but that had happened before. He brought his Whip up blindingly quick, wrapping it around the arm holding his throat. "Go frag yourself."

He couldn't see Mars' eyes behind the helmet, but he knew they were wide. The Titan had frozen instead of shoving his *own* Whip into Odin's brain.

Instead, he lost an arm.

Odin yanked down on the Whip, the three strands slicing through metal, flesh, and bone as if there were no difference between them. Mars stumbled backward and almost fell through the massive hole in the wall, but Freya shoved him just in time. He sprawled to the right, blood spraying across the floor.

Odin realized his mistake too late. His flesh was ripped from his body in three long strikes as Ares' Whip slashed him.

His own blood now spilled, and he fell to his knees. Ares hadn't used the Whip to kill, only injure.

"*ENOUGH*," Ares shouted through his helmet. He brought the Whip down again, more flesh burning away from Odin's body. This time it wrapped around his right shoulder, and Ares let it cut deep, carving into bone.

Odin fell onto his hands and knees. Freya stood in front of him, her gray MechSuit hiding the woman inside. Behind her, and just outside the building, the quadcopter hovered in the air. Wind ripped around Odin as blood leaked from his battered body.

From behind, Ares ordered, "Clip him."

Freya reached to her left leg and pulled out a Clip, which was half a halo that would go on Odin's forehead, rendering his mind and body useless. They couldn't kill him, not in front of all these people. Control would have to change the narrative, though Odin didn't know how they would fix this mess, with Titans missing arms and witnesses everywhere.

You're not done yet, he told himself. *If you're going to die, you're going to do it with Luna.*

He'd been the best once. Maybe he wasn't anymore. Maybe the man behind him slashing his back with a Whip was now the stronger of the two, but Odin could still be the best for a moment.

Freya approached, the silver Clip shining in front of

her. She bent slightly, her Whip now extending only a quarter of the way outside its hilt. Odin's had retracted all the way, giving out as his body did. He felt the warm blood leaking down his chest, some of it his, some of it other's. The Clip was an inch from his head.

He shoved forward, his muscles responding to his commands the best they could, and he flew through Freya's legs. He slid over the edge as she turned around, her Whip slapping down a half-second too late.

Odin reached forward, and his hands gripped the quad-copter's nearest landing skid. The pilot hadn't expected the added weight and couldn't adjust in time. The copter tilted forward and to the right, one of its propellers slamming into the steel wall. Odin could hear nothing besides the *whoop-whoop* of the other propellers. Material crumbled from the wall and hit his already wounded back as the metal propeller bent but kept slapping into it.

The copter started falling, dragging across the building as it did.

Whoop-whoop-whoop.

Odin couldn't look at the Titans above him. All he could do now was try not to die.

The other front propeller was dragged into the wall, and the two together slowed the machine's slide. It'd fallen another fifty floors or so, and Odin's hands were starting to lose their grip. His right side was far too weak to do this much longer, and despite the pilot's best efforts, there wasn't any way this thing wouldn't burn on the side of this building.

He looked down. The drop was still too far. He'd break every bone in his body if he let go.

The copter's tail was swinging, about to collide with the building...and then? He'd burn alive if he wasn't smashed into the steel first.

Odin let go.

The rush of wind immediately replaced the sounds of the propellers. His Whip was still in his pocket, but it was meant to kill, not save. The building was five inches from his body, and if he tried to lean back, he'd drag across it before bouncing off, more of his body destroyed.

One hundred stories left.

Luna, he thought. *I love you.*

Odin's heart was still normal, seventy-seven beats per minute.

He never saw what he hit. He felt a momentary bright pain as if a sun had enveloped his body, then there was blackness.

CHAPTER TWO

*"Those who wish to cause the Commonwealth harm—
these Subversives—must be eradicated at all cost. They
have no place in our society."*

–Aurelius de Finita, First Imperial Ascendant.

"Odin" existed during certain times, those when death sprang from the Titan's hands like water from a fountain. The rest of the time, he was Alistair Kane. After his fall, he was no one. He existed in a world that no one else could see, one of intense pain and nothing else. No knowledge of where or who he was. No knowledge of the past and no hope for the future. There was simply pain.

He didn't know how long he was in that place, but toward the end, he started to hear voices.

Alistair couldn't make out what they said. His mind couldn't piece together what any of it meant. He only knew that it was different from the pain.

Next, he saw a jumble of light, blue and purple, some white. Words, noises, lights.

Until he woke up.

He felt the sting of the slap before he knew what was happening.

"Wake up," a gruff voice commanded. "Wake up."

Smack. Flesh on flesh, the mark of the slap red across his face.

Alistair blinked, once, twice, and then peered into the world. The lights were bright on his eyes, and he kept them narrowed. People stood on both his left and right, but their faces were blurred by Dimmers. They looked pixelated and dark.

"Who are you?" Alistair said, though his throat was on fire and he didn't know how clear his words had come out.

The man on the left responded, "Your guardian angels."

Alistair groaned. No citizen in the Commonwealth would talk about such an ancient concept. He had thought life could get no worse, with Control issuing his death sentence. Now he had somehow been kidnapped by Subversives. How many of them had he killed? How many had he Clipped who were now in cryo? He couldn't count the number if he had untold lifetimes.

Alistair knew what came next: torture. Perhaps years of it, until he had told them everything he knew about Control and the Commonwealth. Until he had made things up that had never existed and never could, but he would say them anyway just to make the torture stop. Alistair had seen Subversive victims before, or at least what was left of them.

"Kill me," he whispered.

The man on the left nodded. "Would if I could, Bub, but it's out of my hands."

The man on the right waved a needle in front of Alistair's face. "We need you to wake up, so I'm going to give you a stim. You ever had a stim before?"

Alistair groaned again, turning his head against the pillow. He didn't know what the man was saying and didn't care. His legs, his chest—everything was on fire as if someone had doused him in gasoline before tossing a match on him.

"Going to feel like someone put a mechheart in your chest," the man said as he continued waving the needle in front of Alistair's face. "You may want to try and attack us, thinking you can get out of here." He looked at the bottom of the bed Alistair lay on. "Your legs don't work no more. They're fragged, and your lungs are only pumping because of this." He tapped a machine to Alistair's right, something he hadn't noticed.

The man on the left spoke up. "So don't try anything, Bub. If we wanted you dead, you would be, *comprende?*"

Alistair said nothing, still not understanding what was happening around him. The needle glistened in the light as it rose into the air. The man holding it spoke once more. "We're hitting your heart with it because we need you wide awake. You won't feel a thing, though, so don't worry."

Alistair barely had time to register what the man was saying before the needle plunged into his chest. If he'd thought he was in pain before, he'd been wrong. Very wrong.

Fire lit across his chest plate as the needle cut through bone, then punctured his heart. The man pressed the button on the side of the syringe, and the stimulant rushed into Alistair. His eyes sprang wide, his mouth opening into a scream that didn't come out. He realized he had no air in his lungs. He couldn't breathe. He sat up, pain breaking out across his lower body, hands grasping at the air.

The man on the left leaned over and swatted him hard on the back.

His lungs opened, and air rushed into them. Relief washed over Alistair. He fell back in the gurney-like chair. The pain in his chest was still there but fading. His eyes focused on his surroundings, years of training taking over without any effort. A light overhead, the rest of the room dark. A single door to his right. Man on his left wore no armor, but there was some kind of small plasma weapon holstered on his hip.

Alistair tried turning around to see the man behind him.

"Don't strain yourself, Bub." The man walked around to the front of the chair, turning off the Dimmer over his head. "I'm not hiding from you, and I don't care if you see my face. You can't trade information with anyone on Earth any longer. Go ahead and tell Control you know who I am. It won't save your life."

Alistair understood now, the stim working on his brain as well as his body. He said nothing, knowing these people were Subversives. There'd be no help here. He tried sitting up again, but the man on the right slammed him back down. "Nuh-uh, Bub. Right where you are is where you shall stay. Now listen to me, and listen closely. Him and me?" He pointed between him and the other guy. "We're the only two things that are keeping you alive right now. Personally, I think this is the worst decision I've ever seen, but I don't got much say in it."

He took a step back and pointed at the door. "Out there is a ship waiting on you. Its only goal is to get you off this planet and out to the furthest reaches of the solar system. As close to safety as you're going to find, now that your life is forfeit. But, Bub, we don't force anyone to do anything. I won't put you on that ship if you don't want to go, so you have to decide if you want to stay on this rock or go to another. You stay here, you'll never see my face again. You'll never see his face again." He nodded at his partner. "We'll wheel you out of here, and then you're on your own. *Comprende?*"

Alistair was taking every word in, understanding it all after the stim. He glanced at the door, wishing he could get up, but he'd seen his legs, which were mangled and completely unusable.

Luna, he thought. If he left, she was lost to him forever.

The man on the left snapped his fingers in front of Alistair's face. "Listen up, Bub. Time is short. Like, real short. Your former friends are searching for you. They aren't gonna stop any more than they stop when they hunt me and mine down. You go to the ship or you..." He looked down at the wreckage of Alistair's body. "See how far you can run on the things you used to call legs."

Alistair laid his head back on the chair and closed his eyes. How had he gotten here? How was this his life?

The thought that made up his mind was a simple one: *If I stay, I'm dead. No Luna. If I leave, maybe there's a chance I see her again.*

It was the silliest of thoughts, one that ignored a galactic empire, a thousand years of law, and the fact that he was now a broken man. Yet the thought possessed him like a virus, rapidly taking over his mind and decision-making capability. Without opening his eyes, he said, "I'll go."

There were a few moments of silence, which caused Alistair to open his eyes. The two men were staring at each other, and Alistair realized that neither of them had thought he would agree. "What is this all about? Why are you helping me?"

The man on the right stepped away from the chair and behind Alistair. When he came back into view, he was holding a gray blanket. "The reason you're in this mess, Odin of the Titan Legion, is because you saved some of ours. The AllMother knows you did, and it means she owes you a debt. The AllMother pays her debts, no matter the cost. Apparently, even if it means saving a cockroach monster like yourself. Don't mistake either of us here. We don't like you. I'd kill you now if I could, but that's not my decision to make." He took a step closer and lifted the blanket. "This is what's going to happen. I'm throwing this over you, and we're walking out of this building. You're not to move because you're a corpse, and we're transferring you. We've got the paperwork in order, so unless you rise from the dead, this shouldn't be a problem."

The one on the left, the man not holding the blanket, leaned close to Alistair's face. "If you do decide to rise, thinking you can somehow save your skin by turning us in, I'm going to slit your throat faster than you and your pretty Whip can possibly imagine."

At the mention of his Whip, Alistair's hand automatically moved to his side, where it was always kept.

"Don't worry, Titan," the man whispered. "We've got it. The AllMother said to keep it for you. Now lay the fuck down, so I don't have to look at you anymore."

Whatever they were doing for Alistair, it wasn't out of love. Their faces held nothing but hate and disgust; they would murder him if they were allowed. Alistair laid his head back down on the chair, and the man on the right pressed a button, allowing the top portion to recline backward.

They draped the gray blanket over him, then the gurney started to move.

Alistair listened with ears that had been trained to detect the slightest danger. He heard every turn of the wheels below him, as well as the footfalls of the men pushing him. He listened for words and other noises, anything that might give him a clue as to where he was. He didn't have any idea how being a corpse was going to get him on an interstellar flight. Off-world body transfers did happen when all of someone's relatives had left Earth, but now? During a manhunt?

The man had lied to Alistair about one thing. They hadn't just given him a stim, at least not the normal kind. His brain was alert, but his body felt numb, so some kind of speedball was in effect. Alistair could only hope they'd gotten the dosage correct.

The gurney came to a stop. Alistair's breathing was as slow as he could make it. This was something Titans trained for, and he was the best at it, with virtually complete control over his bodily functions. All the same, corpses didn't breathe, and if anyone looked at the wrong moment, there wouldn't be a whole lot he could do.

The man who'd called him "Bub" spoke first. "Off-world, Mars."

"Approval orders?" The voice was stern, no-nonsense, and Control wouldn't have it any other way. Interstellar travel was constantly used by Subversives, and they often used interdimensional travel. They all had to start here in the third dimension. Thus, Control made sure only the most detailed-oriented Commonwealth servants were placed in positions to monitor it.

"Here," the man who'd held the syringe said. Alistair knew he was handing over a DataTrack. It would have all the necessary approvals and orders to get them through— or it wouldn't, and all hell would break loose.

Seconds passed, and Alistair could feel the drugs' effects starting to wane. He wasn't worried about brain fog or anything of that nature, but rather, the pain in his legs. He remembered, or at least thought he did, them saying something about his lungs, that they weren't working anymore either. He didn't know about that, but he knew they had to quickly get him somewhere with solitude.

Even *his* mastery of his body wasn't going to be able to shove this kind of pain away.

He tried to think of his wife, to focus on her face, on

her laugh. He tried to think of the way she smiled when she was teasing him, the little curvature of her lip as it pulled up. The way her eyes sparkled when she knew her wit was quicker, and he wouldn't be able to tease back fast enough to matter.

"Is there a problem?"

The question pulled Alistair from his thoughts. He thought Bub had asked it, but he wasn't sure.

"Problem?" the immigration agent responded, his voice sounding like he wasn't used to being challenged, but he was up to it all the same.

"Yeah, Bub, problem. I come and go through Immigration at least three times a year, sometimes more if I'm not going interplanetary. I've never seen anyone take this long over a simple body transfer, and from what I hear on the holosphere, there's a war zone downtown. So yeah, is there a problem? I need to get this body on ice before it starts smelling."

The pain was growing, and Alistair's need for oxygen was increasing.

"If there's a problem," the immigration agent said, "it sounds like it's your problem. You'll wait until I'm ready to let you go."

Alistair's ability to think was fading, his body's need for morphoids and oxygen surpassing anything else.

"Let me see the body." The immigration agent stood up.

One of the men sighed. "You've got to be kidding me."

Alistair's heart rate didn't increase, nor did his breathing, but he didn't know how he was going to fake looking dead. Pallor, skin suppleness, and a dozen other things separated a dead body from a live person, none of which Alistair could manipulate.

Someone grabbed the corner of the blanket, and lifted. Alistair knew his naked body was visible to all. He kept his eyes closed, his breath held inside his chest, hoping against all odds that somehow he wouldn't be recognized. That somehow his damned face wasn't plastered on every holowall in the city.

One of Alistair's men asked, "He look dead enough for ya?"

"Cover 'im up," the immigration agent instructed. "You're cleared."

The blanket flipped back over Alistair's body and the gurney started moving again. The shot they gave him must have done something to his outer body as well as his inner, but he couldn't consider that right now. Alistair waited for a few minutes, then whispered, "Need stim."

"What you need," someone answered from above, "is to not say another word. We're not out of the woods yet."

Alistair's hand bore down on the metal beneath him to keep from screaming as the wreckage of his legs demanded to be heard.

More long minutes passed, then Alistair felt cold air wash over his body. The gurney stopped moving, the blanket was removed, and before he knew what was happening, someone new was stabbing a needle in his arm. Alistair gritted his teeth for a second and felt the soothing morphoid flood his system.

He looked up at a new man, who had a thick beard. "Thank you."

The beard looked at the two men who had wheeled him here. "The AllMother has lost her damned mind."

Alistair tried to keep his eyes open, but he couldn't. Really, that wasn't so bad because unconsciousness had become preferable to sleep.

CHAPTER THREE

"It is through our strength as one people, one purpose, that we have conquered our solar system. We have relegated disease, crime, and poverty to history. We have relegated those who wish to do us harm to the furthest areas of the sun's reach."

–Aurelius de Finita, First Imperial Ascendant

Alistair opened his eyes slowly, blinking multiple times but not really thinking. His brain was dragging from the double dose of morphoids. All he really knew was that he was awake.

He moved his head to the right, taking in his surroundings, and then slowly brought it to the left. A man was sitting on a metal bench. He had a red beard that extended a few inches from his face. His head was bald and his body thick. He had hands that looked like they might be able to bend metal. The eyes that stared back at Alistair were bright red, which sent a chill over Alistair's entire body.

It was an almost iridescent red, something that shouldn't be possible but clearly was. It was outlawed across the entire solar system. Alistair had only seen someone of this kind once, but the man had been Clipped and unable to hurt anyone.

Alistair opened his mouth; his tongue felt heavy and sticky. "You're a mutant?"

The man raised an eyebrow but didn't respond. Alistair blinked again, then figuring the mutant wasn't going to say anything, looked down at his lower body. Everything was covered with another blanket, a different-colored one than when he'd been wheeled through Immigration.

He didn't hurt anymore. It dawned on him that he'd had another dose of drugs, or maybe more than one.

He turned his head back to the mutant. "Where are we? How long have I been under?"

The red-eyed man rubbed his beard gruffly, looking angry. "You're who they say you are, huh?" he asked, tucking his bottom lip under the top and nodding in very slight movements. "You're Odin, the first god. And now you can't even stand up."

Alistair wanted to say something, to respond in some quick-witted way—which was never his forte—but his mind was in such a haze. The only things he could think to say were the questions he'd just asked. "Where are we? How long have I been under?"

The thickly muscled man stood up. "We're on a ship that's heading to a world of ice. You've been under two days, and we're still orbiting Earth. Your little escape has made quite a stir. The Imperial Ascendant actually called for the complete cessation of travel."

Alexander de Finita. It was the first coherent thought not about his whereabouts that Alistair had formed. He thought the name again: *Alexander de Finita.* "He stopped travel?"

The big man's back was to Alistair now, but he nodded. "It seems your death was more important than anyone thought. Certainly more than I thought. Maybe the AllMother knew, or maybe She simply wanted to pay the debt. I don't know." He turned around, his red eyes bright. If anyone boarded this ship and saw those eyes, he'd be put down immediately. Not Clipped, but killed. Even the mutant Alistair had once seen, she'd had her head turned into powder with a close-range MechPulse *while* wearing the Clip.

The mutant put his hands on his hips. "My name is Theos. My red eyes probably tell you that I have no family, nothing so grand as *Finita.*" He whispered the word in mock awe. "But as a Titan, you also have no family name as prestigious. And now, you no longer even have the title of Titan. Odin is dead. Your family name, Kane, is dead." He took a step toward the gurney. "My eyes are red and you call me mutant, but where we're going, you have a choice to make. You will either become like me, a mutant, or fall apart before you ever have a chance to see the ice world."

Alistair closed his eyes tight. He couldn't fully grasp what was being asked. Him, a Pure Born...they wanted to turn him into a mutant? The lineage of Kane may not be anything as prestigious as Finita or Barasam, but he was being asked to throw it all away. Everything, for...

"What..." He opened and closed his mouth a couple of

times, trying to get full use of his tongue. "What are you talking about?"

The big man chuckled, though there was no joy in it. "We're going into the fifth dimension with this jump. Your body, as is, won't be able to survive that, but there's no way we're risking traveling in the third or even the fourth. The only way you'll survive what's coming is if you become like me."

The ice world.

Pluto.

Alistair lay back on the gurney. Tears floated over his eyes, though he willed them to not overflow to his cheeks. How was this possible? How had he gotten here? A week ago, he'd been at home with Luna, awaiting another assignment, but not worried about anything. He'd sat on their porch, sipping whiskey, her at his side. Their lawn had been green, and their dog had been lounging in the grass.

The ice world. Pluto.

All because months ago he'd heard something he shouldn't. He'd *done* something he shouldn't.

Theos walked over to the gurney. Alistair didn't look at him but kept his eyes on the ceiling above. The tears still hadn't fallen.

"You'll get no sympathy from me, Titan. What the AllMother does is beyond my mind. She operates in ways that none of us can understand because she sees the future. I trust her ability to steer us to the future that is necessary, so I do my part, but you..." He shook his head, clearly disgusted at what and who he was looking at. "You are perhaps one of the worst creatures I've ever laid eyes on."

He turned away from the gurney and walked to the

door. He raised his hand to a chip reader, and the door opened by sliding into the wall. "We're making the jump in three standard days. I'll need every second of those three days to even have a chance of keeping you alive. I'll be back in a standard hour. Have your decision ready."

Alistair again shut his eyes hard.

The mutant spoke once more. "The drugs I've been giving you will wear off soon. The AllMother doesn't want you making this choice drugged up. Deal with the pain, Titan, and decide once more if you want to die or keep going forward."

When he stepped out of the room, the door *whooshed* closed, locking Alistair in alone.

The mutant hadn't lied. The pain was back, and Alistair did everything he mentally could to moderate it. His training in pain management was extensive, and when the door opened, Alistair's eyes were closed, and his breathing was a tight twenty reps per minute.

Even so, sweat dripped from his forehead, and his fingers were curling on the metal beneath him, wanting to grab anything.

The door closed behind the mutant, but Alistair didn't open his eyes or turn his head. He couldn't, not if he wanted to keep the pain at bay. The moment he relented, it would flood him like the ocean's tides.

"Have you made your choice, Titan?"

The mutant had been right. He did want to make this choice with a clear head, or as clear as he could get. If he went this route, he was forfeiting the Commonwealth's Contract. He was casting away everything he'd been brought up to believe. Everything his parents taught him as a little boy and everything he and Luna had planned on teaching their children.

Alistair had five more years left with the Titans, then he'd planned on having children of his own.

And he was going to throw it all away. For what? That was the question he'd asked himself in the last hour. Why would he do it? Had he no honor? No sense of duty? Perhaps the Commonwealth had decided he should die, but how many times had he been the enforcer of such a decision?

"Titan," the mutant said, "you know I'm modified. I can tell you're alive, despite your low breathing rate. What's it going to be? There isn't time for games."

Alistair wasn't sure of his answer. Even after an hour, he hadn't been able to get behind it fully, but the thing that kept coming back to him was simple. If he died here, he would never see Luna again. He didn't care how small the chance was that he might get back to her; it was still a chance, and death took it away.

With closed eyes and pain racking his body, he whispered, "Modify me."

So it would be.

THE WRITTEN HISTORY OF THE GREAT INSURRECTION

When people refer back to the man named Alistair Kane, they will undoubtedly talk about his modifications. Even now, it is broadcast across the solar system that he is a mutant, though they capitalize the word to make it sound worse. Mutant.

I didn't yet know the man who I now follow, not when his modification occurred. I was still on a cold, distant planet, waiting for a revolution that I think I knew in my heart would not come. No one attached to the AllMother at that time thought it would come, though we never said that to each other. To do so would have defeated the entire purpose of our lives.

I am second-generation AllMother. I follow in my father's footsteps. To tell my birth-mother what I truly thought, that we would never truly rise against those who kept us in chains? It was unthinkable.

To be modified, at least before Alistair Kane, was an unspeakable idea. The Commonwealth had outlawed it centuries ago, and the penalty for modification was death. If for some freak reason you had to be modified? You were the lowest strata of society. Signs hung in stores that said No Mutants Allowed. To be mutant was to be rejected.

Looking back now, after so much has changed, I can easily see why. The Commonwealth feared Mutants. It feared what they were capable of. It feared that their modifications had made them stronger than we ever could be, and so did the Imperial Ascendant.

The AllMother first saw the truth, and only the future will tell if that truth is worth seeing. I am not there yet; I'm only at the end of the beginning.

I seem to have gotten lost in my ramblings, and for that, I apologize. The focus of this chapter is on Alistair Kane's modification. The Commonwealth hated such people with unabashed fury. They were to be killed, and if that could not be achieved, they were to be thrust from society without mercy. Kane had to face the ingrained idea that by turning into something *different*, he would be evil.

He did it, though.

He had his reasons, but as I said before, this isn't Alistair Kane's story. It is the Insurrection's.

The AllMother understood that after so many generations, we would not achieve victory. We could not, not against something so massive, not as humans. Indeed, I didn't know it in the beginning, but the Commonwealth had engineered something nonhuman—something *different* —that would never let us rise.

So Alistair Kane was changed, and now they call him Mutant, and his Insurrection is considered to have come from the depths of hell.

It's important for history to understand that without his modifications, none of the rest would have been possible.

The winners of this Insurrection will decide if it was a force for good or evil in the world.

CHAPTER FOUR

"No Mutants Allowed"

–Signs on Eighty-Three Percent of Earth Stores

If Alistair had ever thought he understood pain, during the next three days, he realized he'd known nothing of it. He had been a child in the womb before, barely conscious of the matters that now plagued his body and mind.

Lights came and went, voices too. He begged to be murdered, for morphoids, for any and everything that could possibly make this stop. He cursed those he saw, cursed their families and their mothers, but still the pain would not lessen.

When his eyes were open, he saw different people, some new, some he'd already seen, but through it all, the mutant remained. Alistair's body had been strapped down so that no matter how hard he pulled, he could not move. All he could do was scream, yet the mutant never moved his eyes from the task at hand. Sometimes during the pain,

Alistair would try to focus on the mutant's work, looking at the tools in his hand. They changed as the hours did, from scalpel to torch to even a human-sized DataTrack that hung over Alistair. The mutant would stand on a stool, looking down at it.

Alistair saw tools he didn't understand and felt things happening to his body that he hadn't imagined possible.

Injections, corrections, and yes, the final modification.

The mutant said nothing as he approached the table. He held a tube connected to a large egg-shaped container. A syringe terminated the tube.

"No," Alistair pleaded. "I changed my mind. I don't want this. Give me death." Spittle fell on his chin at the last word. Eye clamps now restrained both eyes. From the sides of the clamps, tiny hair-like tubes bled tears into his eyes, keeping them moist. He'd be unable to close them during what came next.

The mutant said nothing in response to his pleas. He stepped next to the table and cocked his head to the side as he stared into Alistair's eyes. After a few moments, he said his only words of the entire procedure. "You will make it."

Without warning, he stuck the needle into the iris of Alistair's left eye, and the machine started buzzing.

"Drink."

Alistair heard the words before he saw who was speaking. He didn't remember closing his eyes or falling asleep. He opened them now with effort since there were crusts in the corners. They felt swollen, as did the rest of his body. A plastic cup hovered in front of him, attached to a massive hand, with something that looked like cow's milk inside it.

"Drink," the voice instructed again.

It hurt Alistair's eyes to move them, but he focused on the person speaking. Red eyes stared back at him, and then he remembered. He knew why his eyes hurt and could guess that his irises were red as well.

Theos tilted the cup forward, and the straw hit Alistair in the lips. He didn't want to touch the cup, but his body understood nutrition waited inside. His mouth opened, and the mutant shoved the straw in. Alistair sucked the liquid while staring up at the man who had changed him. It wasn't milk and tasted like ash, though its consistency was that of water. He drank as much of it as he could before the mutant pulled it away.

"That's enough for now, Fallen Titan." He backed up and sat down in a chair. He was a hulking man, his forearms as big as Alistair's upper arms. Rarely if ever had the Titan Odin been cautious about another man, but staring at this one, he innately understood he wanted nothing to do with him in a fistfight.

Theos leaned back in his chair, resting the cup on his tree-trunk of a thigh. "We're in the fourth dimension now, and soon we're hopping to the fifth. Can you feel it?"

Alistair had never been outside the third dimension except during training modules. He said nothing but closed his eyes and let his senses take over. There was a hum, a buzz that vibrated through his body and brought up memories of how terrifying it had been to jump dimensions while training. Back then, his body had trembled from the pressure, but now it was only a slight rattling.

"It'll get worse when we go to the fifth. You'll feel more pain because of the surgery. There's also something I didn't mention—the dreams."

Alistair opened his eyes. "What are you talking about?"

"It's not a big deal," the mutant said. "It happens to some and not others. I've never gotten 'em, but some do. Your dreaming might change. Most say they're lucid dreams. You know what those are, Fallen Titan?"

Alistair blinked the sleep away. "I've heard of them. You know you're dreaming, and you can control what happens. That about right?"

Theos nodded in agreement. "Some people say the dreams are real, but I've never seen anything like that. Scientifically, it doesn't make a whole lot of sense either. All the same, you might get some lucid dreams. Trust me, it's the least of your worries."

Alistair closed his eyes again. The dreams didn't matter. After a few seconds, he opened them and found the mutant. "Am I like you?"

The big man chuckled but didn't look away. "Do you mean, are your eyes red? Yes, they are. Your irises are the same color as mine and will be until the day you die. How does it feel to be less than what society considers perfect?"

Alistair ignored the question and looked down at his body. He couldn't move, though he didn't feel straps restraining him, and a blanket covered everything from the neck down. "Why am I stuck?"

"You can't move right now, not if you want to keep living. Moving in the third dimension would be catastrophic, but in the fourth and fifth? You would die immediately. The normal human body can handle the fourth dimension, but after what you've been through, movement would end you." Theos stood and put the cup to Alistair's lips again, giving him a few seconds of liquid before pulling it away and sitting back down. "You've been given muscle freezers. You won't be able to move until your body can handle it. Enough of that, though. How well do you understand interdimensional travel?"

Alistair cleared his throat. "Enough to know it's faster and that it's illegal."

Theos smiled. "It is illegal, but we're being chased at this moment. Only the modified can handle fifth-dimension travel. But guess what, Titan—we're going to hit the fifth-dimension, and we're *still* going to be chased. Your Imperial Ascendant uses the modified when he finds them useful, and he *really* wants you right now. There's a team of modified about two standard hours behind us. None of that is important, though. The Hawking Coefficient, have you heard of it?"

Alistair wanted to nod but couldn't. The muscle freezers had him paralyzed from the neck down. "Yeah. I know of it. Allows interdimensional space travel to be something like twenty times faster than regular."

The big man rolled his eyes. "It doesn't *allow* anything. It's what identified the difference. Our reality exists in the third dimension, but there are others—multiples, in fact. When we go up or down the dimensions, time slows or quickens, depending which way we go. With the fifth dimension, we should reach the ice world in five standard days. That's the real reason jumping dimensions is outlawed. It would allow for real war to happen, for the Edge planets to attack Earth. There are patrols that police each of them, mutants like you and me who have been bred to slave for the Ascendant. Their only purpose is to stop this kind of travel."

Alistair's training took over, forcing his next question. "Will we meet one of the patrols?"

Theos shrugged. "We may. We're prepared. The AllMother thought long and hard about this, apparently. More resources than you can imagine have been put into bringing you to the ice world."

"Why?" Alistair asked.

Theos stood up. "Well, if it was my wish, it would be for a public execution that would be broadcast to every planet in the solar system. Perhaps the AllMother is listening and I'll get my wish, but I doubt it. She has something planned for you, so it's my job—and every person on this ship's job —to get you to her safely." He moved the chair to the wall and made his way to the only door in the room. "Rest. It's all you can do right now. We are bound to keep you safe, but we are not your friends, Fallen Titan. Your only friends are sleep and time so your body can heal. I'll bring more food. You drink it and then sleep. Your life has changed, but not as much as it will soon."

CHAPTER FIVE

*"Will the Subversives ever stop? No, I do not believe so.
Some people cannot be happy, thus watching the world
burn is where they find their solace."*

–Romulus de Menuchan, Third Communication
Czar, Academy Graduation Speech

Alistair understood that war had descended on the ship. It
went on for what felt like a long time, though he couldn't
know precisely. The lights shimmered on and off, and the
ship rocked with the blast of lasers hitting it. He didn't
know how deep they cut, only that his body cried out for
nourishment that didn't come. It hurt to be awake, much
worse than it had before, and he knew they were in the
fifth dimension. He tried to sleep, but the pain in his body
and his hunger kept him awake.

    If those chasing them boarded the ship, Alistair would
die. He had no idea if the mutant was telling the truth—if
the Imperial Ascendant used modified humans—but if so,

nothing would stop such strength combined with that of the Commonwealth.

Finally, though, the lights quit flickering, and the ship stopped rocking. The battle was over, and Alistair was still alive.

Theos brought him the ashy white substance, and Alistair could see in his face that to ask questions might prove fatal. He'd seen the look before in other warriors and knew it meant this mutant had lost friends. People this man loved had died, and it was because of Alistair. He drank the liquid and said nothing when it was taken away.

After the mutant left, Alistair was alone. He slept much of the time, and during the rest of it, he thought. About Luna, his wife. Wondering what she thought had happened to him, if she was okay, if Control had decided to take its vengeance out on her. If he ever did get back to her, would she see him as the same man, or only as a mutant? As "less than?" Would she recognize that he'd done it only to see her face again? He thought about his life and how quickly everything had changed in moments. *Mere moments.*

But wasn't that always how it went? The things that moved a person from one point to another, changes that seemed galaxy-spanning, took only seconds to occur. Here he was, in some terrorist's ship, traveling to an unknown planet where hostile forces waited for him, hunted by the very Commonwealth he had spent his life serving.

The buzz in his body changed frequency, pulling Alistair from his thoughts. They'd dropped from the fifth dimension to the fourth.

Then the buzz dropped away altogether. They'd

reached the third dimension, meaning they were nearly to Pluto. Alistair had made it, but what did that mean?

Before his mind could supply an answer, the door to his room opened. Theos stood before him. The ache of battle still claimed his face, but this time he spoke. "We've got our next orders. You're to meet the AllMother."

Alistair cleared his throat. It'd been a while since he'd spoken, and his voice felt weak. "About what?"

"Most likely, she wants to see if you can get her cheaper oysters. Ice fishing on Pluto is a real bitch."

Alistair's eyes opened wide for a second, not understanding, then he saw the tiniest smirk from the mutant.

"I don't know, Fallen Titan," Theos said. "You're smarter than you're acting. I'm not exactly your counterpart, but close enough for Commonwealth work. Did you know everything behind the orders you were given?" The mutant shook his head. "No, and neither do I."

He closed the door behind him, stepping farther into the room.

"What I do know is this, *great Odin*. I've never met the AllMother. I've served her for a decade and never once been blessed by her presence. This is a precious honor being bestowed upon you, and though I know you don't recognize it, someone should tell you. She is the closest thing to a god the human race now knows, and she's wiser than you can ever imagine. If you lie to her, Titan, she'll know."

Alistair stared at the man, feeling the almost palpable reverence he held toward this AllMother. He didn't know how to respond. He was trapped on a table in a body he couldn't see, one that wasn't truly his, floating just above a planet that was as alien to him as any foreign galaxy. All he could find to say was perhaps the dumbest thing, a simple, "Okay."

The big man looked at the deck. "Do you know where that term comes from, Fallen Titan? Back before the Ascendency, there were great wars on Earth. In one of them, one they called the First World War, they used primitive means to communicate—but even then, the death of their loved ones mattered. The United States empire used a code, and every morning their soldiers would wait on words to come through a certain code known as morse. The code they wanted to know was the number of people killed, so any time it came back as zero-k, it was a good morning. It was an 'okay' morning." He looked at Alistair. "It hasn't been okay for me and mine for a long while, Alistair. Prepare to meet the AllMother, and hope she didn't bring you all this way to make an example of you."

The ship landed at the planet's only dock without any problems. Alistair didn't get to see it; indeed, they didn't come for him until the ship had been emptied. He was the last one to disembark, and of course, it was Theos who came for him.

"Come on, Fallen Titan. It's time to get you to the ball."

He stepped to the back of Alistair's chair. The former Titan couldn't see what was happening, but he heard the touch of fingers on a keypad, then the release of compressed air beneath him. The chair rose a few inches off the ground, surprising him some. He probably shouldn't have been shocked—given that these outlaws had just jumped dimensions—so clearly they had some technology—but this seemed a bit gratuitous for those being hunted.

How well have you *been hunting them, Allie?* his wife's voice whispered inside his head, using her secret name for him—the one she always used when playfully mocking. *Have you been doing such a good job if they've got toys like this?*

The mutant stepped back around to the front of what was obviously an airchair, but he didn't pause. He moved to the door and pulled it open, then stepped through. The chair beneath Alistair started moving, appearing to follow the mutant. "Woah, wait a second. Wait. Stop."

Theos turned around, red eyes gleaming with secret knowledge.

Alistair's chair stopped too. "How did you do that? Is it following you?"

"What do you think, Titan?"

Alistair saw it then, the metallic twinkle in his red iris. The right one. It said the mutant's mind was communicating with the piece of equipment beneath Alistair. Not just that, but controlling it. It took something that was already wrong into the realm of grotesque. "Did you do this to me?"

"What if I did?" the mutant asked. "Would it matter?"

"*Yes,*" Alistair spat. "I'm not selling my soul for survival."

"What do you think you've been selling all this time, Fallen Titan?" The metallic dots in his iris twinkled in and out. "You certainly weren't selling sweet buns. If I were you, I'd hope you have some soul left to bargain with. Otherwise, this life may get even more unpleasant for you than it already has." The mutant turned to the corridor and started walking through the ship again, Alistair's chair following.

He didn't know if the mutant had given him the same capabilities. He could only hope that it wasn't so. A bastardization of the grandiosity of men, never happy with their place but always wanting more. Not content to control the solar system, but now wanting their mind to control things it had no business controlling.

The chair wound through the ship. Alistair could see where it had been breached by railgun projectiles. The oxygen must have been sucked out of large areas of the ship, and vacuum protocols had activated. He realized again that people had died to protect him—or at least, died to follow their AllMother's directives.

The mutant didn't attempt to put a hood or mask on Alistair's face. He let him see everything, including when they exited the ship. They were in a large hangar, the only ship docked inside it. Alistair didn't *know* why that was, but there were multiple possible reasons: distance of Pluto from other planets, the need to hide such ships from him, etc.

There wasn't anyone waiting for them in the hangar, just Alistair and the mutant crossing alone. Alistair took in everything around him as quickly as possible, his training kicking into gear. The hangar was sealed since the ice world's climate would kill humans without the proper attire. Alistair knew that Pluto had been partially terraformed, but not nearly to the level of Mars or other moons in the solar system.

Truthfully, he didn't know much about this place and

wasn't sure if those who lived here did it above or under-ground. Pluto had been such a small part of his life, it might not have existed at all.

They left the hangar and entered a small corridor. The chair moved at a constant pace about ten feet behind Theos. He never once looked back to check on it, but Alistair knew he didn't need to. It was all inside his head, a corruption of the human brain.

Alistair paid attention to the slant of the corridor, which told him they were going slightly down. Rather than terraforming the surface, it appeared these Subversives had made their home inside of this ice and rock.

Eventually, the mutant came to a stop. There'd only been one passageway the entire time, and it was small, Theos' head nearly scraping the ceiling. Perhaps they had dug into the world, but they were sparing with their efforts.

The corridor continued on, but Theos stood in front of a single skinny door. It looked like Alistair's chair would barely fit through it. "This is where I leave you, Fallen Titan. Your future lies behind that door, however long it might last."

"What's in there?"

The mutant shrugged. "Never been inside." He reached forward and scanned his hand on a panel to the left. The door slid into the wall. "My security clearance would not have worked here before. You're special cargo, Odin."

The chair started moving and in a moment's time, Alistair had passed the plane from hallway to room. The door shut behind him with enough speed to chop a man in half.

An octagonal tower stood in front of Alistair, touching

both the ceiling and the floor of this new room. A man was leaning against it, staring at Alistair. His eyes weren't red but the cold ice-blue of someone born on Pluto. Alistair had only ever seen one Plutonian before; they were strange-looking humans when compared with Earth. They were taller and lankier due to the decreased gravity on the smaller planet, and over generations, their DNA had altered significantly from their Earth brethren.

This man was a little over two meters tall and held his arms crossed over his chest. He was taller but thinner than Alistair, or at least the body the former Titan remembered. He had no idea what this thing beneath the blanket looked like.

"Why am I here?" Alistair asked.

The man said nothing in return, only appeared to be studying him with a disdainful expression. As if he didn't want Alistair to be important, but since he was, he'd like to know why.

Alistair sighed. He glanced down with his eyes, still unable to move from his neck down, and stared at the unknown lap that sat beneath the blanket. "Look, I didn't ask for any of this. I don't have any control here. Either tell me why I'm here or kill me or throw me on the tundra outside. I'm tired, and I'm tired of not knowing anything."

The tall man swallowed and straightened. He kept facing Alistair but put his thumb on a panel behind him. It lit up red as it scanned his print, then flashed green. The sound of quickly moving air filled the room, and Alistair finally understood what was behind the tall man—an elevator, though one powered by different mechanisms than Earth's.

The octagon's walls slowly folded in on each other until only a platform remained. The man stepped out of the way, making room for Alistair's chair to float onto the platform.

"I'm not sure what all they've told you, but I'm not exactly capable of moving right now, so you're going to have to help out here."

The Plutonian didn't seem annoyed as he walked behind the chair. He briefly touched the datapad behind Alistair's head and the chair moved toward the platform, then he followed, standing at an angle so he could look at Alistair.

No weapons, the former Titan observed, which meant that they were confident he wasn't a threat to him. Wherever they were delivering him out here in this icy wilderness, he couldn't touch them.

The platform started rising, which wasn't what Alistair had expected. He'd figured they would go deeper into the planet. As they passed through the room's ceiling, Alistair saw dark ice surrounding him on all sides. The insulating material between him and it was more technology he didn't understand—but otherwise, he would have frozen to death immediately—the air in his lungs expanding so fast his chest would have exploded through his ribcage.

A small white light shone down on him. "Where are we going? Are you taking me to the AllMother?"

That caused his tall companion to laugh, but he didn't respond otherwise. Rather, he let the silence return, and the elevator continued to rise. Eventually, it passed the last of the ice and came to a stop on what appeared to be the planet's outer crust. Alistair's eyes widened as he looked around. The elevator was encased in a bubble. Though that might not have been the correct word, it was the first thing that came to his mind.

He didn't know what the material surrounding him was, nor the technology that kept the cold outside, allowing him to sit here with only this blanket covering his broken body.

As he looked around, he realized he was actually in a room. There were couches to his left and a fire pit in front of them, where flames licked artificial logs. Alistair was lost on how ventilation occurred inside the bubble. A wet bar sat to his right, though the furnishings were mostly lost on him. Only the trained killer part of his mind kept up with them; the active part of his mind stared *outside* the bubble.

He'd only seen images of this world and a few videos, but none of them did *this* justice. In the far distance, he could see lights from some outpost. He looked to his left and saw something similar on that side, and between those two barren points of light? A world of black ice. The light from inside his bubble cast out a few hundred meters, allowing Alistair to see a ragged world made not of rock but of frozen nitrogen and other chemicals. He saw no farms, no terraforming, nothing that could sustain life on this cold, lost planet.

Alistair had momentarily lost track of the man who brought him here, but his mind wouldn't allow it for long. He caught him out of the corner of his eye, the man having moved to the edge of the bubble. His eyes hadn't left Alistair.

"Do you like our home?"

The voice that carved those five words into existence

sounded as if it had never known pain or heartache. As if the cold ice did not exist outside these transparent walls.

Alistair tried to jerk his head around to see where the voice came from, but his body still wasn't responding to his commands. All he could do was move his eyes to the side, but the woman who spoke was too far behind him for him to see.

"It's a bit different than the place you were born, yes? I've never been to Earth. I've only seen what holovids show us. I'm curious what your thoughts of this place are so far."

Alistair still wanted to see what kind of creature could speak in so lovely a voice on a world so fierce, but it was useless to try to turn his head. "How many people live on this planet?" he asked.

"Oh, you Earthers call us a planet now?" The woman laughed. "I thought we were just an asteroid. News travels slowly out here, but I suppose it would make little sense for Earth to need to have dominion over an asteroid, thus Planet Pluto. There are about fifty thousand people that live here."

He got it, or at least thought he did. "Most of the travel occurs beneath ground. Even the dock we arrived on, it's beneath the ground, isn't it?" He looked at the lights in the distance. "Those areas out there are only a very small subset of the people who live here because regardless of how hard it is to terraform underneath the ground, living on this tundra would be all but impossible."

The woman clapped. "Not all brawn. That's a good sign." Alistair heard her footfalls cross the room until she circled around the platform he still sat on. He focused on her, taking in each detail as he would in a combat zone.

She was tall for a woman, though shorter than the male at the edge of the room. Her hair was red, combed straight, and fell to her shoulders. She wore clothes that were different from any he'd ever seen in person, from a past that was long dead. Two straps held the piece of cloth to her shoulders, and the rest draped down her body. He couldn't remember the name of it, though he'd seen holos of them before. "My ancestors carved out this place after the Fleeing. We don't have a WorldBreaker, or at least not the kind the Commonwealth uses, but we've made do. You're told that Earth made its way outward from Mars and Jupiter and so on, but that isn't true."

She turned around and looked outside the bubble, though it was impossible to tell where her eyes landed.

"You're wrong about one detail, though. We didn't build beneath the ground out of ease. We did it to hide. If the Imperial Ascendent had seen my ancestors here, he would have destroyed the whole planet rather than allow one single *Subversive*, as they call us, to live." She turned back around. "Do you know why?"

Alistair couldn't tell how old the woman was, not exactly. He understood that lower gravity allowed people to live longer, but she appeared to be younger than him by twenty years—or at least what his body *used* to look like.

The woman snapped her fingers, her friendly countenance suddenly turning cold. "Do you know why they wouldn't have let one of us live?"

He blinked, coming back to the present. "Be...Because you would take lives. You would kill others. The same as you do now."

The woman's cold expression melted, and a warm

smile took over. She moved gracefully to one of the couches on Alistair's left. "No, Titan. It has nothing to do with murder. It's because we are a virus, but not of the body. Of the mind." She tapped her temple with her right index finger. "If even one of us was allowed to live, we would spread. And spread we have, and perhaps they saw that one day, someone like you would end up here with us."

"Are you her?" Alistair asked. "The AllMother?"

The woman laughed, looking more like a girl as she did, and flicked her eyes to the other man. She held his gaze for a moment before looking back at Alistair. "No. You could say I'm something of a right hand to the AllMother. An envoy, if you like."

Alistair's eyes narrowed. "The mutant said I was meeting her. Who are you, and why am I here?"

The woman's smile didn't die, though malevolent fire lit behind her eyes. "I'd be careful how you throw that word around. You have been told what we want you to know when we want you to know it. You will not see the AllMother until she deems it appropriate, and she has not yet. Be glad you are in the room with either of us, for it is more than anyone on this planet thinks you worthy of."

Alistair swallowed. He'd forgotten his eyes were red. He'd forgotten the monstrosity that lay beneath these blankets. "Who are you? Who's your errand boy behind me?"

The fire in her eyes died and the sweet smile returned, but Alistair knew the honey was laced with poison. "My name is Servia. The man behind you is Thoreaux. While I do wish he was my errand boy, I cannot claim such."

"Why did you do this?" Alistair asked. He searched the

room with his eyes. "Why did you do all of this? Bring me here? Turn me into this monstrosity?"

Servia rapped her knuckles on the cold steel armrest. "No, no. We did nothing. We gave you choices, and you made decisions that led you here."

"Why?" Alistair practically yelled.

The woman turned her head and looked outside the bubble again. "The AllMother thinks it is time for our virus to finish spreading. She's ready to finish what she began."

Alistair heard the man's—Thoreaux's—footsteps as he walked over to the couch. He didn't sit down but found Alistair's eyes. "We need to show you the truth, Titan. Before anything else happens, the truth must be shown."

"I want to be able to move before anything else happens," Alistair responded. "I'm tired of living like this."

Thoreaux looked at Servia. She studied Alistair for a moment, then glanced at the outside world again. "No. You will see the truth first, then you can decide if you still want to be fixed."

Alistair wanted to jump out of his chair and throw this lady through the reinforced bubble around them, yet his rage was useless. "Then show me now, because I will not abide being an invalid any longer. I'd rather be dead."

Servia gave a wicked smile. "You may get your wish sooner than you'd like."

CHAPTER SIX

"History doesn't exist. Reality is what the human mind says it is, and programming the human mind is something we've become exceedingly adept at."

–Romulus de Menuchan, Third Communication Czar

Thoreaux obviously had no connection with inanimate objects like the other mutant, and that gave Alistair a bit of relief. He wasn't dealing with totally insane people who'd all sacrificed their humanity for power. Alistair's chair proceeded according to its programming, and Thoreaux stayed behind it as the two moved through the underground passageways. The tunnels were small, as the first one had been, and Alistair didn't see another soul.

His pain was well-managed, and the chair kept to a pace that didn't put any stress on his joints or muscles. He couldn't move, but he didn't feel like he was dying either. Thoughts of his wife Luna tried to force their way

DAVID BEERS & MICHAEL ANDERLE

into his mind, but he knew he couldn't entertain them now. Not here in this underground world with people who seemed undecided about whether he would live or die.

"You're not much of a talker, huh?" he asked his silent escort.

"What is there to say?"

The chair took a left.

"You must have some thoughts you'd like to express," Alistair responded.

"Not to you. Enough ideas will be imparted to you shortly."

Alistair gave up on conversation. Whoever this man was, he'd give up no more information. Alistair could admire that.

They eventually reached another hollowed-out room with an elevator. It opened up, and the two got on. A minute or so later, they were in another bubble, though this one completely black. Alistair realized he wouldn't have been able to see it from the first one. It was invisible on the black ice. How many of these bubbles existed, the ones that couldn't be seen?

The chair continued floating forward without being told. Thoreaux moved to the other side of the bubble until the entire room separated them.

"Holo on," the tall man told the empty space.

The room turned into a holovid. Only a foot of space separated Alistair from it, and he could no longer see Thoreaux.

"Everything you think you know is a lie." The Plutonian's voice boomed across the room, louder than Alistair would have thought possible. "This is history as you've been told it."

The holovid flashed to a city of old. Alistair thought he recognized it from his history lessons, the New York, or something like that. The buildings were tall by historical standards, though they were almost miniature by modern day.

Alistair knew what came next. Everyone alive did. The holovid zoomed out, the city and its surrounding neighborhoods growing smaller. Something burned across the air, streaking toward the city. The hologram zoomed out again, and the vast sky was filled with missiles streaking back and forth across continents. When they hit the ground, mushroom clouds burst upward, dotting the holovid like gray fungi.

Thoreaux's voice filled the room again. "You were told that Demockracy caused this. The move to Demockracy across the planet caused the rise of individualism, reinforcing nation-states that warred with each other for sparse resources and land."

The holovid zoomed in again, back to the city that had been shown before. Gone were the towering buildings and cars jammed on the roads. Smoke and shattered structures filled the view. Bodies littered the streets, flesh burnt off the bones. Child and adult skulls were the only traces that humanity had ever walked this place. Not a single bird flew through the sky.

"Civilization ended in nuclear war, in which the world was pushed out of most of its major cities. The world population was reduced by fifty percent in a single week. It was then that the first Imperial Ascendant rose out of the ashes, a phoenix to save mankind." His voice was mocking as the holo switched to a government-produced video.

The Primus Imperial Ascendant. One hundred years after the massive destruction of the world, Aurelius de Finita rose, taking the name of his Roman forebears. In the holovid, he was the image of perfection, blond hair swept to the side, jawline cut from granite, eyes showing a fierceness that it seemed impossible for man to possess.

The holovid showed the words that every school-age child on Earth had memorized. "One People. One Purpose."

A Whip hung from Aurelius' right hand, its red tentacles waving.

Thoreaux spoke again. "Primus Imperial Ascendant and Primus Titan. He saved mankind, and since then, everything has been perfect, except for the pesky 'Subversives' who want Demockracy back so we can begin subjugating people again. So we can restart the Great Devastation." His chuckle made its way across the room as if to shame Aurelius de Finita. "And since then? Since mankind's savior died? His bloodline has continued, ruling humanity as it conquered the solar system and now prepares to move farther into the Milky Way."

That was exactly as Alistair had been taught. He knew the face in front of him, knew the pledge that all Earthborn said: One People. One Purpose.

The holovid ended, and Alistair blinked. He looked across the room and saw Thoreaux standing with his hands crossed in front of him. His eyes glowed in the dimming lights. "It's all a lie, Titan. Nearly all of it, at least. Aurelius existed, but the man you just saw in front of you, the statues built to him? They aren't him. They're myths created to prop up the Commonwealth."

Thoreaux moved his right hand to the side, palm facing Alistair. "Would you like to see the truth, Odin of Earth?"

Alistair was not Odin right now, not even a quarter of that man, but that wasn't the question. Did he want to see the truth? As if this all wasn't their propaganda, and he was going to buy it wholesale.

The holovid lit up again, filling the room and blocking out Thoreaux. This time it wasn't a single image that he saw, but a multitude of them. There were scenes of war, scenes of peaceful protests, scenes of mothers and their children. Alistair watched as all of humanity's emotions played out in front of him.

"There was war, yes, but there was also peace. There was hatred..." next was a scene of a dark-skinned man being hung from a tree, "and there was love." A dark-skinned man at a pulpit of some kind stood outside with thousands of people in front of him and a rectangular pool in the middle. It was an image Alistair had never seen before. "The war that supposedly took place never did."

The image changed to a street with buildings on either side. Thoreaux was at the end of the street, and he walked into the hologram, coming closer to Alistair. "Do you know how many cities were allegedly attacked with nuclear weapons, Titan?"

"Twenty-five."

Still inside the hologram, Thoreaux nodded. "That's right. Twenty-five major cities across five world powers. Do you know the death toll?"

"Eighty percent inside each city."

"You've been a good little student," Thoreaux said with a smirk. "Though I know every man and woman on Earth has been taught these things since birth. It's necessary to keep the power structures in place." The hologram moved from a cityscape to a desert. Alistair could see nothing but sand in every direction. The Plutonian looked to be standing in the middle of it, the hologram adapting to his shoes, making the sand wrap slightly around them. "Do you know anyone who's ever been to one of the attacked cities?"

Alistair laughed. "Of course. I've been to two of them myself."

Thoreaux looked down at his feet. "Do you know anyone who's been to every one of them? All twenty-five?"

"No. That's impossible. Five of them still haven't been opened. It'll be another hundred years, at least."

The holovid morphed from sand to nuclear-created rock, and Thoreaux kept staring at it. "Yes, that's what you've been taught. Some of the sites were worse than others, the nuclear bombs stronger, the fallout worse, the ability to contain the radiation less. Five cities remain untouchable. Do you know what they used to be called?"

"No," Alistair responded.

Thoreaux rattled them off. "Beijing. Washington, DC. Moscow. Brasilia. Jerusalem." He looked up. "No one in a thousand years has gone to those areas and returned, and you believe it's due to radiation. Look." The hologram changed again, this time showing an aerial view of Quadrant One on Earth—a satellite viewpoint. "I'm standing where Washington, DC used to exist. This is what you're told it looks like from space. It isn't." The gray, diseased circle on the eastern side of Quadrant One faded away, replaced by a black hole. "This is what it actually looks like from space, or at least what it looked like ten years ago. We were able to hack the satellites, and you can't see anything inside those five cities. No gray, no green, no lights, only this blackness you see before you. They patched the hack, so we don't know what it looks like now, but I don't need to tell you what makes a black hole like this. We both know it's not nuclear warfare."

A StealthBlanket, Alistair thought. "That's not possible. They can't make one that large, and not over five cities."

Thoreaux shrugged. "Then why was it the only possibility your mind came up with? And why is the area black?" The holovid faded, leaving a pale blue light just below Thoreaux. "Everything you know is a lie, and even after a thousand years, we don't know the truth, Alistair. There was no nuclear war. There was no destruction of humanity, at least not the way you were taught. The de Finita family lineage rules because of a lie, and they rule with force. They rule through people such as you."

Thoreaux walked forward and stopped a few feet in front of Alistair. "That's the truth as we know it. There's more—more details, more information, more convincing evidence—but that's the overview. What you choose to do with it? That's up to you."

Alistair stared at the blue glow that had just created the grand piece of propaganda. "I'm supposed to believe all this? Your sales pitch?"

"What got you into this situation?" Thoreaux asked. "Why are you here?"

Alistair looked at the Plutonian's pale blue eyes. It was

the one thing he hadn't considered since this started. He'd been too focused on surviving, on Luna, and on this hellish modification. "You know why. It's why you got me off Earth. Because I let some of *your* kind go."

Thoreaux chuckled. "*My* kind. What happened to One People, One Purpose?" He waved away the question. "What did they tell you, Titan? What made you let them go?"

Alistair blinked and glanced outside the bubble, staring at the other little bubbles of light in the distance. "It was a couple. They showed me a holovid. They showed me their kids, two of them. They said their kids were waiting on them to come back to Europa. Back to Jupiter's moon."

Thoreaux squatted so that he was nearly eye-level with Alistair. His Plutonian body was still a bit taller, but it was close. "I thought it was a suicide mission, Titan. I told the AllMother that myself. Sending them to be caught by you in order to tell you *that*? I said we were killing our own for something pointless because you wouldn't listen. You wouldn't care. The AllMother ignored me and sent them anyway."

Alistair wanted to shake his head, but he couldn't. That didn't make sense. "You're saying you planned it? You sent two people to Earth to get caught in some makeshift Subversive terrorist attack just to see if I'd let them go because they had *kids*? What kinda bullshit do you think I'll believe?"

Thoreaux's face was deathly still. "I planned nothing. The AllMother did. She sent them and they went, knowing they'd probably die, killed by the greatest Titan's hand without a care. They did it because *she* asked, and you let them go. Tell me why you did that."

"I don't know."

"Yes, you do. Now tell me."

Alistair wanted to spit on this man for questioning him. "Because their kids had nothing to do with *this*." Vitriol dripped from his words. "Because their parents might be cretins, and I might be a killer, but those kids..."

He shook his head, his teeth gritted. "Those kids are neither. Not yet, and if I killed their parents, where would they end up? Probably just like them, just like you—murderers. I did it because I've killed a lot, and maybe not killing two nothings could make the universe a bit better."

He looked down, coming to grips with what he'd done. With all he'd lost. Perhaps even thrown away. And for what reason? "I don't expect someone like you to understand it. If I killed their parents, those children would grow up to be the same. They'd grow up to hate me and the Commonwealth. They'd grow up and probably fight my progeny one day. I let those two Subversives go because I thought maybe two parents living and raising their children would be a benefit to the solar system."

Alistair looked up, the anger returning. "I *certainly* didn't do it out of any belief in you or your Subversives. I didn't think I'd get caught. I thought the room was clean, but I should have known better. They *did* catch me, and I fucking lost everything. My whole life, because I let a few of you live. I deserved what the Commonwealth did to me. I betrayed an oath and a code. The *only* reason I tried to escape was that I love my wife."

He paused.

"I did it because I want to see her again, and if I had

died in that building, that chance died with me. I'll do almost anything to see her again."

Thoreaux dropped his eyes. "Love is a funny thing, isn't it? It'll make good men do evil things, and evil men do good." He looked up. "Which one are you, Titan?"

A month ago, Alistair would have had an answer. Now he opened his mouth to speak, but no words came.

THE WRITTEN HISTORY OF THE GREAT INSURRECTION

It is probably necessary to describe the economics behind the false narrative that is the Great Devastation. Throughout human history, despots have risen and tried to enforce slavery or harsh nationalization of private enterprise. These types of economic systems can only last very short periods and only in very specific circumstances. Namely, when there are new worlds to be discovered, and thus new resources. My history of the human species is not as constrained as the Earthborn, so I recognize that much of England's rise in the Middle Ages had to do with their ability to extract resources from other lands. The nationalization of Germany's economy during the twentieth century was only successful when there was a war to fight.

Eventually, though, on a single planet with limited resources, slavery and the eradication of most private enterprise will end in economic disaster.

What allowed the de Finitas to hold on to power so long has as much to do with the time they came to power as it does with the method they used to indoctrinate humanity. If not for that very specific timing, their rule would have collapsed under their ironclad control of the economy.

However, space travel became almost commonplace shortly after Aurelius de Finita took control of the planet. The desire to discover what existed on other planets beyond probes or landers took the world by storm, and when de Finita-189 was found, humanity's destiny changed.

It is worth taking a moment to discuss de Finita-189, if not in a technical sense, then at least with its effects.

In short, and without any dramatic flair, de Finita-189 allowed for unlimited energy, as long as the element could be mined. Unfortunately, it's in short supply on Earth, and thus it wasn't discovered until we began colonizing Mars. At that time, terraforming was extremely slow, and the Commonwealth was showing signs of cracking. I cannot imagine the stress Aurelius de Finita must have felt, racing against time to find something—anything—that would continue his reign.

And then like manna from heaven, terraforming revealed de Finita-189, a simple molecule that was found in abundance on Mars, and even more so inside the gas giants. The need for fossil fuels, solar, wind, or any other type of energy dissipated almost overnight.

It gave the de Finitas and their benefactors a stranglehold on Earth. As long as de Finita-189 flowed, the economic crash that should have come never did. In fact, the Commonwealth's economy soared, not for one year or ten, but for a hundred, and then another hundred. Mars' terraforming allowed for not just space exploration but colonization, and de Finita-189 sped it up. From there, Jupiter's moons were colonized, and more de Finita-189 was found. The farther out humanity went, the more they found. To this day, superdreadnoughts fly beneath the swirling gasses of Jupiter, collecting the molecule.

What is not known is how Aurelius got so lucky. No scientists, no explorers, *no one* had predicted the discovery of such a radical fuel source, yet when de Finita's world seemed to be crashing around him, he stayed on course.

It is a mystery to all of humanity how he knew he'd find something as valuable at such a crucial time.

CHAPTER SEVEN

Q: "When will people be able to return to the few radioac-tive sites still remaining?"

A: "There are no plans to return to those sites. Perhaps in another thousand years, but as of now, they are off-limits to humanity."

–Question and answer with reporter and Alexander de Finita, Current Imperial Ascendant

They kept the drugs coming; Alistair remained immobile and yet was not in much pain. The mutant stopped by to check on his wounds and laid him on a cot in his small room.

"How does it look?" Alistair could only stare at the ceiling.

The mutant was silent as he moved up and down his body. "It's not great."

Fear slipped into Alistair's brain. The lack of pain had

made him forget about the damage that had been done to his body. "What do you mean, 'Not great?'"

Theos straightened up. "It means you're going to need to make your choice soon. You need the oxygen tank, or your body isn't going to survive, which also means *you're* not going to survive."

Alistair stared at the mutant's red eyes. "What choice?"

"You know what choice," Theos answered. "We've never modified anyone as old as you, and we've never waited this long for an oxygen tank. Very few survive without a tank, and none as old as you would have survived even if the modifications had been done *inside* one. Your body, as you well know, is special. However, nothing is perfect. You'll need to decide what you want to do before your body makes the decision."

"I don't understand," Alistair said. "You said this was the only way to survive the dimension jump, but now you're saying it's going to kill me?"

The mutant nodded. "Your bone structure is now ten times stronger than that of anyone born in Earth's gravity. It's a hundred times stronger than a Plutonian's who isn't put in a gravity room as a child. Your limbic system had been enhanced to a degree ordinary humans can only imagine. All of that made it possible for you to handle the crushing pressure of extra dimensions, but your body didn't *heal*. The modifications were too much for it to repair itself. Soon, your body will devour itself for resources to try and heal this damage, and in the end, your heart will give out. No amount of nutrition will stop it. Only the tank, but they're not going to give it to you until you make your choice."

"What happens if I choose to say, 'Frag the lot of you?'"

Theos shrugged, his face unconcerned. "I imagine the AllMother will give you the tank anyways. It wouldn't be much of a choice if you had to join her or die."

"And after that?" Alistair asked.

"Man, I don't know. Those are decisions I have nothing to do with. All I do know is if you don't get in a tank soon, you're done."

Alistair sighed. "Send one of her two *envoys* in. I want to talk to them."

Theos shook his head, chuckling. "If you weren't broken, I'd throw you through a wall for commanding me."

Alistair smirked. "Maybe you would, but I guarantee you're going to send them in. Now do it."

Alistair listened as Thoreaux entered the room, the door closing behind him.

"Do you know what's happened to my wife?" Alistair asked.

The tall man didn't walk into the room but remained at the door. "I do."

"Can you show me? I won't take you at your word."

Thoreaux flashed his hand over a sensor on the wall, and the lights dimmed. He lifted his wrist to his mouth and said into the holowatch, "Show me the Titan's wife." He pointed his arm at the ceiling, and the holovid sprang to live.

Luna was sitting on their porch. The sun was setting behind the house, and she sat on a rocking chair. The grass had grown too high; Alistair should have been there to cut it. She always told him he should just get a bot to do it, but he enjoyed yard work. Luna stared at the lawn, holding a cup in her lap with both hands. He couldn't see what was in it, but from her red eyes, he thought it was alcohol of some sort.

Probably vodka.

The chair wasn't rocking and the door to the house stood open, as if she'd just forgotten to close it. She slowly raised the cup to her lips, her hands shaking as she did.

A tear dropped from her eye and rolled down her face.

"Enough," Alistair demanded. "Turn it off." His own eyes were wet. "How is that possible? How can you see her from here?"

Thoreaux dropped his arm and the holovid ended. When he spoke, his voice was soft. "It's not live. The data is sent via laser. It moves almost at light speed, so there's only a slight delay. We have drones on Earth. We can see most things that are in the open if we have coordinates and even some that are closed off. What you just saw is a miniature drone at one hundred times magnification. It's real, Alistair. That was your wife around five standard hours ago."

"What are they saying about me? What is she hearing?"

"You're dead," Thoreaux whispered. "You were killed at the building we caught you at. You died a hero at the hands of Subversives. They're showing an Earth-wide broadcast about your life in two days. She's supposed to be honored at it, but she still hasn't responded to the request."

In the end, that was what made the decision for Alistair. If he was dead, he would never see Luna again. If he lived, he might be able to touch her face once more. She, who'd helped change him from the Titan the world feared to a man that a woman could love.

"If I join you, do you think I'll see her again?"

"I don't know, Titan," Thoreaux answered. "I know that if you don't join us, you won't."

Alistair blinked, his own tear falling onto his face. "How long will it take? How many years?"

"I don't know the AllMother's schedule."

Alistair sighed. It wasn't a choice, not with seeing Luna still a possibility. He'd conquer worlds to be with her, even if only for a moment.

"Let's get started," he told the Plutonian.

The elevator opened, and Thoreaux stepped into the bubble, which the Plutonians called igloos. The lights were off, which was how he preferred them. Sunlight wasn't plentiful on Pluto during the best of times, so it was safe to say Thoreaux had been born in darkness.

The Titan had understood things quicker than Thoreaux thought he would, coming to grips with the duality of life above and below ground on this distant rock. That didn't mean much to Thoreaux, not really.

It was rare that he slept in an igloo, preferring to be in the larger pods underground where rooms were shared. At twenty-eight, he understood that to have risen so high so early in life bred jealousy. Being close to those who had reason to hate him made it harder for them to do so.

Tonight, though, Thoreaux needed some separation from people. To call the day long would be like calling the universe big, a bit of an understatement. Also, things were changing faster than he felt he could keep up with. This plan...Thoreaux hadn't been aware of it until a standard week earlier, though the AllMother had put it in motion a long time ago.

Thoreaux placed his jacket on the chair and then froze. "Were you going to let me completely undress before saying something?"

Servia sat on a couch to the far left, and Thoreaux's exhaustion had allowed his training to slip. He hadn't scanned the room. If Servia were an enemy, he'd be dead by now.

"Just testing you," she said. "Wanting to make sure you're not going soft on me. I must admit it took you longer than I expected."

Thoreaux sat down in the chair, his jacket hanging off the back. He slid down it, wishing he could just fall asleep. "I'm too tired for verbal jousting, Servia. I need to sleep. The Titan agreed to come aboard, and we have the AllMother to talk to tomorrow. Can this wait?"

Servia ignored his question. "What do you think of him?"

He sighed and tilted his head at the ceiling. "I think the AllMother may have finally lost her edge."

"Blasphemer." Any levity in the woman's voice disappeared.

Thoreaux turned his palms upward in a surrendering gesture. "You asked me my thoughts. Don't get pissed when I give them to you. I have no idea what she sees in this man and no clue how he's going to further the cause. He's another body, but the number of man-hours wasted getting him has probably amounted to ten total lifetimes."

Servia stood. "What exactly are you saying, Thoreaux? That the AllMother should no longer lead us?"

"I'm saying I don't know what he's supposed to do or what I'm supposed to do with him. Don't show up here asking me these things this late at night if you don't want an honest answer."

"Will you be this honest with the AllMother when you're in front of her?"

Thoreaux didn't answer for a few moments. He was tired and grumpy, but would it extend through tomorrow? Did he really believe the AllMother's leadership should be called into question? "I'm tired, Servia. I'll tell her I think we've wasted a lot of resources if she asks, but do I still love her? Do I still follow her? Of course."

She sat back down on the couch, which was exactly what he *didn't* want to happen.

"Would you have left if I told you I would call for the AllMother's replacement tomorrow? If so, I retract my statement and put forth that one instead."

Servia waved away the comment. "I think he's the one."

Thoreaux raised his head to look at her. "He's a bit old for you to be falling in love with, or is this one of those daddy-issue things people talk about?"

"Go frag yourself. I just see more clearly than you. The AllMother is right. He's going to reverse the tide."

Thoreaux let out another sigh, relaxing his head once more. "Fine. I hope so, and if it lets me get some sleep, I'll even agree with you. He's our savior."

DAVID BEERS & MICHAEL ANDERLE

Servia stood up again and made her way to the elevator. Thoreaux would be the first to admit she seemed inexhaustible. The woman was a force of nature. His eyes tracked her as she walked, and when she reached the elevator to head below the surface, he spoke. "Hey. I hope you're right. Sincerely. I hope the AllMother is right. We need her to be."

Servia smiled, and Thoreaux understood why so many would die for her. He could forget it when he was tired and irritable, but in the radiance of her smile, it was impossible to not remember. "She will be. Get some sleep. Tomorrow we bring the Titan back from the dead."

THE WRITTEN HISTORY OF THE GREAT INSURRECTION

I've said before that this written history isn't about me; it is simply fact. However, when this is finished—and that is coming quickly—I do think some mention of my family will be important.

My father's name was Nero, and he came from a family of prestige. He would not have liked to have his family name associated with him in the written form, however, so I will not place it in here. My father would have wanted it to be forgotten by history that he came from that lineage, and I imagine that the rest of the family wants the same.

He was the only one to join the AllMother. The rest of his family disowned him, some even turning him into the Commonwealth. Luckily, my father had the resources to make it off Earth and to a friendlier planet.

He was younger than me when he did that, only twenty-four. He left his fortune, his loved ones, and everything he had ever known behind. I'm not sure I could, or would, have done the same thing. To leave a life of privilege for one of hardship, a life whose mission had very little chance of succeeding?

He met my mother in the AllMother's ranks. Her name was Allison, and she was perhaps more militant than my father.

I didn't grow up with them because they refused to leave the AllMother's side, which meant they refused to leave Pluto except for missions. It was her base of operations during those years, but she refused to allow children or the elderly on the planet. That meant my parents had to ship me to a foster family on one of Jupiter's moons. They came to visit a few times each year, but I didn't really know them.

The AllMother did. She's told me stories of both, but they're almost like strangers to me. Not quite legends, though to many in our movement, that is exactly what they would be termed.

Perhaps I write this brief chapter out of selfishness, simply wanting my parents' names to be remembered. They died before the Insurrection truly started—before Alistair Kane's name had ever been mentioned. They were killed off-planet, doing something the AllMother hadn't sanctioned. It was their single greatest failure as her generals.

I will dedicate more time to this point later, but the AllMother has been hunted her entire life, not only by the Commonwealth but by...*others*. My parents went to find them, the others who hunt our leader, and they were killed. At least, they never returned. Would they have left me? Probably. But the AllMother?

Not a chance.

It's a brief history, but that's it. They served and they died, and through their legacy, I have risen high. I am second in command under Alistair Kane, and before that, under the AllMother.

Yet, I feel their final sin lies across me. They went on that unsanctioned mission to save the AllMother from further threat. I sometimes wonder if it's in me, that willingness to disobey a superior if you feel it's for the right reason. I think the AllMother believes it is.

I wonder what he thinks, Prometheus? Alistair?

CHAPTER EIGHT

"Demockracy was tried. It failed. Humanity seeks strong leadership, and that is why the Imperial Ascendant will never disappear. My lineage will last as long as humanity."

–Aurelius de Finita, First Imperial Ascendant

Alexander de Finita sat with his back against the chair, one leg crossed over the other. He had ordered the lights to dim because of what he would do after this meeting. He didn't want his eyes to have to adjust when he left here. A group of three stood before him, the man in the middle a few feet forward, while the other two remained behind him. Outside, the moon was rising, another of its almost endless trips. Sometimes Alexander felt jealousy toward the moon, as silly as the thought might have been. It had an unending job, but it was a simple one. It was the simplicity Alexander envied.

"Given that you three are standing here, I imagine the words you're going to tell me aren't what I want to hear."

Only one of the three men kept his head raised, the one in the middle. The one Alexander had pinned so many of the Commonwealth's hopes on. Ares. "No, my liege."

"Go ahead and tell me of your failure then, young Titan. Do not make me guess."

"Our intelligence reports that Odin—"

"*No*," the Imperial Ascendant snapped. "He no longer holds that name, and if you use it once more in my presence, you will join him in being stripped of that which you've earned."

Ares nodded. "Yes, my liege. Our intelligence reports that *Alistair Kane* made it to Pluto. All evidence conclusively shows it was a Subversive mission. The ship we attacked in the fifth dimension scanned as the same one which left Earth under the guise of body transfers."

"Pluto..." Alexander let the word linger in the air. He didn't remove his eyes from Ares. The boy wonder. Barely twenty-six years old, yet lethal in a way that had never been seen in the human species. "And pray tell, Ares, what plans are in place to retrieve the traitor or to have him killed."

The Titan blinked. "Pardon, my liege? To retrieve or kill?"

Alexander broke eye contact and looked around the room. It was circular, with floor to ceiling windows, and it was so high in the sky, its occupants hung amidst the clouds. Against the walls, standing six feet apart, was his Praetorian Guard in full MechSuits. Alexander raised his hands to show off those around him. "Do you think these men and women in attendance on me are here because I'm a person with a lot of time?"

"Excuse me, my liege, I do not understand."

The Ascendant's eyes went back to the man in front of him. "Do you think I have a lot of time, Ares? Do you think my position allots me the blessing of idleness?"

"No, my liege."

"When you ask me to repeat myself," Alexander said, "you are inherently saying my time is like that of a child's. I assure you, good sir, it is not. So please answer my question."

Alexander saw the rage rise in the young man. He had as much arrogance as talent, though the Ascendant would snuff out at least one of those. To the Titan's credit, his voice was controlled when he spoke. "There are no plans, my liege. Pluto is seven billion kilometers from us, and even if Alistair is a mutant now, there has been no threat from the Edge planets. Their docks are virtually nonexistent."

Alexander placed his arms on the chair's armrests. "Hear me, and hear me well, my young Titan. Whatever it takes to destroy this man, I want it done. If the planet of Pluto must be burnt, every inch of it razed, then that is what we shall do. How long will it take you to have the First and Second Fleets there?"

"Fourth-dimension travel, two standard weeks."

"Then in fifteen standard days, I want you to report back to me either that you have proof Kane is dead or that Pluto no longer exists. Do you understand me, young Titan?"

Ares dropped to one knee, lowering his head. The other

two Titans followed his lead. "Yes, my liege. As you wish, so it shall be. One People. One Purpose."

"One People. One Purpose," the Ascendant repeated. "You are released."

The three stood and did an about-face, then walked out of the room, their royal blue capes billowing slightly behind them. As the doors closed, silence fell across the room. Alexander was virtually never alone since the Praetorians guarded him twenty-four hours a day, but he no longer saw them. They were more or less furniture to him. His entire life from birth until this very second had been preparing him for what was to come. Those who just left the room might see what he was doing as insanely cruel, and very shortly, he would begin a messaging strategy with the communication Czar to ensure the Commonwealth's compliance.

The truth of the matter was that the Ascendant's next decisions would be the most important he ever made. Indeed, he above anyone else understood the importance of what had just happened.

It had always been a possibility that the Subversives would attempt to capture Kane, but the Prediction Algorithms showed it at a very low percentage. Only now, only after the Titan's escape from Earth, had the algorithms increased its likelihood.

Eighty-seven percent.

The AllMother, Alexander thought as he rose from his chair. *The old bitch finally made her move, and during my reign.*

He walked down the steps in front of his throne and

headed to the back of the circular room. The Praetorians remained frozen. None but the Imperial Ascendant could enter the next room.

He reached the edge of the circular room and stepped onto a square roughly twice as large as his two feet. It looked like any other polished stone in the room, and even if someone knew where it went, it wouldn't matter. Once on the square, the Ascendant knelt and placed his right thumb on it. He felt the particles moving beneath him, swiping the tiniest bit of his DNA to verify for admission.

He stood, his DNA the only one in the entire galaxy that would open the next door. It would be that way until his son rose to be the Imperial Ascendant, then Alexander's access would be denied. It had been so since the Devastation and would continue until the end of time if Alexander had any control over it.

The block beneath his feet turned neon-purple, then rose. Alexander didn't turn around to look at the room behind him but continued staring out the window as the block took him to the top of the room. Just before his head collided with the ceiling, the surface shimmered and disappeared.

No Praetorians glanced upward. They stared forward as if nothing had changed.

The block paused on the other side of the ceiling. It shimmered once more, a twinkling thing, then Alexander was on a solid floor. He stepped off the block, alone in a room that his ancestors had built and now entrusted to him.

There were no windows. The walls were the royal

purple of his family, though they were completely bare. This room was as holy a place as someone in the Commonwealth could step, yet only one thing was inside it beside the Ascendant.

Alexander knelt, bowing his head. "My Lords," he said to the room's only other occupant. "We are moving forward with the traitor's execution. One way or another, he will never make it off the ice world."

The voice that returned in answer sounded human in a certain way. It was as if nine humans were speaking the same words at the same time.

Because they were.

"For the sake of us all, I hope you're right, Imperial Ascendant."

Basara xi Simpose met the Imperial Ascendant on the patio. The patio was one hundred floors up at the Imperial Ascendant's personal residence, and Basara never liked being called here. He paused for a brief moment as he stepped out onto the terrace, looking at the Ascendant sitting alone at a glass table. A salad plate had been pushed to the side, most of it finished, the fork and napkin lying across the top of it. Basara immediately recognized there was no second plate of salad, so this wasn't a leisure call.

"Salve, my Communication Czar. How does the day treat you?" the Ascendant called without looking over his shoulder.

"Well, my liege. Thank you for asking. And you?" Basara walked across the terrace. Praetorian Guards stood around the edge at about fifty paces. Each one wore a MechSuit, and Basara could see their HUDs outside their helmets. It was the Ascendant who had decided the HUD should appear outside rather than in the helmet. He wanted to know when they were on.

"I'm vexed, Basara." The Ascendant crossed one leg over the other and pointed at the empty chair on the other side of the table. "Please, sit."

Basara took the chair and turned it as the Ascendant had his turned, looking out the glass-windowed terrace. The clouds were parting in front of them, and Basara could see the buildings surrounding this one. None were quite as high, but all were a testament to humanity's strength.

"You're a true believer, aren't you, Basara?"

He cocked his head to the side. "In what, my liege?"

"The Commonwealth." The Ascendant didn't turn to look at him but continued staring forward. "I know you fear me, but that's to be expected. You didn't go through the Foundation like my Titans or Praetorians. Your path to the top was strictly intellect, no brawn."

The Ascendant waved a hand as if to say such a thing didn't matter.

"It's a perfectly respectable way to get to the top. The Commonwealth takes all types to run it so efficiently. Your fear is perfectly acceptable, but your loyalty to the Commonwealth is absolute, am I right?"

Basara was stunned. The two of them had never spoken about his fear, nor his route to Communication Czar. Nothing got by the man. Basara didn't know about his intellect, but he understood a ruthless cleverness rested inside the man's head. To lie to this man would mean death.

"Yes, my liege. The Commonwealth has given me everything. It has given humanity everything. I—we all—owe it our lives, and anything less would go against everything I've been brought up to believe."

The Ascendant nodded. "That is what I thought. It's good. It's why I've called you here today, if you need to know the truth, Basara. If I didn't think you could do the job I'm going to put before you, I would have you removed from office." The Ascendant met his eyes. "You understand that, right? I would have to do it for the Commonwealth's sake?"

Basara nodded, though he didn't know what Alexander was talking about. "I understand, my liege."

Again, the nod. Basara thought the man was considering something, but he said nothing. He waited in silence for the leader of the human race to tell him what this meeting was about.

"We are going to burn Pluto to ash, Basara."

The Communication Czar's lips opened slightly. He never wanted people to know what he was thinking, but he couldn't help it now. He blinked twice. "Pluto, my lord?"

"You heard of Alistair Kane's demise, yes?" the Ascendant asked.

Basara nodded, not understanding.

"It was a lie. He didn't die. He lives and is en route or has made it to Pluto. He has become a Subversive, and while everything I know doesn't concern you, burning Pluto does." He leaned over the table, his eyes boring into Basara's. "What I need from you is to construct a narrative, a story that will get the populace behind this act. There's no way to hide it from them, not on Earth or any other planet, yet we cannot tell them the truth as I'm sure you see. I'm charging you with developing that narrative and disseminating it throughout the worlds before the destruction happens."

"H-how..." Basara closed his eyes and took a deep breath, then let it out slowly. He'd never done *anything* like this in front of the Imperial Ascendant. When he opened his eyes again, he had more control over himself, though the Ascendant was still staring at him. "How is it going to burn, my liege?"

"Most likely plasma and nuclear warfare. A mixture. Is that important?"

Basara nodded, his mind naturally finding the words and reasoning that had allowed him to rise so high inside the communication channels. "The populace will hear what weapons we used, and the more severe they are, the stronger our reasons must be, my liege."

The Ascendant smiled and leaned back in his chair, his look softening. "That was what I wanted to hear, Basara. Is this a narrative you can create? Do you think the populace will believe it?"

"When do we need it by?"

Still smiling, the Ascendant said, "Yesterday."

"With all due respect, my liege, I ask to leave this meeting then. There's a lot of work to be done."

The Ascendant rubbed his hands together. "Very well. I look forward to seeing what you create, Basara."

"Thank you, my lord." Basara stood. His mind was focused because the Commonwealth needed him. Some might call Basara an ant, someone scurrying around to feed the queen, sacrificing his life for that of the colony. Basara didn't care what such people said, though, because if you weren't willing to sacrifice for the Commonwealth, you weren't worth the air you breathed.

CHAPTER NINE

"Will we ever let Mutants apply to the Academy? Would a wolf ever let a hyena into its pack? Mutants made their choice to step outside the human race, and they can live with the consequences."

–Marcus de Reespen, Current Primus Academy Director

Alistair lay inside a glass tank with a plastic mask covering his mouth and nose. A tube was attached to the mask and wound its way behind him so that he couldn't see what it was attached to. The things he could see in the tank, he didn't want to.

No one had told him anything when they put him in it. He imagined pure oxygen filled the space, helping accelerate tissue growth and repair, thus the reason for the mask. Pure oxygen would have made him pass out, which would have halted the process.

Alistair wanted nothing more than to be unconscious.

Metal spiders crawled on the inside layer of the tank. He could see his body now, lying naked the length of the tank. He didn't want to see it or the things the spiders were doing to it, so he mostly kept his eyes closed. When he *did* open them...

Terror and disgust.

Perhaps a hundred spiders about the size of his palm *click-clicked* their way across the glass. How they saw, Alistair didn't know, but their hind parts would spit out some sort of webbing, then they'd drop down to his body. Their metal legs felt like tiny pinpricks on his skin as they scurried to open wounds.

Then their mandibles would get to work. Lasers and needles. Salve that Alistair didn't understand, looking like frothy spit as the metal creatures rubbed it into his wounds. Their needles sank deep down to his bones, reinforcing them to a strength that could only have developed on a world with gravity twice as heavy as Earth's.

He didn't know much time had passed. He closed his eyes and tried to block out the pain. He tried to ignore the tiny *click-clicks* from the spiders and the feel of their metal legs running across his body. Alistair's mind went to his wife, seeing her on the porch, drinking and crying. Did she believe he was dead, or did she know something more sinister was taking place? Was that why she hadn't responded to the Commonwealth's funeral requests?

Would he see her again, or would he die before he got the chance?

Would she want him like this? A mutant?

There were so many questions that he couldn't answer,

and he found himself wondering once again how he'd gotten here.

It didn't seem like it had been step-by-step. No, everything had been normal until it suddenly wasn't. Wasn't that how the worst things in life happened? The ones that brought you to your knees and had you looking at the sky and begging for help that wouldn't come? One minute the one you love is at your side, and the next, they're gone forever.

She's not gone forever, he told himself. *You will see her again.*

Alistair no longer heard the spiders crawling above him. He felt no more needles pressing on his flesh.

The tank split open, the sides falling away and the mask releasing from his mouth. His body tilted upward as the metal that had held him inside the cage rose. Alistair hung upright, and Theos stood in front of him.

He studied the former Titan's naked body. He leaned forward, pressing on his thigh where the tiny spiders had walked to and fro. The mutant turned Alistair around and focused on his hamstrings and glutes, inspecting his back muscles as well. The former Titan felt like a stockyard animal being judged before auction.

"Do I pass muster?" he asked.

The apparatus moved him to face the mutant again. Alistair tried to find an answer on his face, but it was as if Theos wore a mask. He showed nothing. He didn't attempt to meet Alistair's eyes but rather kept studying his body.

After what felt like an eternity, the mutant finally spoke. "You may be my finest work, Fallen Titan. You may be the best work I've ever seen."

Alistair blinked, not knowing what to say. Theos' red eyes twinkled, and the apparatus holding Alistair lowered him to the ground, then released him. He stood on his own two feet for the first time in what felt like ages.

"Careful," Theos said as he stepped up and grabbed Alistair's shoulder. "Your body is very, very different now, and your mind is not ready to use it. You're going to feel a bit like... Well, a bit like you're learning to walk again. Or maybe riding a hoverboard if you ever did that as a kid."

Alistair took a step forward and found out what the mutant was talking about. The neural connections that had worked for nearly forty-two years felt *off*. His foot slammed down on the floor, and his other one didn't automatically pick up to follow it.

Theos laughed. "Oh, I forgot how funny this can be."

Alistair gave him a glare. "If I could, I'd hit you right now."

Theos was still chuckling. "Calm down, Fallen Titan. You'll end up hurting yourself, and I've no desire to see this magnificent art I've created damaged. At least not until it's on the battlefield. Now, come look at what I've done for you, and then you can tell me all about how mutants are disgusting creatures that should be removed from society."

The two slowly walked across the room. Alistair paid no attention to his surroundings, just concentrated on making his body work the way it should. If he could only control himself like this, he wouldn't be worth a damn to these people.

"It'll get better," Theos said as if reading his mind. The two had reached a holographic mirror that came up from the floor next to the far wall. It would be far too expensive to get glass this far out on the Edge.

As Alistair looked at his body, the economics of glass fell away like the shards of a shattered mirror. What he saw disrupted all his other thoughts. At forty-two, Alistair had easily been in the top one percent of physical fitness for his age group. His body had been hard, strong, and capable. Perhaps one or two Titans edged him out in physical abilities, but he retained the majority of his capabilities.

The man he saw before him now dwarfed who he used to be. In size and muscularity, his new body was something the Greeks used to carve as statues. "Did you lengthen my legs?"

"And your arms, Fallen Titan," the mutant responded. "You're one and a half meters taller. Your arms and trunk had to reflect that growth for you to remain symmetrical."

Alistair's chest muscles bulged, and his thighs were like tree-trunks. Veins crisscrossed his forearms like rivers on a map.

He looked into his eyes and saw the red irises. He leaned a bit closer, and Theos held onto his shoulders to keep him from falling. He put his right finger just below his eyelid and pulled. "Why are they red?"

"The first creator of mutants hated us. That's not a rumor, it's a fact. He created us because the Ascendant wanted to test fifth-dimensional travel, among other things. Every other creature including man had broken apart inside the fifth dimension. However, he nor the Ascendant wanted us to be able to blend in with society. They wanted something that would mark us, and our creator had just the thing. There's a chemical that mixes with your blood now, Fallen Titan. Your cells don't reject it, and it does a miraculous job of healing you quickly, but the double edge to it is your eyes. The chemical turns the iris red, and there's no way around it."

"What's the chemical?"

Theos smiled. "The creator named it after himself—his little tribute to his genius, marking us for all to see. 'Argenio.'"

"You can cover it up, though, right? There are lenses that can mask it?" Alistair kept staring at his irises. He no longer doubted anything the mutant said.

"We can, but there's a technology that sees through it. You have to know that most streets on Earth have iris scanners."

"But why don't you try to hide it out here?"

"Because," Theos answered, "frag them. I'll not hide what I am from any man. Unlike you, I didn't have a choice in this."

Alistair glanced at the mutant. His face was hard, lined, and serious. The former Titan nodded, understanding what he meant. "Frag them."

CHAPTER TEN

"At best, she's a myth. And if she's real? The AllMother? She's an old woman who sends ill-prepared soldiers to die at the hands of our Titans. You're more likely to die by a lightning strike than at the hands of her Subversives."

–Alexander de Finita, Current Imperial Ascendant

Thoreaux walked into the simply adorned room with the same reverence as he had the first time. To him and Servia, the room was sacred. Despite his exhaustion last night and continuing doubt in this plan today, the woman who lived in these quarters was the closest thing to a god Thoreaux would ever meet—or ever wanted to meet.

The AllMother.

Thoreaux had heard rumors of her age, though he'd never dared ask. He did sometimes wonder why someone as young as he was allowed direct contact when so many older brothers and sisters, all better tested, were denied.

Perhaps it had to do with his parents, but again, he didn't dare ask.

The AllMother preferred living beneath the surface of their planet, though today she had picked for their meeting place a distant igloo in the fourth quadrant. There weren't any other igloos for many kilometers, meaning that they were alone. Thoreaux knew the AllMother well enough to understand she was pensive.

Her back was to them, and she stared at the rising sun on the horizon. Thoreaux had never been to Earth, but he'd seen holovideos of it, and this was sad in comparison to what the Earthborn were accustomed to. The view was hazy, the light dispersed over the billions of kilometers separating the sun from this ice orb. Thoreaux focused on the AllMother. Her white hair was long, falling to the middle of her back, and her body was far too fragile to be in charge of the might she controlled. Her hands were folded in front of her, and she said nothing as he and Servia stepped off the elevator.

The two remained at a distance of ten feet, waiting for her to start the meeting.

Eventually, she did, her voice much stronger than one would think by looking at her body. "They tell me the Titan decided to join us."

"That's true, Mother," Servia replied. "He finished his modifications this morning. Theos is working with him right now."

The AllMother still didn't turn around. "What do you both think?"

"I think he's going to be a benefit to our forces." Servia

looked at Thoreaux with a sly smirk. "Thoreaux thinks this path might not be the right one."

The AllMother gave a slight nod. "Let him speak for himself."

Thoreaux didn't bother tossing a glare toward Servia, though he wanted to. "I don't see how one man, even a mutant, can change the tide of this war, Mother. I think we risked a lot and consumed a lot of resources for him. We've never done that before, and I don't understand why he's different."

The AllMother turned, and her red irises fell on him. "You think I've wasted our resources?"

He thought about his words carefully. "I believe they may have been inefficiently used."

The AllMother nodded, then slowly walked to the couch. She lowered herself onto it and crossed one leg over the other. She wore a long dress of a style no one else used anymore, a garment from before the Great Devastation—before the Commonwealth came into existence. He'd never asked her why she continued to have these types of clothes made for her, assuming it was a silent refutation of the current rulers.

"They are coming for him," the AllMother stated.

Thoreaux blinked, not understanding. "Who?"

The AllMother turned her face to the sunrise again. "The Commonwealth. The Ascendant. He's sending his forces to get him, the Titan I wasted resources on."

Servia stepped in front of the AllMother's couch. "What do you mean, Mother? They lost him in the fifth dimension. It would be pointless to come out here looking for him. We would shut down the igloos and cave in the docks if need be. They would lose millions before they breached the surface. It'd be a suicide mission for them."

The AllMother chuckled, the wrinkles on her face making her look grandmotherly. "I love it when youth tells me my business. Have I mentioned that before, Servia?"

Servia dropped her eyes. "I'm sorry, Mother. It's just—"

Thoreaux stepped forward and came to a stop next to her. "It's impossible, Mother. It's never been done. The Sanctum stays away from the Edge, at least this far out. Why would they risk so much for him?"

The AllMother kept smirking. "Perhaps I didn't waste as many resources as you thought. Not if they're willing to waste more to ensure his destruction."

Servia shook her head, then dropped to her knees, forcing the AllMother to look at her. "They won't be able to find him. They must know from drone scans the extent of our penetration of the planet. Every one of their men will die searching for him."

The AllMother cocked her head to the side. "Are you trying to convince me that the intelligence reports I received this morning are false?"

"You're sure of this?" Thoreaux asked.

She nodded as she looked at him. "Yes, my son. Why else do you think I brought this Titan to us? Did you really believe I so misjudged his value?"

Servia placed her hands in the AllMother's lap. "This was part of your plan? To have them come here? For him?"

She took Servia's hands in her own. "My sweet girl, they aren't coming to find him. They're coming to destroy him and all of us in the process. They're going to burn the entire planet until there's nothing left."

Thoreaux's mouth suddenly felt dry. He tried to swallow but was unable to. He opened his mouth to speak, but his tongue felt like sandpaper. He looked at Servia, whose blood had drained from her face. She was in the same place as him.

"What..." He paused, trying to regain his composure. "What do we do, AllMother? How much time do we have?"

"They'll be here in two weeks."

Servia stood, taking her hands from the AllMother's. "We have to begin evacuation measures. We have to disperse amongst Jupiter's moons, maybe Venus as well. Some will have to live aboard ships, at least for the time being. I don't know how many we can get through the Portal, but we've got to start looking there." Servia glanced at Thoreaux. "How long will it take to get other ships here?"

Looking outside again, the AllMother said, "There will be no evacuation."

Thoreaux blinked. "What?"

She shook her head. "We're not evacuating, not one single person. Your parents served me. You two grew up playing at my knees, and even after all this time, you don't understand. This is the beginning of the end. This is where we make our stand, my children." She met their eyes. "Many will die, but I want them all to realize there is no going back. I've purposely made it so there are no children on this planet, that they're dispersed. It wasn't by accident. This is where we fight. Now, go prepare for war, and make sure that the Titan is ready for it as well."

Thoreaux didn't move, and neither did Servia. He knew he'd heard her correctly, but he couldn't process her words.

Thoreaux's father had died protecting Pluto, and now they were going to lose it all? And their lives? They were going to lose the Insurrection before they ever had a chance to win it?

The AllMother stood and gathered Servia's right hand, then Thoreaux's left. "You have followed me as loyally as your parents did. Can you do this now? Can you trust me? If not, I understand, but I will need to quickly replace you both. The Commonwealth will be here in two weeks, my loves. We will need to be ready for war when they arrive. Can you two get me ready?"

Servia answered first. "Yes. I'm sorry, Mother. It's just a lot to take in at once. Of course I trust you."

"And you, Thoreaux? Are you with me?"

He took a deep breath, hardly able to process everything he'd heard. The question before him, though? The answer had been programmed into him long ago. His parents had pledged their lives to this woman. Would he not do the same?

Much later, when things had gone so far beyond what he'd ever imagined and many more lives had been lost, Thoreaux would question the wisdom of those words.

At the moment the question was posed, though, there was only one answer he thought possible. He dropped to one knee and felt the AllMother's hand touch his head. "Yes, Mother, I'm with you until the end."

The AllMother was alone, Servia and Thoreaux having left her.

She remained in her igloo, sitting on a couch that faced the setting sun.

The AllMother had been born with a name, but that had been a long, long time ago. She didn't think of herself by that name any longer, and only a few other people in the universe knew it. When pressed, she thought of herself by the name given to her by her followers: AllMother.

Sitting alone in the igloo, watching the sun descend beneath the horizon, she allowed herself to feel something she normally forced away. She was tired, more tired than she'd ever been. After all these years of fighting, of struggling, she knew she was finally weakening.

Is this the end for you, old lady? she wondered. *Have you finally grown too frail to do the job?*

She chuckled quietly, a smile forming on her ancient face. Had she thought she would live forever? No, not really. She'd never been that vain. She'd prepared well enough, though few others saw it yet. Servia, perhaps, but Thoreaux? He thought she was losing it, bringing this Titan here.

A lot of pain was coming for her children, and very soon. Many would die, and for the AllMother, this was the hardest decision she had ever made. Retrieving the Titan had been much easier than what would come next because she would need to sacrifice so many of those who believed in her. Those who followed her would die in huge numbers, but it was necessary.

They had to see with their own eyes what she already knew.

This Earthborn Titan would be their savior. The AllMother had watched him for years, though no one knew her eyes reached so far. She'd seen him growing as a child, starting right about the time the whispers of his superiority started. Her eyes had fallen on him and stayed, for his physical skills were necessary but not sufficient. There had been many before him who possessed the ability to kill, but without the ability to feel in equal measure, they would never be able to do what she needed.

If it was only a killer she needed, she could go to the AllSeer and try to get him to listen.

No, it was the heart that concerned her the most, so she had watched him at the Academy. She had even risked going to Earth to see him once, though of course, he'd had no idea she was there. She saw him graduate from the Academy, knowing that he would become a Titan and perhaps the most feared ever to exist—those who hunted her kind down and killed them without benefit of judge or jury.

Still, she didn't make any moves. There was always the chance that the Titan would die during her planning period, but that risk had to be taken, so she continued watching and planning. The AllMother saw him grow as a human, and he fell in love with a woman who gradually became even more important than the Commonwealth to him.

Finally, she had acted. She'd sent people on a mission they thought was suicide, to be caught by this Titan. He would either prove to her that his heart was what she thought or that her decades of preparing had been for nothing.

He's the one, she thought to herself. *And just in time, because I'm growing too tired to hold this together any longer.*

The AllMother had been alive for a long, long time. She often wondered if the gods existed and were watching her. Judging her. Were they doing the same to the Ascendant and the AllSeer? Each of them had their own motivations and were moving toward a goal that was in direct opposition to hers. Did the gods care? Or did they not exist at all?

Those were the questions the old woman asked as she realized her life might be coming to an end. She was alone as she asked them, but then again, she'd been alone most of her life.

He, this Fallen Titan, would make sure that those who followed her would not be alone during *their* lifespans. He would give them hope. He would give them belief. He'd give them a fighting chance.

CHAPTER ELEVEN

"de Finita-189 is the lifeblood of the Commonwealth. Without it, none of what we've accomplished would be possible. If it dries up, the solar system as we know it will drastically change."

—Reestine de Teerenese, Tenth Energy Czar

"You going to tell me what's going on?" Alistair asked. People were moving to and fro down the hallways with a franticness he hadn't witnessed since he'd arrived on the planet. A day had passed since the oxygen tank, and Alistair was controlling his body much better. Thoreaux came to get him, waking him from a deep slumber. The Fallen Titan had been dreaming about his wife, a dream he hoped he would never have again. He'd been tied up tightly, his limbs stretched out and a Whip coming down on his back over and over, but with only fifty percent power. Blood streamed down his body while his wife cheered in front of him.

Because of the monster he'd become. Because of his red irises.

The wake-up had been more than welcome.

Now the two of them were heading to a mystery room that Thoreaux had refused to tell Alistair anything about. People were passing them both ways in the hall, hurrying with barely a glance at the two.

"The Commonwealth is coming," Thoreaux finally answered.

Alistair stopped walking. "What?"

A few feet in front of him, Thoreaux stopped as well. "The Commonwealth is coming to Pluto and every second counts, so even stopping in this hall is a problem."

Thoreaux had been taller than Alistair a day ago, but now he was a few centimeters shorter. He still acted as if the Titan was the size of an insect, however. "They're coming *here*? Why?"

"It's none of your concern, Titan. All that matters to you is helping us defend our home."

Alistair shook his head. "Defend? I saw one of your docks. There's no defending against what's coming for you—

"Coming for *us*, Titan," Thoreaux interrupted. "Now, I know you've followed orders before, killing *Subversives*. I'm gonna need you to follow orders again. I'm in charge of making sure you're ready, and I've got about two weeks. You've already wasted four minutes asking questions and telling me what we should do. You want to waste another four gabbing, or do you want to meet the man who's going to train you?"

Alistair ignored the question momentarily. "You despise me, don't you?"

Thoreaux's eyes narrowed, and he opened his mouth to respond but paused before any words came out. After a few seconds, he found his voice. "Love or hate isn't important. Your mere presence here has created everything you see around you, and a lot of those I *do* love are going to die. Whatever the AllMother sees in you, *I* don't, yet I've been charged with getting you up to snuff. So, your questions don't matter, and you can stop asking me."

The Plutonian began walking again, assuming that Alistair was going to follow. Alistair no longer needed to worry if he was alone here, if not physically, then in every other way imaginable. The man walking away from him was apparently his main connection to life, and he wanted nothing to do with him. He spoke to him only out of duty, and not duty to Alistair, but to this mysterious AllMother.

He started after the Plutonian. He wasn't concerned with catching up but focused on why the Commonwealth would come here. As far as he knew, it had never been done. It was unprecedented, and for what reason?

For me? he wondered as they took a right into another busy hallway. It made no sense. Perhaps he was the greatest Titan, but the greatest Titan was nothing compared to the Commonwealth's greatness.

He wanted to ask questions, but he knew the answers he'd get, every one of them basically telling him to keep his mouth shut and do what he was told. It was not much different from when he'd first started out with the Titans, and Thoreaux was right about at least one thing: Alistair knew how to follow orders.

Thoreaux stopped at the end of a hall in front of a hangar bay door, if a miniature one. He flashed his hand over a panel on the right, and a green light read his palm. The hangar door rose into the ceiling, and the two men walked into the room on the other side.

Thoreaux waited until the door closed behind them before speaking. "Your body may be different, Titan, but so is fighting on Pluto. Our lack of resources has kept us from terraforming the planet's surface to any real degree and enforcing greater gravity across the planet, but it's also created a natural defense. I know you Earthborn don't train to fight on Pluto, so when your Commonwealth arrives, invading us will cause them some issues. Your first task is to learn how to fight here." He pointed to the right. There were SkinSuits hanging on the wall. "You worn those before, Titan?"

Every time Thoreaux said that word, Alistair could hear the condescension dripping from it. He let it be and focused on the SkinSuits. "I have." They were modeled after scuba gear and fit tightly, and while they wouldn't block thermal signatures, they created enough heat inside to keep the wearer from immediately freezing to death in space. The hood grew out of the neckline when the user put it on, and just like the rest of the body, it hugged the flesh tight. The eye system was a curved black panel. "These versions have HUDs?"

"None that you'll be training with," Thoreaux answered. "You need to learn to walk before you run." He reached into a pocket on the inside of his jacket and pulled out a red Whip, looking down at it as he spoke. "Before you, I'd only heard of these. Is it true what they say, that they're sentient? Only you can open it? Even now, it's looking for you?"

Alistair's eyes widened as he looked at his Whip. They'd told him they had it, but he'd thought it was a lie and that the Whip had been lost forever. He nodded. "Yes, it's true. It is sentient, but not like you or me. Do you know what a hawk is?"

Thoreaux nodded without looking up from the weapon.

"It's like a trained hawk in its sentience. It can often read what its master wants before the command comes, and it's able to feel fear or anger from its master as well."

Thoreaux gripped it harder. "It's warming up."

"It's very sensitive to its master's DNA. It can sense I'm here, most likely through water droplets in my breath when I speak."

Now Thoreaux's eyes widened, and he looked up. "It wants to come back to you?"

"The same way a hawk does its master."

Thoreaux didn't hand it over but held it close to his own body. "I'm wary of giving you this, though I've been instructed to. I know how dangerous you are with one of these things, and even though you're still adapting to this body, I imagine you could cut me down without any problem. If I give it to you, are you going to let me live?"

That pulled Alistair's eyes away from the Whip. "Is it my honor you attack, Plutonian?"

Thoreaux shrugged. "It's an honest question, to which I want an honest answer."

Alistair discarded his desire for the Whip and straightened to his full height. "Kane might not be a highborn name, but I rose to be the greatest Titan to ever walk Earth. My honor, while something you might not understand, was unscarred until a single moment when I let *your* brothers and sisters go free. That is the only scar on it. I have pledged myself to your cause—for your reasons or my own, it doesn't matter. I would not scar my honor to kill you or anyone who stands with you. Your death is not worth it."

Thoreaux held his gaze for a moment, then looked back down at the Whip. "Don't get all pissy, Titan. It's a magnificent weapon." He handed it over without another word.

Alistair held it, feeling reunited in a way that most other humans would never understand. The Whip could sense him, and the heat that had been growing in it died, its anticipation fulfilled.

"I've tried turning it on about a hundred times," Thoreaux said. "Will you do it?"

Alistair smirked. "You sure you trust me?"

"After that monologue about your honor?" Thoreaux raised an eyebrow and gave his own grin. "You better not even hurt an insect that flies in these rooms."

Alistair chuckled. "Well played, good sir." He closed his eyes and gripped the Whip. His DNA had activated it, and now the Whip understood his desire. The three strands shot into the air before turning into endlessly curving circles.

"It's an amazing weapon," Thoreaux said as he stared at the red lasers extending from the hilt. After a moment, he glanced back up to the wall. "Go ahead and pick out a SkinSuit. Your trainer is waiting."

Alistair's eyebrows drew together. "You're not training me?"

"No, Titan. I said I'm in charge of making sure you're up to snuff. Your actual trainer is a different person, and they'll be reporting your progress to me." Thoreaux pointed at the wall. "Now get a suit. You know how to fight in Earth's gravity. Let's see how good you are in space."

The suit kept most of the cold out, but Alistair could still feel it. It was a blood-freezing cold that somehow sunk beneath the SkinSuit and down into his bones. Alistair stood on ice that was ocean-black. Four boxes formed a square about sixteen meters in each direction. The boxes glowed a dull white, casting enough light for Alistair to see inside the square and a bit outside as well.

He pulled in a deep breath. The suit was continually making oxygen from a tiny rectangle that sat on Alistair's spine. If it was damaged, he would suffocate within a few minutes.

He held his Whip in his right hand, though it was not activated. He didn't know what to do out here, and the man sitting on the side of the square had said nothing so far. He was facing the opposite way, his legs folded beneath him.

"Are you from Pluto?" Alistair called loudly enough to be heard across the ice. The man, even sitting, didn't look tall enough to be Pluto-born. Perhaps Mars, or maybe even Earth.

"No." The stranger didn't look over his shoulder as he

spoke. "The ice adopted me. She's a cold parent, but she does love me."

The man hopped up quicker than Alistair thought possible. He moved elegantly, spinning in the air so that when he landed, he was facing Alistair. "You're the one I have two weeks to train, is that correct?"

Alistair could see nothing of the man. The SkinSuit was a deep blue and hid every inch of the man's skin. All Alistair could tell was that he was shorter and lacked reach on him as well. He was thin, lithe, and wouldn't be able to overpower Alistair if it came down to a wrestling match. "Yes, I believe so. My name is Alistair."

"I know who you are." Any emotion the man's face might have given away was hidden beneath the mask. "Everyone on this planet knows who you are. You've killed my friends, *Odin*. Isn't that your callsign? A god greater than all the rest?"

Alistair thumbed his Whip, saying nothing.

"Do you still like to be called Odin? Do you still like to be thought of as a god?"

"I didn't give myself the callsign," Alistair responded. "I've told you my name—Alistair Kane. If that is not good for you, then perhaps you should close my mouth so I don't tell you any more names."

The man squatted and picked up what looked to be a blue metal pipe. Alistair had missed it, the color having blended in with the ice beneath it. The man squeezed the middle and metal shot out to either side, creating a pole and a weapon. "Perhaps I will shut your mouth, *Odin*. If I do, I get to give you a new name. Does that work?"

"And my weapon?" Alistair asked.

"You use that Whip that you keep rubbing." The stranger looked down at Alistair's waist.

"You'll die if I do. I'm not here to kill the trainers. If you prefer I fight you with my fists, that's fine by me."

The stranger chuckled and began spinning the metal pole with his right hand. It twirled by his shoulder, moving faster with each rotation. "I think I'll be fine, but if you do kill me, just have them replay my microphone inside my hood. They'll see I asked for it. So, do we have a deal? I shut your mouth, I name you?"

Alistair didn't know what to think or say. He didn't want to unleash his Whip on this man. Regardless of where they were fighting, forms used, or anything else, the man had only a *metal pipe*.

He watched as the stranger moved forward, the pipe now a blur as it moved by his shoulder. "Speak, Titan, or I'll make it so you never do again."

The threat pushed Alistair over the edge. "Name me if you can." His Whip came to life, the red lasers blazing out of the hilt. The gravity here was about a quarter of that on Earth, so Alistair wasn't quite sure which form to use, but he knew he could adapt quickly if needed. He took on the Elemental's Whisper, counting on the decreased gravity to increase his speed at the sake of power.

His Whip curled into the air like a serpent, forming a single lash as the three strands wrapped around each other.

"Elemental's Whisper," the stranger said, and even though Alistair couldn't see him, he knew there was a smile beneath the mask.

He knows Earthborn forms, Alistair thought as the stranger circled him, remaining inside the square.

Alistair moved right, slanting toward the trainer, and his Whip continued its serpent-like twirling as he flashed toward the man. For Alistair, this was already over, and he'd have to explain that he had killed the person they'd sent to teach him.

He slung his Whip forward, decreasing the power slightly as he did, hoping that an injury would make the man stop.

Alistair didn't want to kill him.

He felt the pole at the base of his skull and blinked. He was face-down on the ground, and his Whip had been slung across the ice. His arms and legs were spread out, and if the pipe was pushed down, it would quite possibly snap his spine in two.

"So, *Odin*," the stranger asked, unseen now as he stood above Alistair, "is your mouth sufficiently closed?"

Alistair looked across the ice at his Whip, now inactive and too far away to be reached. He could try to flip over, but just as he thought about it, the pipe pressed down harder.

"Have you been bested, Titan?"

He didn't know how he'd been beaten so easily, but he couldn't deny it. "Yes."

The pipe came off his neck, and Alistair climbed to his knees. The stranger walked around to his front so that they could look at each other. "My name is Linc Hipwrite, also of Earth. Your name, until you earn another, is now Phaethon. This is your first lesson, though there will be many more over the two weeks we have with each other. If we somehow survive the coming disaster, I imagine I will teach you for a long time. Your first lesson may be the most important, and it is right that you're on your knees as you learn it. You know *nothing*, boy. Since you want to be a god, do you know the story of Phaethon?"

Alistair shook his head. He wanted to reach for his Whip to keep it near him, but he knew he might pull back a shattered arm instead.

"Phaethon wanted proof he was the son of Apollo. He asked to drive the sun god's chariot, but when he did, he couldn't control it. He was not powerful enough, and the chariot nearly crashed into Earth, which would have burned the world to ash. Zeus had to kill the arrogant boy with a lightning bolt to save the world. You are that boy, Phaethon, trying to control something you're not strong enough for."

Alistair stared up at the man in the dark blue SkinSuit, unable to remember the last time someone had spoken to him so. Maybe in the Academy, but even then, he had been so far ahead of his class, the professors had understood what he would become. Here, though, he finally understood. All the shit-talking and all the hate up until now...He sat on his knees, a man with nothing more than a metal pole having disabled him—could have killed him.

"So," the masked trainer said, "learn your first lesson well. Tomorrow, I expect a better start. Pick up your Whip on your way down. I wouldn't want you to lose such a *deadly* weapon."

Linc walked out into the icy wilderness, leaving Alistair to stare at the most sophisticated weapon ever created while remembering the sarcasm that had dripped from the stranger's voice.

CHAPTER TWELVE

"The Academy trains the best of us to be better. Without the Academy, humanity would decay from within, a rot that would end up turning cancerous and eating us alive."

–Marcus de Reespen, Current Primus Academy Director

The Academy had been the toughest experience Alistair had ever gone through. It was a two-year-long school only the most elite tested into. Inside the Commonwealth, the Academy was the great equalizer. It did not matter who your family was or whether your house was great or small. The Academy looked at all equally, and the best rose to the top.

At least, that was supposed to be the truth of it. Of course, as with any institution, politics ruled much of the day. It *could be* the great equalizer, but somehow the top ten percent of each class just happened to come from the top ten percent of the great houses.

Except when Alistair went through. He was an unstoppable force, closer to a storm than a human. For a solid two years, he worked harder than he thought possible. The rest of his life had been measured against those twenty-four months: how hard was such and such compared to what he went through at the Academy?

Until he met Linc.

The two weeks he spent in preparation for a hopeless battle surpassed the Academy by many long, long kilometers.

He was up at four Standard Time. His breakfast was sparse, dried meat and vegetables that had been shipped from some other planet. He didn't ask what the meat was, though he thought the vegetables were probably cabbage. Alistair had ten minutes to eat, then Linc showed up. He was much older than Alistair had thought possible, given how easily the man had disarmed him.

He had gray hair, the sides shaved and the top long but kept in a bun near the back of his head. It was the style for battle on this planet, apparently, because Alistair saw more people with the same cut.

The first morning after he was renamed, Alistair had paused as he brought a piece of dried meat to his mouth. When the old man entered the room, Alistair couldn't help but stare. He rubbed his eyes with his left hand. Perhaps he was seeing things.

Linc's hands were folded in front of him, the metal pipe he'd used beneath them. "Something wrong with your eyes, Phaethon?"

Alistair sighed and looked back down at his food.

"Something's wrong with my body if I lost to someone your age."

The old man chuckled. "You're not the first person I've met trying to drive a chariot that was too strong for them to control. Let's see if we can get your arms a bit stronger, yes?" His pole shot out and knocked the food from in front of Alistair to the floor. "Fastbreaking is over at four-ten Standard. It's four-eleven now. We're late. Suit up. I'll see you surface-side."

The old man left Alistair to clean up the mess.

He met Linc in the same place as the day before. A second man was there this time, though he stood outside the light boxes. He wore a SkinSuit as well and said nothing, not even when asked.

Looking at Linc, Alistair said, "He's a friendly one."

The trainer shrugged in response. "Might be a she. We don't take kindly to sexism on this planet."

Alistair rolled his eyes, though it was a wasted response behind his mask. "What do we learn today?"

"You're aware of the two sets of fighting forms?" Linc asked.

"There are hundreds of fighting forms."

Linc shook his head. The blue mask showed nothing of his face, though Alistair imagined he was smiling. "Forms? Yes. I'm discussing sets, boy. There are two sets, and they both grew from their birthplace. The Sanctum set, which you pathetically showed yesterday, and the Edge set, which you saw a bit of with me."

Was that why he had been defeated so easily? Some form he wasn't aware of?

Linc continued talking. "You can use the Edge or the Sanctum, but not both."

"Why not?" Alistair asked.

Linc squeezed his pole again, then shoved the bottom into the ice before leaning on it. "You ask a lot of questions, boy."

"You say a lot of things that don't make sense, old man."

Linc chuckled at the retort. "The sets don't complement each other. In many ways, they're the exact opposite. You cannot perfect both, but only one."

"You know both," Alistair said. "How can you know both but tell me I must pick one?"

The masked man sighed. "Phaethon, I need you to listen to me. I may *know* the sets, but it doesn't mean I can fight with them both. My life has been studying them, and I pray to the gods that it wasn't only to teach you. If you are my greatest student, then indeed, life is too much work with very, very little reward. Now focus, boy. I can know the Edge and Sanctum sets, but I have only mastered the Edge. You may be tempted to try the forms you see with me. Do not do it. Out here, with me, you will only end with bruises. If you try such a thing in battle, you will die. Master one set, and be the master of it. Do not become greedy. That is where men meet dirt."

"I understand," Alistair said.

"Good, good." Linc popped his pole up so that he held it between both hands. "I can tell you're not yet an Overlord. Am I wrong?"

An Overlord was the highest anyone could achieve in the fighting forms. It was a level of mastery only a few gained, and it included all Whip forms as well. Alistair had been close to gaining it, but there had been no point in the end. He was unstoppable, and with the weight of the Commonwealth behind his every move?

"No, you're not wrong," he answered.

"Why not?" the trainer asked.

"I didn't learn to be the best. I learned to do a job. I was the best without mastering the forms, and my jobs were always completed."

Linc twirled the pole once. "Have you ventured outside this solar system, Titan?"

Alistair shook his head.

"I thought not," Linc responded. "I have. What's coming for us now, and what's sure to come later if we survive *this*? They will require you to master the Sanctum's forms. You will not master them here with me, but it's something to remember, Phaethon. Now we learn how to fight in low gravity."

He swung his pole with a speed that was barely visible to the naked eye. Alistair dodged it, missing his jaw being shattered by an inch.

"Good," Linc said. "Never let your enemy's droning on put you off your guard. It doesn't only happen in bad holovids, but in real life too."

The training started in earnest then. The same time every day. Alistair learned how to use the AirSoles. They manipulated the gravity around him, allowing him to float up and down in the air and to speed up and slow down. He learned how to control his Whip in the low gravity. To turn, to feint, and to defend.

He went to sleep nightly, bruises across his body, his shoulder feeling like it was out of joint. Linc broke two ribs on the fourth day, and Alistair had to sleep in the tank that night. Theos had watched as they lowered him in. "Already breaking my glorious creation. I thought they taught you Titans how to fight better."

"I hope you fight him one day," Alistair mumbled.

Theos gave him a wink. "I did. He gave me a better name than Phaethon, though."

On the twelfth day, Alistair was pushing his chair in, his morning fast-break finished, when Linc opened the door to his room.

"On my way, master," Alistair joked while reaching for his SkinSuit.

"No training today."

Alistair paused and looked at Linc. "We've two days left."

"Not all brawn after all," the trainer responded. "You have a bit of brain in there, too. Tomorrow you'll be introduced to your legion, and most likely your contingent."

Alistair's hand still hung over his suit. "Our time is done then?"

"I own you for today, and the rest of your time in this universe will depend on what the AllMother tells us. I serve at her leisure, as do you and everyone else."

Alistair straightened up, dropping his hand. "So, what's the plan?"

The old man smirked. "Put your suit on. We're going for a walk surface-side."

Alistair stared at him, nonplussed. "Had to wait until I thought I was staying inside, huh?"

"I only have another day with you. Give an old man his fun. I'll see you upstairs."

The stranger in the black SkinSuit walked behind the two of them, saying nothing just as he had on the other days he'd ventured outside with them. He didn't volunteer any information when Alistair tried verbally sparring with him. He was like a ghost, staying two hundred meters behind them.

"You going to tell me who that is?" Alistair asked as they walked across the ice.

Linc shook his head. "If he *or* she wanted you to know, they'd tell you. Perhaps it's the AllMother herself, checking up on you. If so, how do you think you've done?"

"Well, given that I only laid hands on you twice, I imagine she's regretting her decision to save me. Especially given what's coming."

The two of them had walked well beyond any igloos, their soles at twice the usual gravity, which allowed them to move quickly but remain in control. They covered a kilometer every four minutes or so, with neither of them needing to breathe heavily.

"Okay, here we are." Linc slowed his AirSoles down, bouncing a few steps. Alistair went beyond him a bit before slowing his down, but he was finally starting to look graceful as he did it.

"Where are we?" he asked as he approached his trainer, the masked stranger still in the background.

Linc didn't look at him but rather stared into the hazy sun. "Do you know what they're calling this down in the barracks?"

"No. I've only seen you and Theos in the past two weeks."

"Pluto's Stand," Linc responded. "It's growing into legend already. The men and women down below, many of them haven't been to war before. Did you know that?"

Alistair thumbed his Whip absently. "I suppose I did. The last real rebellion was on Mars, and what was that, two hundred years ago? No one really thinks about it much anymore."

"You think you've been to war, don't you?"

Alistair was quiet for a moment as he stood shoulder to shoulder with his trainer. "I suppose I do. I've been in over a hundred ops."

"That's not war, boy. That's you in a metal suit raining down hellfire on people who dare challenge the Commonwealth. That's nothing like war."

Alistair shrugged. "I imagine you haven't been to war either, then. If that's the case, I would imagine no one in this universe has been to war."

Linc chuckled behind his mask. "The universe is a large place, Phaethon. Larger than you can possibly imagine. I've been in war, and I'm here to tell you it's like nothing you can possibly imagine."

Finally Alistair broke his stare on the horizon to look at his trainer. "How is that possible if the last war was two hundred years ago?"

"There are other worlds than these, boy." Linc looked down at his pole. "Many other worlds. There are worlds you can't even conceive of, but I've seen them. I've fought on them."

Alistair took a step back, creating a little more separation. The masked stranger in the distance couldn't hear their words, but he didn't move. "You called me out here to lie to me, Linc?"

"I'm not lying, boy, and I'm telling you this now because a time may come very shortly when you have to utilize those other worlds. War is hell; there is no other word for it. You watch the men standing next to you shot down by railguns, their bodies cut in half, their intestines smoldering and spilling across the ground." He paused for a moment. "Were you scared when you were chasing down Subversives, as you call them?"

"In the beginning, yes," Alistair whispered. "But not for a long time."

"You'll know fear again shortly. I've seen the Commonwealth's fleet, their legions of Titans, and their mutants they bring out of their chains to hunt those who refuse to bend the knee. All of those are coming here, Phaethon." He looked at Alistair for the first time. "The AllMother sees something in you. Perhaps I see a little something too, though not as much as she does. She has decreed that we're to fight the invaders, but when they drop unlimited nukes on this ball of ice, I don't see how much we will be able to fight. We will burn, then this planet will burn, and the Insurrection will be over. Do you understand what I'm saying?"

Alistair studied the man's mask, wishing he could see the face beneath it. "We're all dead. This was a dream that you and your people are about to wake up from."

Linc laughed, turning his head to the stranger as he did. The person remained silent and unmoving. Linc shook his head, still chuckling, and looked back at Alistair. "No, boy. I didn't train you for two weeks to fight on this godsfor-saken planet because I think we're dead. I think some will die, yes, but there are reasons all of this is happening. I won't sit here and tell you I know them, only that I trust in the AllMother. For years, she has not allowed children on Pluto. If you have a child, you're shipped off-planet. Now I know why. She had been planning for this very thing.

"Now, enough with your questions, boy. It's time for you to answer mine because each second you spend yapping is a second during which the fleets grow closer. Are you aware that there are planets outside this solar system that are occupied? That have humans living on them?"

"Everyone hears rumors," Alistair said. "But that's like hearing rumors of a haunted house when you're a child. It's all nonsense that kids pass around."

Linc looked over his shoulder for a moment. "Show him."

Alistair followed Linc's eyes to the stranger, who had pulled a small round object out of his suit. There was a single red button in the middle of it, and the stranger pressed it down.

Linc pointed to his right, and Alistair's eyes followed. On the edge of the horizon, *something* was happening. Sparks were streaking into the sky and the world seemed translucent, as if reality was falling apart to reveal some-thing beneath it.

"You've got a StealthBlanket over it?" he asked. A Blanket reflected the natural world, and when you draped one over an inanimate object, it was nearly impossible to detect.

"I think you'll come to see that we're not nearly as primitive as you imagine."

Alistair stared as the Blanket fell away, the translucent reality thinning until it no longer existed. In its place was something impossible. "That's not real. It's a mirage." His eyes were huge behind his mask, his mouth hanging open. His hand had dropped from his Whip.

"Real or not, what do you think is in front of you?" Linc asked.

"It's an Intergalactic Portal."

"You know what they used to call them? Stargates. I like that term better, but the Commonwealth thought it too plebeian."

The arch stretched five hundred meters in the air, and the two ends were well over two hundred meters apart. You could walk hundreds of people through it shoulder to shoulder. The arch appeared to have nothing in the middle of it; it was just a standing structure made of cold metal. Ice crystals ran up and down it, and on the other side? More of Pluto—ice as far as the eye could see.

"It's real?" Alistair asked, unable to pull his eyes away from it.

"It is."

"Where does it lead to?"

Linc hit the ice with his pole. "That's the wrong question. The right one is, why don't you know these things exist? Why do you think they're fairytales children spread? And if we have one here, how many others exist? Because to build one without a sister site somewhere else in the universe would be pointless. For years I questioned a motive for putting it on Pluto. There are more populous, less harsh moons we could have used, or so I thought. I understand now, though. Even the construction of this..." he waved his hand at the arch, "was the AllMother thinking about you. About what was to come here."

Alistair had no words. Every time he felt he had a grasp, even a weak one, on the situation, his world shattered further. His *universe* in this case. The Portals weren't supposed to exist. Humanity had conquered its solar system but had not gone much farther. It couldn't be done; that's what they taught. The science so that humans could survive moving from one Portal to another just wasn't possible, yet—

"You said..." Alistair swallowed. "You said you'd been in wars, and there were other worlds than these. Are you telling me you've traveled through these Portals, and there are other galaxies with humans in them?"

Linc turned away from the Portal and placed his hand on Alistair's shoulder. "My good sir, I am telling you that your entire life is a lie. That there is nothing you can trust from before you woke up with those red eyes. I'm also telling you this, and perhaps it's the most important thing you'll hear from me: whatever happens, there's a way off this planet. That Portal is operational."

"Why are you telling me that?" Alistair asked.

"Because some here, those that haven't been in war, might say it's cowardice to run. I'm telling you what you already know. We can't win this battle, and if we don't survive it, there is no possibility of winning the war." He pulled his hand off Alistair's shoulder. "Do you understand?"

Alistair nodded; he understood completely. Regardless

of what the AllMother thought or told these people, the force coming for this planet was unlike anything they could imagine. If the Commonwealth wanted to, they wouldn't need to drop a single bomb. They could invade and lose tens of thousands without blinking an eye.

"Good," his trainer said. "Then let us go back beneath the surface. There's plenty more to be done."

THE WRITTEN HISTORY OF THE GREAT INSURRECTION

He trained, the man known as Alistair, Odin, and Prometheus. He trained for two weeks in an environment that was as strange to him as land would be to a fish. A harsh, cold, desolate place, one where the gravity was completely different than both his body and mind had learned to deal with.

He did it while being treated as something *less than*. He did it while the woman he loved had been ripped away from him and the life he'd known sat in smoldering ashes behind him.

I watched him at night after the day was finished. He didn't know I was watching, and I don't regret it. I had to understand the man I was being forced to integrate into an army I'd spent three years training. He crawled into bed, his body bruised and exhausted, then he stared at the ceiling. He cried sometimes, silently, without bothering to wipe his eyes.

I never had to ask him what he was weeping for—his stolen life.

But the next morning I watched him stand, dress, and go prepare for war. Linc was the greatest hand to hand fighter I've ever seen, but I knew immediately that Alistair would surpass him. On this world or any other, the man was going to be a killer like none seen before.

He moved like water, his body capable of changing direction—almost changing shape—in ways I didn't think possible. He fought using the Sanctum's forms, but even Linc saw him starting to adapt them. Small things; Linc cursed him out about them, saying they would get him killed, but it was like Alistair simply couldn't help it. He did what was necessary.

He never won against Linc during those two weeks, but he never gave up, and he never took a loss as anything other than an opportunity to learn.

Earth's greatest Titan fell again and again in front of me on that ice world, and each time he got back up determined to do it better. To *be* better.

That was when I started to believe in him. I said nothing, not to Alistair or the AllMother. I just watched silently, and my heart started to change. I don't know if hope was the right word. There is no hope in war besides that it might one day end, but belief?

Yes.

I started to believe that someone might be able to bring us light.

CHAPTER THIRTEEN

"The Commonwealth's Fleet is unparalleled in human history. Its capabilities can defend us from all enemies. Truthfully, anyone who wishes the Commonwealth harm should quake in fear at the power our Fleet wields."

–Veena de Ragnimus, Primus First Fleet Captain

Veena de Ragnimus stood on the bridge with her hands on her hips. She didn't stare at those in front of her, but rather, she looked through the panels that showed the ships outside. It felt like overkill to Veena, though she would never voice that aloud to her superior. She'd received her orders: bring the First Fleet to Pluto and use whatever means necessary to ensure Alistair Kane's death.

If his body wasn't recovered, the planet should be burned in its entirety.

Veena was Primus General of the Commonwealth's Interplanetary Fleets. She would follow her orders as she had her entire career, but this seemed...

Off.

She had a host of Titans on board five of the ships, those that would initiate the invasion. Their Primus Ares was on this one, and he'd just entered the bridge, according to the comm in her ear. Veena's capo didn't need to speak aloud since his neuro-connection synced with the ship automatically, thus the immediate relay when the Titan entered the bridge.

Veena had informed her capo that she wanted to know where Ares was at all times, and especially when he was moving. Veena had never met the Titan before this operation, but she didn't like the young man. His arrogance was born from something Veena didn't understand because it wasn't purely talent-based. She'd heard rumors about him, like everyone in the military—Aurelius de Finita reborn. The only thing that would keep someone of his might from rising to the Imperial Ascendancy was his bloodline. A single family could hold that spot, and it wasn't his.

All the same, Veena didn't trust him, so she had her capo monitor him almost constantly.

"Salve, Ragnimus," the Titan said as he approached from her right.

Veena didn't look his way but said, "Salve, Ares."

The Titan was strong yet had a svelteness that whispered of deadly speed. Veena didn't like standing next to him because she knew if she had to fight him, she would fall hard.

"What brings you to the bridge?" she asked after a moment.

"Tired of sleeping. How long do you stay here? All the time?"

"Negative. I need sleep just like you do. Regulations say unless we're under attack, I have to take a break once every sixteen hours. I follow regulations."

"Hmmm," the Titan mused in a way that Veena didn't like. "We haven't really talked about what's to come. How do you feel about it?"

Veena glanced at him before gesturing at the crew. "What's wrong with you? You see what's in front of me."

Ares waved away her frustration. "They're all harmonized with the ship. They're not paying attention."

Veena could have slapped him right then, but she remained outwardly calm. They'd gone this far without a blow-up, and on the eve of an attack, the leaders couldn't be arguing in front of the crew. "Come with me."

Veena walked away from the forward bridge, entered the back hall, and then took a right into an R&R room. The crew currently in it jumped to their feet and saluted with their hands over their hearts. "Commandeering the room. We'll be done shortly."

"Yes, ma'am," the five crew members responded as one before flooding into the hall.

The door closed behind the last one, and Veena let her facade of peace fade. "First, never ask me a question like that in front of my crew again. Second, never question my judgment in front of my crew again. It doesn't matter to me if you're a Primus or not. This is my territory, and you're a guest here."

Ares smiled and shrugged. "My apologies, Primus." He walked to the floor-to-ceiling window that showed space from the ship's side. Five dreadnoughts were visible, their lights beacons in the sea of darkness. "I just realized today that we hadn't discussed our thoughts about this mission, only the technical pieces of it. I'm curious how you feel about what we're going to do."

"My thoughts are inconsequential to the operation. I know what I've been commanded to do, and I'll do it."

Ares nodded with his back still to her. "That's a very militaristic way to view it. Very soldier-like of you, Veena. To me, this seems like a very *drastic* move to find Odin."

She didn't know where this conversation was going, but she didn't like its direction. "I'm unsure what the point of this is."

"Just two soldiers getting closer to each other before a war. That's all. They call you the Hawk. Why is that?"

"I don't know who 'they' is," Veena said, "and I don't pay much attention to what people say."

Ares touched the glass with his right hand. "It was on a Mercury mission about twenty years ago. Isn't that right? You were piloting a single-person corvette and storming one of the Subversives' strongholds. I forget the name of it, but they say you were like a hawk in the sky, and the Subversives little more than field game that you picked off one by one. They *say* the battle would have gone the other direction if you hadn't been there. There aren't too many soldiers who can claim that."

"Odin was one, wasn't he?" Veena asked.

Ares glanced over his shoulder, his grin gone. He said nothing, just held Veena's eyes.

"Were you there for that?" she asked.

He returned to looking out the window. "For the last one, yes. He saved my life."

"Does it bother you that you're going to take his?"

"Didn't you say our thoughts on this subject don't matter?" Ares responded.

"Just trying to follow your lead, Titan."

He turned around and leaned against the window, finding her eyes. He was a strikingly handsome man. Veena imagined he had his pick of any woman back on Earth or any other planet he arrived on, except perhaps for Pluto.

He shook his head. "No. It doesn't bother me, even if I think the effort we're extending is overzealous. All it takes is for one brick to begin cracking, and before long, the floods have broken through and drowned the peasants."

"He was your mentor, wasn't he?" Veena didn't know why she was pressing this, but she couldn't stop herself. "How many years did you work beneath him?"

Ares leaned his head back against the glass and stared at her for silent seconds. "I studied under him for three years. Why wait until now to ask me these questions?"

"Need I remind you that you came to my bridge, Titan? Call me curious." She moved over to one of the tables and pulled out a chair, then sat down and propped her feet up on the table. "Do you think you and your men will be able to find him, or are we going to have to turn the world into a furnace?"

Ares drummed his knuckles on the glass. *Knock, knock, knock.* "What makes you think I'll be with my men?"

Veena opened her mouth to speak but found herself too stunned for a few moments.

"You won't be invading with them?"

Ares smirked at her as if she were a child who had just asked something incredibly cute but unfathomable. "Why would I invade a planet you just said you might turn into a furnace? My men will invade, and hopefully, they have enough time to return to their ships. I shall command them from here."

Veena shook her head. "If you decide to stay in orbit, you will not be here. Placing two Primuses on one ship is far too dangerous to the health of the overall Commonwealth. One strategically placed missile may kill us both. I've allowed you to stay here until now because scans show nothing incoming on our route, but when we arrive, they *will* attack."

"Noted," Ares said. At least he listened to reason, though had he not, Veena would have ensured he was gone before the first shot was fired.

"You're saying you can't stop him, right?" Veena smirked as she leaned farther back in the chair. "Otherwise, you'd be down there with your men? I am curious...what happened at that tower on Earth when you were supposed to kill him?"

"The Subversives took him before I could finish him." Ares' face had grown very still, like that of a granite statue.

He didn't like this conversation. Killing Odin would have made him the greatest Titan ever. Instead, he'd failed. "But you have a chance to finish him now. To go down there inside the ice planet and root him out. You don't want to take it?"

"My honor is intact, Primus."

"And your glory?" she asked.

"History grants true glory, and I won't risk my history being cut short if one of your crew has an itchy trigger finger. If I have a chance to kill him, I'll take it, and I will succeed. He ran last time. There was a reason for that." He turned to look at her. "I would be careful how you speak to me, Primus. Remember how many years it took you to reach the station of Primus, then remember how many it took me. I am but twenty-six years old, and we stand in the same place on the same mountain."

Veena nodded, still smiling. She'd seen his weakness, and it lay in his arrogance—an attempt to cover up an underlying insecurity. "You would do well, Primus, to remember that I've been on this mountain a lot longer than you. I know where the pitfalls are and how hard the wind blows over the cliff faces."

Ares was alone on the ship. He was waiting for the transfer pod to take him to his new dreadnought. Veena hadn't been kidding about it, and while he knew the decision was the right one, he still thought her a royal bitch. The Subversives were going to attack them, and he hoped the Primus ended up dead.

She'd asked him why he wasn't going down to the planet with the other Titans? Because Ares knew *she* wouldn't wait for him to get back up here before she let the fire rain down. Sure, there were meeting camps for the Titans to get back aboard their pods, but he wasn't dumb. He knew the chances of him dying down there were greater than two in three, and he wouldn't have his bones turn to ash on the ice rock. Ares didn't see *her* volunteering to go in his stead.

No matter. If she died, she died. If not, hopefully he wouldn't have to deal with her again once this mission was finished. They killed Odin, and all of this was done—the whole nasty business.

Ares kept his emotions to himself, something he'd learned as a child from his father. The lessons had had painful consequences, for which he was grateful for now. The world saw what Ares wanted it to; it saw the Titan. It never saw Romulus. He wasn't sure most of those he came in contact with even knew which family he was from because he made the world see the god of war.

He would never have gotten himself in the situation Alistair did. Even now, over a month after the original incident, Ares didn't understand it. How could the man have been so dumb? So *weak*? It was a mistake Ares would never have made. Bodies would have hit the floor before Ares *ever* showed weakness like that.

He let them go, the Titan thought as he shook his head. *He did this, not me. He put me in this situation.*

Ares had no desire to be here on this ship so far from home. Truthfully, he didn't want to kill Alistair, regardless of what he portrayed to the outside world. Alistair—Odin —had been his mentor. In some ways, he'd been a second father.

What choice did he have? His real father, Magnimus, had taught him as a boy the importance of serving the Commonwealth *and* serving yourself and your family. They were one and the same because when one served the Commonwealth well, their family would see their name on banners of triumph. He had no choice. To deny this mission would be to deny his family, his legacy, and his unborn children's legacy.

He served, and he served honorably. Alistair was the one who hadn't done that.

Ares remembered the first time he'd met Alistair. He'd been twenty-three years old and went by his birth name, Romulus de Livius. He knew of Alistair Kane, Odin the Primus. Someone from Ares' lineage had never served under such a base name—*Kane*—but he knew this man was not like any other on Earth. At thirty-seven years old, Alistair Kane was a legend, both within and outside of the Titans. He'd been Primus for a decade, the longest-serving Primus Titan ever.

It had been a privilege to meet him, let alone serve under him.

And now?

Ares loved the man he was going to kill.

Deep in the place that Ares never let the world venture to, he didn't want to see the man dead, though that didn't matter anymore. Alistair *would* die, and it was his own fault. His own decisions.

You caused this, and I hate you for it, Ares thought.

CHAPTER FOURTEEN

"One People. One Purpose."

–Max de Aurelius, Seven-Year-Old Student, First
Day of Class

Alistair sat up. Something smelled different in the air.
Theos hadn't told him that his olfactory senses would be
different, but they were, and whatever was in front of his
door was different from anything he'd smelled before. It
didn't even smell human.

Alistair's right hand found his Whip beneath his
mattress. His eyes never left the door. There'd been no
alarms or sirens, no outside word that anything was
wrong, but Alistair knew something was different.

He stood up, and the door opened. His Whip unfurling
as it did.

"Calm yourself, Titan," Linc said. "I brought you a little
friend."

Alistair's face grew confused. "What the hell are you talking about?"

Linc stepped into the room and to the side, revealing what was behind him.

Alistair found himself staring at the largest dog-like creature he'd ever seen. It sat on its haunches, gazing at him with cautious eyes. The width of its shoulders nearly filled the doorframe, and Alistair knew that if the creature stood on all fours, it would be taller than his waist. Smooth black hair covered its body, while its eyes were the pale blue of most Plutonians. The dog, or wolf, or *horse* didn't move, only sat peering at the new human.

"Linc, what in the hell is that thing?"

His trainer was looking at the dog when he asked the question, but he flashed angry eyes at Alistair. "First, it's not a *thing*. He's a breed of animal not from this galaxy, and he's a pup."

"That thing is a pup?" Alistair couldn't take his eyes off the creature.

"I'm going to bat you upside the head if you say that again." Linc turned to look at the creature again. "They're called Drathes. He's a pup and will be for another ten standard years or so. They live a little more than a human's lifespan. He's three." The trainer looked at Alistair again. "They're linguaphiles, Phaethon."

Finally, Alistair pulled his attention away from the Drathe. "What are you saying? Do you want to speak Common, or should we continue speaking Old English?"

Linc shook his head, obviously not impressed. "If our hopes are pinned on you, all is lost. Drathes are linguaphiles. Some say their ability to learn languages surpasses that of humans. They can't speak, at least not in words, but they understand what you say. This one here is well versed in Common, so when you call him a *thing*, I'm sure it hurts his feelings."

Alistair squatted so that the two were eye level with each other. There was intelligence in the creature's eyes, a deep-seated sense that brought the word "wisdom" to mind, though Alistair would never say it aloud for fear of sounding ridiculous. "It have a name?"

"*He* does," Linc responded. "I didn't know it at the time, but apparently I was naming him after his future owner. 'Obstinate.' I call him Obs for short. He's just as stubborn as you, Phaethon."

Damn it if the Drathe didn't look up at Linc then. The dog didn't quite glare, but it was close. Alistair's eyes widened. "Did he understand you?"

"Of course he did." Linc stepped forward and patted the Drathe's head. "He knows he's stubborn. Come on, Obs, this your new home." The dog whimpered and didn't move. Linc smiled and patted his head. "It's okay, boy. I know he looks mean, but he's harmless. Go on now. You knew I couldn't keep you."

The huge dog-like creature got up on all four legs, dwarfing Alistair as he remained squatting. The Drathe walked to the doorframe but didn't step into the room.

"He's waiting for you," Linc said.

Alistair stood up. "What is going on here, man? You bring this bear to my room and say I'm supposed to keep him? I'm going to die tomorrow."

Still smiling, Linc gave a shrug. "Maybe you won't. Maybe you'll lead us to glory. Doubtful, but maybe." There was a gleam in his eyes. "Either way, this Drathe was never meant to be mine. He was meant to be yours, and that's why I'm here. If you die tomorrow, then it's too bad you just met, but fate doesn't seem to care about such things."

The Drathe still didn't move. Alistair's eyes narrowed. "You want to tell me what the hell you mean instead of all this cryptic talk?"

"There's the asshole I know and love." Linc kept smiling. "A Drathe matches with one owner. It's why they're such linguaphiles. On their planet, they're looked at as magical creatures, and truth be told, our solar system can't explain how they do the things they do. I was on their planet when a shaman brought this one to me and said I'd find his owner one day. That was about two years ago. I liked the little guy, so I took him, plus I wanted to see if the shaman was right." He looked down at the top of the Drathe's head. "Turns out, he was."

"How do you know I'm his mythical owner?"

"Because the stubborn bastard has been trying to get down here since the moment you arrived. He paws the door at night and whines when I leave in the morning." Linc shook his head as if mystified. "At first I thought he was going crazy, but then I realized what was happening. He led me the whole way here, not stopping until I opened the door. Apparently, Obstinate is also shy."

The Drathe didn't look away from Alistair. If he understood what was being said about him, he gave no indication. Instead, his head was tilted up slightly, and he stared at Alistair's face. "I gotta say I'm mesmerized myself," Linc said. "He's never acted like this."

"What does it mean if I'm his owner?"

"The myth is that they follow their owner to death. If you die, he dies, and he'll do anything to keep you alive. They won't even mate if there's a chance their owner might be in danger. They won't leave your side."

Alistair raised an eyebrow. "So basically, you're killing this creature by giving him to me? Because we both know no one is making it out of here once the Commonwealth arrives."

Linc put his palms in the air. "I didn't make this decision. Obs here did."

The Drathe looked at him then, and this time his glare couldn't be mistaken.

"So look, I've got things to do." Linc ignored the Drathe. "You want him or not?"

"If I don't take him?" Alistair asked.

"I'm not a shaman, Titan. Apparently, they can only have one owner. I imagine he'll just sit outside until you let him in."

The Drathe looked at Alistair again, lowering his head slightly.

"He dangerous?" he asked.

Linc sighed. "All these damn questions. What do you think, Phaethon? He could rip out both our throats in a heartbeat. He weighs three hundred pounds. Yes, he's dangerous."

Alistair rubbed his hand through his short brown hair. "You're killing me, smalls."

"Huh?" Linc asked.

Alistair shook his head. "Nothing. Whatever. If I die during this invasion, you're probably dead anyway, Obs." He turned to his side and waved his hand. "Come on in."

The Drathe darted forward, quick for such a huge animal. In one bound, he leapt onto Alistair's bed.

"Never done that before either," Linc said. "Always slept on the floor in my dorm."

Alistair glared. "Great. Anything else?"

"Nope, that's all I got. Enjoy, good sir." Linc left the room, the door standing open. Alistair continued staring at the animal, a beast of mythical proportions.

"None of that shit is true," he whispered while he silently closed the door. "But come tomorrow, it probably doesn't matter who your owner is. Not once the Commonwealth gets here."

Alistair walked into the room, feeling as stupid as he ever had before. The Drathe stood and walked to the foot of the bed, leaving room for Alistair at the head, then laid back down. The cot sagged almost to the floor. "You really picked a dumb time to find your master. You know that?"

The Drathe looked at him with expressive eyes.

"You trying to tell me I don't know as much as I think?"

Obstinate gave a low rumble in his throat and laid his head down, then closed his eyes.

"Did you really understand me?" Alistair asked.

Another low growl, but this time it turned into a sigh. The animal didn't open his eyes.

"Well, I'll be damned."

Alistair was dreaming, and he knew it. His mind had taken him somewhere peaceful, somewhere he wanted to be, rather than the hell his life had become. He didn't want to stop dreaming. He didn't want to wake up, wishing he could exist in this place forever.

The edges of the world were hazy, as dreams usually were, but the focus of this particular one was extremely sharp.

Is this what the mutant was talking about? he wondered. *Are these the dreams he meant?*

It had to be because this was a dream unlike any he'd ever seen.

He was staring at his wife, at Luna.

She sat on the other side of the table from him. It was their second date. The first one had been awful. Alistair hadn't known what to say, and looking back on it, he'd barely been a man back then. He'd been twenty-two when he exited the Academy and twenty-three when he'd met her. He had over fifty kills to his name by then, had graduated as *Rex* of his Academy class, and still had choked up when it came to saying anything to the beautiful lady.

On the first date, when their AirTaxi had dropped her off, she'd turned around and looked at him for a long moment. "I'm going to assume you came down with some rare disease that makes you mute for twenty-four hours instead of assuming that you don't like me. That means I'm going to give you twenty-four more hours to get over this sickness, then I expect you to call me and ask me out again. Do you understand all that? It could also be that you're incredibly dumb, and if that's the case, I'm beyond frightened for the Commonwealth. Do you understand what I'm saying, Mr. Kane?"

Alistair's eyes had widened, and he'd simply nodded. He'd tried swallowing, but his mouth had been dry.

"Good. I will expect the call tomorrow when your vocal chords start working again."

She'd walked inside, and the door had slammed shut behind her.

Had he fallen in love then? It was cliché or something out of a sappy holovid, but yes, he'd known then. No one had spoken to him like that since he'd graduated from the Academy. He was destined to be a Primus one day, and sooner rather than later, yet the woman had verbally slapped him for being a flat-out idiot.

And the second date? What he now stood in, the weirdest dream of his entire life?

"I'm sorry about the other night," he told her. A week had passed before she'd been available, despite him calling the very next day. "I...I took some vitamin D shots, and I think the disease cleared up."

She gave a slight grin, her beer just below her lips. "It speaks." She took a sip and put it back down, still grinning. "They not teach you boys how to talk to the ladies in that Academy?"

He hadn't known what to say then and felt himself about to fall all over his words. It was a miracle of the gods that he managed to say anything and that what he said wasn't that bad. "They're not like you."

She raised an eyebrow, that devilish grin spreading on her face to an outright smile. She half-stood from her chair, leaned over the table, and looked at both sides of his head. "Checking to make sure you don't have an earpiece in. Someone telling you sweet things to say. No way the lug I met last week could have managed that one."

She sat back down, still grinning. Some guys might

have hated that and felt her teasing was making fun of him. Not Alistair. He'd loved it, and in this dream that felt *almost* like reality, he still loved it.

"I get lucky every once in a while," he said as he drew his finger around the mouth of his glass. He looked down into it. "They aren't, though, you know? The women in the academy." He looked up. "That's why I asked you out. You're different than anyone else I know."

"You've only known me a week, so what do you really know, Titan?"

He shrugged and glanced back down at the glass, his finger still resting on the rim. "I just know."

Alistair hadn't kissed her that night, but he'd asked to on the third date. She'd told him he had to wait for one more because their first date didn't count. It'd been too awful.

The dream moved from that bar to the end of their fourth date. He'd been standing outside the AirTaxi, the platform to her apartment extended and the AirShields up to keep them from being blown to the street a hundred yards below. "Can I have that kiss now?"

She stepped forward, tilted her head up, and their lips had met. Alistair had kissed women before, but he knew right then, at twenty-three, that he would never kiss anyone else again. She, Luna, was perfect. Perhaps not as a person, but perfect for him, and that was what really mattered in this life.

Alistair had wanted to relive these moments, so he'd let them flow. Now, though, he wanted to say something. He wanted to change the past, and while that wasn't possible, he could change the dream.

He pulled away and gazed into her eyes, his hands resting gently on her small hips. "I'm coming for you, Luna. I'm coming back. I promise. No matter what it takes, I'm going to see you again."

The woman who would be his wife stared back at him. "Why did you leave?"

"I...I didn't have a choice."

She nodded as if that made sense and she believed him. "You're going to come for me, though? You haven't left?"

He stared into those eyes. He knew this younger version would change, that the skin around her eyes would wrinkle some. She would get a few pounds heavier. But those eyes...they never changed. They had the same beauty on the last day he saw her as on this one. "I'm coming back. You have my word."

"I'll be waiting," his dream wife told him.

CHAPTER FIFTEEN

"Not conquering the Subversives in their entirety isn't a question of power but of economics. It simply isn't worth the cost to kill bugs that are so small. If they bother us, we destroy them. If they stay away, they'll be well."

–Aurelius de Finita, First Imperial Ascendant

Alistair stood inside a massive auditorium. Its size made him realize the immense capabilities of the men and women who had come to this planet before him. They had fled the Commonwealth and come here to dig through the ice. Now he stood in the wake of their greatness.

Standing to his left and right, as well as in front and behind, were the men in his Legion. He could hardly see where they ended—ten thousand men, all serving under Thoreaux. Alistair was just another face in this crowd. Well, almost. His modifications made him stand out, and he'd seen a few others like him, including Theos. Despite his size and red eyes, no one had paid him much mind.

Everyone was focused on what was coming this evening. As the sun set on Pluto, the Commonwealth would arrive.

A stage stood at the front of the room. It was unadorned, exhibiting none of the pomp and circumstance Alistair had come to expect from the Imperial Ascendancy. A line of leaders stood shoulder to shoulder at the back of the stage, and Thoreaux stepped to the front.

Many of the men and women standing around Alistair were grizzled veterans. Some were young, though, fresh faces that had never seen trials and tribulations, only heard about them at their parents' knees. Sure, their hands were rougher than those of the people on Earth. Growing up on an inhospitable planet was different, but it wasn't the same as fighting for your life.

Alistair looked closer at the untested youths than the grizzled vets. Even those standing behind him looked like they had seen more violence, and that made him wonder again why Thoreaux had been entrusted with so much responsibility.

There was a comm in the leader's ear, and when he spoke, the whole room heard him. "You all know me. I'm not one for stirring speeches, and I'm not going to blow smoke up your asses either. Tonight, our enemy comes for us. They come for your lives and the lives of those you love. They come for your mothers and fathers. Many of you were born here, and make no mistake, they're coming for your homeland. They will see you dead and this place an inferno. You are all that stands between them and the destruction of everything you know. I say that so you understand what's at stake. Our AllMother has decided this is where we make our stand. We shall not run. We will fight, and they will hear our war cries."

Thoreaux paused and looked down at his feet.

"Tonight, we will launch you at their fleet. Many of you will not make it back." He looked up. "Many of you will die in glory, and there will be songs sung about you far into the future. Your children's children will speak about the Great Insurrection and where it all started, and they'll say, 'My family stood. My family didn't kneel.'"

He took a step toward the front edge of the platform.

"Make the AllMother proud. Make your family proud. Make our insurrection proud. No matter what happens, the universe will not forget your sacrifice."

After Thoreaux's speech, Alistair met his contingent. They were a group of eight, including the leader. The man wasn't Plutonian but had the regality of someone born on Saturn's moons. His name was Brenyo, and he had a scar that went from his temple down to his jawline. It could easily have been fixed—Theos could have repaired it in his sleep—but Brenyo had apparently decided to keep it.

He told the company what the plan was, and to Alistair, it sounded insane. He'd heard of strategies like this, and he'd also heard how badly they'd failed. The company of eight would board a special kind of ship referred to as a Spider. Fifty of those would be flung into the air, each moving at a speed that would break the bones of their inhabitants if not for the internal mechanisms. The Spider would rapidly fill with an oxygen-equivalent liquid, both inside and outside the bodies of its passengers. The OEL allowed the soldiers to breathe and also not lose their lives due to the rapid increases and decreases in speed.

The speed was necessary because the Spiders would be targeted by the enemy. Not all would make it to their destination, but it would be tough to hit them.

The best part?

The Spider would crash into its predetermined enemy combatant ship, creating a massive hole to drain soldiers and equipment alike into space's vacuum. The Spider then took on its namesake, thick webbing filling the hole it had created in seconds as the OEL inside drained from inside. The webbing *hopefully* spread fast enough to stop the ship's vacuum protocols, leaving it possible to traverse the vessel's hallways.

But wait, there was more, according to Brenyo. *Then* the eight soldiers from the Spider would exit the ship and try to take the bridge.

Alistair said nothing, just let his leader talk. The others in his group had obviously trained for this sort of mission, but Alistair had spent all his time learning how to fight on a world he wouldn't even inhabit during the battle.

Brenyo had given them an hour's break before they needed to suit up. Alistair went back to his room, thinking that none of this made sense. Obstinate was waiting on him, and he lifted his head from the bed as the former Titan entered the room.

"At ease." Alistair went to the cupboard and started pulling out everything inside—dried meat, dried fruit, and vac-sealed cheese that didn't spoil. He laid it on the table while the Drathe cocked his head in confusion. "Look,

Obs," Alistair said as he continued pulling out food. "I just realized everything I've done the past few weeks was pretty much for nothing and that the people in charge of this endeavor have as much sense as this pack of jerky. I'll be dead before this rock does one more rotation. I don't know if anything Linc said was true, but if you do somehow live longer than me, you go ahead and help yourself to this food." He opened another cabinet. "And look, there's a portal on this planet. I'm going to leave the door cracked, and you just follow people to it, you hear?"

He hadn't heard the massive animal hop off the bed, but he felt the cold nose on his palm.

Alistair looked down, and the Drathe stared at him. When Alistair didn't move his hand, Obs pushed it onto the top of his head, forcing the man to pet him. Alistair dropped down on his ass then and leaned against the cabinets as tears filled his eyes. Obs pushed his way between his legs and laid down.

Alistair looked at him for a second before petting the beast. It'd all been for nothing. This whole thing—what he had done to his body, and sacrificing his soul to become a wretched hybrid creature. He'd never see his wife again; it had been only fool's gold to think he might. The people in charge of this thing, including the AllMother—if she even existed—were incapable of fighting a war against the Commonwealth. The Spider was going to smash into its chosen ship, and all eight of its passengers would be cut down within minutes.

Obs put his head on Alistair's ankle, resting it there.

"I did this to get her back, but I was a fool," he whispered as he wiped his eyes.

The door opened, and Alistair's head snapped up. His eyes were still red, so he couldn't hide that he'd been crying.

"Dry 'em, Titan," Thoreaux said, shutting the door behind him. He moved in front of the table, staring at all the food. "It's really not a good idea to eat before launching into space. You're going to vomit as it is."

Obs growled but didn't raise his head from Alistair's ankle.

"Ah, it's for the mutt," Thoreaux said, nodding. "In case you don't make it back?"

Alistair wiped his eyes hard. The only person who had ever seen him cry was Luna, and even then, it'd only been once--on rising to Primus Titan. He didn't want this stranger who looked down on him seeing it. "No one is making it back. That plan of yours is insanity. If the AllMother made it, then she's a better mother than a strategist. Attacking with Spider ships is only going to end in death for everyone involved."

Thoreaux leaned forward and placed his hands on the table. "Is that why you're crying? Scared of your own mortality?"

"Frag yourself."

Thoreaux stared at him for a few moments, then straightened back up. He dropped his hand to his pocket and pulled out a dull black rectangle with what looked to be a button in the middle of it. He tossed it on the table, where it hit a package of food. "That's for you. Whatever happens, you're not dying tomorrow, Titan."

Obs moved without being told to. Alistair stood and picked up the small rectangle. "What is it?"

"If you're in trouble at any point tomorrow, you press that button, and a Rover will come get you. So long as you have that receiver on you, the Rover will be within five minutes of a pick-up. It's stealthed and will be in position for where your Spider is targeted."

Alistair turned the receiver over in his hand. "How many people can fit in the Rover?"

"Just one. It's for you. The AllMother says you're not expendable, so you're not."

Alistair looked up, his eyes narrowed. "You want me to leave my contingent if things get bad? You want me to desert them?"

Thoreaux took a step back and sat on the bed. Obstinate moved around the table and sat, his eyes on the new man. Thoreaux glanced at the beast. "Linc showed the Drathe to me a few years ago, but I haven't seen him since. Lots of myths about those animals." He turned his attention back to Alistair. "You're still not getting it, Titan. It doesn't matter what you or I want. We do not have a say in this. We are troops in a war, and our general is the AllMother. You can ridicule her decisions if you want, but you *will* follow them. You are in my legion, and I command you to use that receiver if things get bad. Get in the Rover. Go where it takes you. Your job tonight is to survive."

"And if I say I won't?" Alistair asked.

Another growl came from Obs' throat, and his upper lip peeled back to show white teeth.

Thoreaux didn't look at him. "You'll use it. Don't ask me questions that aren't a possibility. I have a lot to do." He stood up and started making his way to the door.

"No," Alistair said. The Drathe bounded to the door, cutting Thoreaux off.

"You've got to be kidding me." He stared at the hulking beast, knowing he wasn't going to be allowed to exit as long as Obstinate stood at the door. He turned back to Alistair. "You do realize we're at war, right? That you're wasting time and probably costing lives?"

Alistair placed the receiver back on the table. "I won't leave anyone to die while I take an escape pod. I'm not sure who your AllMother thinks she's recruited, but that isn't me."

Thoreaux's face got very still. "Then I suggest you figure something else out, soldier, because your instructions are to survive. If you don't want to leave those around you, then develop a plan to bring them with you. *Your* orders aren't changing."

"Just so long as you know I won't leave people. You can tell that to your AllMother too."

"Move the animal," Thoreaux said.

Alistair didn't take his eyes off the man as he said, "Obs, to me."

The Drathe growled once more, then padded to Alistair's side.

Thoreaux left the room, closing the door firmly behind him.

Alistair looked down at Obs. "Good dog."

The Drathe lowered his shoulder and swung his body into Alistair. The Titan fell on his ass, his eyes wide.

It took him a moment, but he started to laugh and couldn't stop, not until tears were streaming down his face. He grabbed the animal and hugged him.

CHAPTER SIXTEEN

"To everyone who went along with this farce, who has contributed to my death and all the other world leaders' deaths, eventually you will pay a price. You will not wash your hands of this blood."

–Charles D. Winnaker, the Last President of the Geographic Area Formerly Known as the United States of America, Moments before Being Hung

The Spider was a black vessel that looked almost nothing like its namesake.

It was a disc about six meters tall, with a diameter of ten meters. All in all, the thing was tiny when Alistair thought about what it was going to be crashing into. However, looking at the ship, he felt slightly better about it. He reached up to touch the edge of the ship.

"I wouldn't if I were you."

It was Servia.

"It'll take your finger right off, Titan," she said with a

little grin. "That material is the sharpest material in this galaxy, and when it slams into the Commonwealth's dreadnought, it's going to be superheated to near-plasma levels as well as vibrating at a frequency that will slice through any shields the dreadnoughts have."

Alistair let his hand drop to his side. He'd been about ten centimeters from losing his index finger. "Thanks for the info. You coming with us?"

She shook her head as she turned away. "No, of course not. I'm much too pretty to risk scarring this face. Just wanted to see how you looked in our army gear. Too bad I'll miss you in the suit. Nice ass, spaceman."

Servia left the dock. Alistair's eyes were wide and his mouth was slightly ajar. After a moment, he grinned and turned back to the ship. "So it's going to cut our way in."

Alistair heard footsteps behind him.

"Time to suit up, Titan," Brenyo called as he and the rest of the contingent walked in. Alistair looked at the crew. He didn't know all their names yet, though they knew his. It seemed like everyone on this forsaken planet knew him. There were five men and three women, and all except for Brenyo and Alistair looked to be in their mid to late twenties and untested, another thing against them.

That wasn't Alistair's lookout, though. "Yes, sir. What are we wearing?"

"One," Brenyo said, "never call me 'sir.' Not here, and not in orbit. I don't know how long this contingent will be together, but we may end up doing something a bit more clandestine than smashing into an enemy ship. If that's the case, an errant 'sir' could get us all killed. Aces?"

Alistair nodded.

"Good. Suits are on the ship. Skins and soles for this one." He pointed at the descending ramp. "Go time is in one hour, so suit up, get into your places, and pray to whatever gods you believe in."

Alistair watched the men and women walk past him. There was a bit of playful talk and some light shoving, which Alistair had seen before in people going to battle. *These people know each other*, he thought. *They love each other.*

Like he used to love Ares—another person he'd lost that he hadn't grieved yet. Would he see Ares again? And if so, what would he do?

"Come on, broth," someone said as they slapped him on the back. "Name's Relm. Glad to have you with us. Heard you're a demon with that Whip."

Alistair looked at the young man and realized he'd seen him before: bright blue eyes and shorter than most Plutonians. Relm winked at him. "Stick close to me, broth. I'll protect ya."

Relm laughed at that and then walked up the ramp. Everyone seemed to have a snarky comment for Alistair today, but he offered not a single one back. He reached into his pocket and felt the receiver. Thoreaux was expecting him to leave this group if it meant *he* lived.

Not happening, he thought. *I may have sacrificed my body to see my wife, but I won't give up my soul.*

Alistair strode up the ramp and entered the Spider. The inside was black, with twenty pods on the walls. In the middle of the disc sat a column with tiny holes dotting it. That was where the Oxygen Equivalent Liquid would come from, and maybe the webbing when they finally landed.

"Come on, broth. Saved a pod for you," Relm called as he dropped his clothes and started putting his skin on. There were more than enough pods for him to not be near anyone, but there was Relm, pointing at the pod next to him.

Alistair walked over and looked at the SkinSuit inside. Black; they were all going as the color of night. Weapons were fastened to the outside of each pod. Each person had a MechPulse, a smaller StarBeam, and an eight-inch diamond blade in case hand to hand fighting was necessary. Alistair hoped they didn't run into any Titans. These weapons would matter about as much as a breath in a hurricane.

Alistair dropped his clothes. He'd undressed with men and women alike before, and he was glad to see it didn't bother anyone else in the contingent. It meant they'd trained together like this. He reached for his skin but paused. He still hadn't gotten used to his new body. The strength of it. The muscles that rippled his torso, legs, and arms. Without any vanity, he knew he looked like he'd been carved by the gods.

"Aye," Relm interjected. "That mutant did a pretty good modification on ya, huh?" The word "mutant" didn't seem to have any negative connotations for the young man. He'd said it as he would have "fellow."

"You know Theos?" Alistair grabbed the skin and started to put his legs in.

"Sure I do. Theos is a good sir, no doubt about it. Earthborn hate mutants, and even a few Plutonians look down on 'em, but not me. Dad was a mutant, actually. Wish he'd been able to give me some of them genes."

Alistair constantly forgot the color of his eyes, but everyone in this crew knew he'd been modified, regardless of whether he was naked. "Thanks." He didn't know what else to say, so he shoved his hands into the suit.

The crew was spread out far enough that no one could hear them as they spoke, but Relm leaned in. "You scared, broth?"

Alistair looked at the skin hanging off him. Fear hadn't been discussed much, and no one in the contingent had mentioned it. He nodded. "Yeah, I'm scared."

"Of death?"

Alistair shook his head. "No. Pain? Probably. Death? It's just the taking of the living from us, but once we're there, I'm not sure we even know it. Once the living have already been taken from us, there's not much else to fear."

Relm chuckled, then straightened back up to finish putting on his suit. "The Titan is an intellectual. What's got you scared, then?"

"That I'll never see the living again."

Relm paused. "Got someone you're hoping to come home to?"

Alistair pressed a button on the beltline of his suit. The back melded together, covering everything but his head. "Someone I'm hoping to find."

Relm nodded and pressed his own button. "So, you are scared to die, but for a different reason than most, maybe. How about this, broth? How about if we make it out of this, you tell me who you're hoping to find?"

Alistair looked up. It was the first sign of friendship anyone had given him since Ares had told him about his death sentence. "Sure. I'll do that. Are you scared?"

"Me?" Relm leaned against the wall, checking his weapons. "Dripping hell, yes, I'm scared. I was born scared, broth. Only thing that helps me face it is saying it out loud. I'm scared of those Earthborn ravaging me, but that doesn't mean I gotta let it rule, am I right?"

Alistair almost finished it with, "*As the Commonwealth,*" but caught himself. "Yeah, that's right."

"Check your weapons, broth. I don't trust the men who put 'em on here because they haven't shared blood with me."

Alistair went through the checks, but the only weapon he counted on using was his Whip. The pulses and beams wouldn't work well in a ship's small corridor. His Whip would lay waste to his enemies.

Everything was in order, but Alistair realized he'd made a mistake. He was almost completely suited, but there was one more thing to do. He took his left arm out of the skin, pulled the diamond blade from the waist, opened it, and lowered his head while turning his left arm so the palm faced down.

"What ya doin', broth?" Relm asked.

Alistair didn't listen to him. It was the ritual all Titans performed, one he wouldn't discard just because he'd discarded *them*. He'd grown up performing this every time he went into battle, and it was as much a part of him as his Whip. These people might have changed his name from Odin to Phaethon, but the same heart beat in his chest.

"I do not kill for glory," he whispered, not caring if anyone heard him. "I do not kill for malice. I kill because it is right. Because if I do not kill, those who seek to harm me and those I love will do so."

He took the blade and cut a circular wound across his arm. The blood started dripping immediately and fell to the floor beneath him.

"I do not fear the enemy. I do not fear death. I only fear living without protecting those I love. I only fear cowardice and hiding from my duty. As this blood flows, so will I. I bleed now so that I will not later. I bleed now so that those who sow harm against me know that blood does not frighten me. I bleed now because it is this blood that will conquer anyone in my path. See it and fear. See it and die."

Alistair placed the knife on the floor. Using his right hand, he wiped off half the wound, then brought the blood up beneath his right eye and smeared a line. He repeated the same for his left, then jammed his arm back into the suit.

He retrieved the knife and straightened. The entire contingent stood before him in silence. They were all dressed in their Skins, their heads uncovered.

"Gods protect me," one of the women said. "Is that what you Titans do every time you try to kill us?"

"Any time we face enemies, yes," Alistair answered.

"Broth," Relm said from his side, "new part of the deal. We make it out of this, you're teaching me that. Aces?"

An urge to tell him no came, but Alistair recognized where it had originated—from a group that tried to kill him. He'd bled for the Titans, but they would be on the other end of his Whip until he stopped breathing. *This* was his new family. "Aces."

"You're a weird one, Titan," Brenyo said. "Get into the pods. Countdown is in five minutes."

The contingent departed without anyone saying another word. The time for war had come. Alistair hooked himself into the pod, and its see-through ballistic glass enveloped him as soon as he was situated.

The minutes ticked down, and suddenly someone new walked into the disc. It was too late for anyone to get out of their pods, but this stranger was already in their skin. It was impossible to tell who they were, but Brenyo made no movement to get out of his own pod. Alistair didn't understand. No one had mentioned a ninth, but there wasn't anything that could be done now.

Alistair watched the stranger hook into a pod.

A loud *beep* came over the speakers—the countdown.

10...9...8...

Alistair closed his eyes. The enemy was upon them.

7...6...5...

Let me be true, he thought.

4...3...2...

Luna, I'm coming.

1...

CHAPTER SEVENTEEN

"They'll find out."

"If they do, it'll be too late. You'll be dead long before then anyway. In fact, you'll be dead before nightfall."

–Final conversation between the last Russian President and the First Imperial Ascendant

Two things happened at once, both of which amazed Alistair.

The Oxygen Equivalent Liquid began pumping from the column in the middle of the disc as well as from the pods. It came out fast and filled everything. Alistair thought he was going to choke when it hit his mouth and nose, and his body immediately tried to reject the substance. It couldn't be stopped, though, and it flooded his mouth and throat, his sinuses, everything.

He felt like he was suffocating until it hit his lungs, then he simply breathed in and out, in and out as if nothing had changed. The liquid was clear, so he was able to see through it, yet he couldn't move. He tried to raise his arm, but the substance had only the slightest give. He understood now that it was to protect him from both the speed and the "landing."

The second thing would have taken away Alistair's breath if the liquid hadn't already filled his lungs.

The Spider suddenly became transparent. The outside metal disappeared, and everyone inside the ship could see the world around them. It was obvious why such a thing would happen—not for aesthetics, but so the warriors could understand that nothing was as peaceful as things seemed inside the ship.

Alistair looked out in despair, unable to believe so much had been sent for *him*. The Ascendant had spared nothing; the entire First Fleet was here. Superdreadnoughts were scattered throughout the sky, corvettes flashing from them, carrying death to Pluto. Burners raced across the sky, smaller ships that were much harder to hit with ground weapons. They would carry Titans, valuable cargo that, once unleashed on the ground, would wreak havoc.

Are you here, Ares? Did you come to finish the job?

Inside the ship, everything was silent. Outside, bombs streaked from on high, ready to obliterate the ground-based railguns that were already targeting the fleet. Alistair realized that Linc had been right: this was war. Alistair had never seen anything close to it.

The ship they were heading toward grew larger as the Spider raced through the black sky. Since they were cloaked within a StealthBlanket, the ship wouldn't detect them until it was too late.

The beeping began again. The dreadnought was nearly at their windows, and they still hadn't turned opaque yet.

Alistair saw the edges heat to white-hot, then the Spider hit the ship, cutting through metal as if it were bread. Men and women flew out into space, their lungs exploding as they tried to suck in air. Equipment and furniture alike emerged into space's vacuum. Sirens blared loud enough to be heard inside the Spider.

Webbing started shooting from the outside of it, coating the ship's opening. The webs moved so quickly that Alistair couldn't keep up with them. One moment, objects shot out of the ship, and the next, oxygen and pseudo gravity were being restored.

The OEL had started draining immediately, and by the time the hole in the ship was repaired, Alistair was free of his pod. The ramp lowered, and three of the eight were ready with their pulses, firing at two men trying to rush on the ship. Their bodies flew back against a far wall, chests crushed.

"*ON ME!*" Brenyo commed, and the contingent responded.

They moved from the Spider to the destroyed platform where they'd landed. Sirens were still blaring, but the Skin-Suit dampened the noise that reached Alistair's ears as the contingent spread out to clear the area. Alistair had left his pulse on the ship but hooked the smaller beam to his waist. He unleashed his Whip as he moved through the wrecked room. Everyone but those two men had apparently been sucked out.

Brenyo raised his arm to look at the DataTrack embedded in the skin. His voice came over the comm in Alistair's hood. "Heading left. Enemy incoming. Phaethon, you planning on using that Whip the whole time?"

"Yes," he responded.

"Then you're our tank. We'll cover from behind. Try not to get your ass shot."

Alistair thought it might be the smartest direction he'd been given so far. He used his soles to boost him to the front of the line. The door in front of him was closed and double-barred with reinforced steel. "Going to need a charge."

"Watch out, broth. I got it." Relm stepped around him, then knelt and placed four charges at the four corners. As he stepped back, he tapped his temple with his right index finger. "Sorry, broth, brain got scrambled a bit in the crash. I'll have 'em ready for you next time."

Alistair nodded, and the group stepped back as one. Relm hit a receiver in his hand, causing the charges to give off a low whine. Ten seconds passed, and the door melted as the charges heated up.

"Stand back," Brenyo commanded. He brought his pulse to eye level and fired and the door flew back, boiling-hot metal hitting the group of soldiers on the other side. They shrieked as it melted their metal armor and reached their skin.

Alistair went forward, automatically calculating the number of enemies in front of him and the forms he would need to take to get through them all. He thought nothing of those behind him, nor of what might be farther down the hall.

The here and the now were all that mattered.

His Whip flashed right as his body moved left. He slammed an elbow into a woman's nose, and the bone slipped into her brain as the Whip lashed at a heavily armored soldier on his right. His right arm came off at the shoulder and blood splattered the face mask of the man behind him.

Alistair continued, the Cold Space fighting form propelling him without his muscles having to do much work. His mind was a silent place of action and focus.

A man came up on his left and slashed a BeamBlade through the air to get to Alistair's gut. He stepped back, letting the blade get within a centimeter of his skin as his Whip curled around the man's neck and decapitated him.

Alistair's body had never before moved like this. His strength, speed, and mass were too much for these Earthborn. They fell around him as if they were crops being cut down by a farmer.

Four minutes later, the corridor was empty. Alistair was at one end, his contingent at the other. Dead men and women lay between, blood and body parts strewn around as if they were some psychopathic toddler's toys.

"Broth," Relm came through the comm. "I don't know if anyone's told you this before, but you've got a gift for this killin' business. We might actually make it out of here alive."

"Nice work, Phaethon," Brenyo said. "Let's move forward. We've got to make it to the bridge or none of this matters."

Alistair no longer existed inside the suit. He was a creature who had once been called Odin. He moved through the passages, hearing the directions given to him from behind. Enemies came and enemies fell, their screams only echoing as long as he allowed them to.

"You sure he's a man?" someone said over the comm at one point. "He looks more like a god."

None of it mattered to Alistair. His mission was to reach the bridge, and at last, he did.

Sirens were still blaring down the corridors. Dead men and women decorated the deck, and a broad semi-circular door stood in front of the contingent. Alistair stepped to the side as Relm moved to the front of the pack and scanned the bay-like door.

"They've got this thing reinforced both vertically and horizontally. At least twelve bars run through it."

"Can you melt it?" Brenyo asked.

"We gone try, I suppose," Relm said. "Titan, you have any tricks that might work here?"

Alistair was thinking hard. He hadn't spent much time on ships since the Titans mainly made sure Earth was secure, leaving the Fleets to protect the rest of the Commonwealth. "I don't think so. This isn't my domain."

Relm smiled as he stared at the massive door. "No, I don't imagine so, broth. Can't become an expert in killing and spend time learning spaceflight. Brenyo, can you see anything with your track on the other side of this door?"

"Notta. Door's too thick, and they've cut off our comm."

Relm sighed and started pulling charges out of the pockets of his skin. "This thing is probably gonna melt halfway through, but the door is gonna hold. You're all gonna need to use pulses for us to have a chance to get through. Never imagined it'd be this well reinforced. They might have someone special behind there because this door ain't normal in the least."

He finished placing twelve charges across the barrier. Alistair didn't know why he'd picked the places he had, but he imagined they lay over the metal bars that reinforced the door.

Relm hit the receiver, and the charges started. It took longer this time, but eventually, the metal did begin to melt. Alistair stepped behind the contingent as they all raised their pulses, including Relm.

"On me," Brenyo said over the comm. "Five...four... three...two...fire."

The pulses slung their invisible ions at the door. The reload came quickly, and again the ions punched into the metal door, then a third and a fourth time.

It finally looked to be weakening. Relm's voice lit up the comm. "It's got one more in it. Be ready for enemy fire the moment it falls."

"Switch to beams," Brenyo commanded. The Mech-Pulses were overheating, and they wouldn't be operable on the bridge, not until they'd had time to cool down.

The pulses hit the door a final time, and the dripping metal flew inward. This time it didn't hit anyone because no one was close enough.

Incoming fire slammed into the team. Someone caught a plasma bolt on their leg that burned away the SkinSuit and melted through their flesh. Everyone heard a brief but agonized scream through the comm before Brenyo cut it off.

"Pull her back into the last hallway. We can't waste a medic on her right now, so get your ass back up here."

The rest of the team retreated, firing their beams and trying not to get hit. It was hard to see where the fire originated, but Alistair understood they were dead if something wasn't done quickly. He'd been stupid in his rush to get here, not realizing it was exactly what the enemy wanted. He could kill whoever he wanted outside these doors, but on the bridge, it would be a shooting gallery.

"Permission to enter," Alistair said into his comm.

"And do fuckin' what?" Brenyo hollered back. "They'll cut you and that Whip to pieces before you make it ten feet inside."

"Permission to enter," Alistair repeated. His voice was calm, his pulse not above eighty. The tears he'd shed earlier had come from a different man.

"Permission-fucking-granted," Brenyo said as a hole opened in the wall next to him. "For the love of the gods, do something."

The tall stranger who had joined them at the last minute stepped up next to Alistair. His voice came over a private comm—Thoreaux's. "What do you think you're about to do?"

Beams and ion shots filled the hall, destroying the carefully constructed metal and inching closer to the contingent. "I'm going to keep everyone alive," Alistair replied over the private comm. He looked at Thoreaux, challenging him to say something else.

Instead, he gave a slight nod. "Stay alive."

The Fallen Titan stepped into the corridor and quickly found the sources of danger. It wasn't only his reflexes that were faster, but also the neuro connections from his eyes to his brain. He leapt toward the bridge, his head nearly touching the ceiling before his descent started. He felt the heat of a shot burn close to his neck, but it didn't penetrate the skin. The combatants were pointing their weapons at him, ready to obliterate the incoming warrior.

Alistair tucked his head and hit the deck in a somersault, then shot upright, his Whip slashing. The strands cut a man in half.

Lasers hit the deck around him. One obliterated the upper half of the dead man as Alistair used his AirSoles to take off and flew forward like a heat-seeking missile while spinning in the air. He extended his arm and let the Whip work for him, slicing into the largest group of weapon-wielding enemies. He cut them down to nothing, and their guns fell from their lifeless hands to the deck next to their bodies.

The contingent moved in behind him and covered his assault with their beams. Alistair's feet hit the deck, and he turned to the forward position on the bridge. The crew remained focused on their terminals, not turning around to the assault. They were all synapsed into the ship, and losing their focus could mean death for them and everyone else in the dreadnought.

Pulse and beam shots flew past Alistair as he paused, not believing what he saw. This was the reason the ship's bridge was so reinforced: to protect one person, though Alistair could hardly fathom it.

He turned his comm off, and when he spoke, his voice carried across the bridge. "You let your Titans go fight while you sit here on high?"

Ares stood ten meters away, his MechSuit covering every inch of him except his head. The helmet remained retracted into the suit. He held his Whip at his side, the red lasers slowly twirling. "This is a fortuitous turn of events, I must say."

Alistair went forward, wondering how out of all the starships in the atmosphere, they would end up on the same one. "Where did I go wrong, Ares? You sit here while your men die? This isn't what I taught you."

He forgot about the battle blazing around him as he approached his erstwhile protege.

"What did you teach me, *Alistair*?" He purposely didn't use the Fallen Titan's old callsign. "You betrayed your oaths, and then, instead of turning yourself over like a man, you fled. You joined the very thing we swore to destroy." He shook his head. "Look at you. I don't need to see the red of your eyes to know you've been modified. You disgust me, Alistair. Everything we stood for, you threw it all away. You sold your soul, and for what? You're going to die here. You gave up your very soul and got so little in return. A few extra weeks of life."

Brenyo's voice came over his comm. "We need to get control of the pilots."

Alistair ignored him as he raised his Whip and brought it down across the deck. Sparks shot into the air. "You fooled me. You made me think you were a *worthy* heir to my legacy." He saw the contingent moving to his right, using their weapons on the dwindling enemy fighters while making their way to the pilots. The best fighters had been sent to the ground; these people here weren't meant to take on an elite team. Ares shouldn't be here either, but Alistair now understood that he didn't plan on dying, whatever else might happen.

"Why don't you come to me, Mutant, and we'll see who is worthy of what?"

Alistair's anger rolled through him. The Titans had been *his* command. He had taught them to be honorable, and now their Primus hid in the sky while they went to battle beneath. He brought his Whip down again, raking the steel from the deck and leaving black snakelike gouges in its wake.

Alistair stepped forward as the sparks floated around his black mask.

Ares' helmet rose above his head, his MechSuit fully enveloping him.

Thoreaux came over the comm. "Alistair, *no*. Retreat. We will cover." He knew what the MechSuit could do, just like every Subversive. It was a deadly weapon that amplified the wearer's movement, strength, speed—everything.

Alistair ignored the command and watched as Ares took his form—the Cliff Breaker. It was a smart choice, prioritizing strength over everything else. He planned on beating Alistair into submission.

A beam streaked in front of Alistair's face. One step forward and his head would have been obliterated. He didn't flinch. Again, Thoreaux's voice came over the comm. "You fucking idiot. He's drawing you in."

Alistair heard it before he saw it. He'd been focused on Ares' form, on battling a MechSuit, and the *tick-tick* of metal on metal was almost lost in the noise of battle. Alistair looked up, seeing the grotesque creature for the first time—if it could be called that. It hung from the bridge's ceiling, its five hundred eyes staring at everything all at once.

As Theos could modify human bodies, there were others like him, often called butchers, who did the same to other species. The thing hanging above Alistair was neither insect nor robot but an unholy mixture that combined the worst of both species into a killing machine.

It dropped from the ceiling, not needing to flip over, its metal legs simply shifting downward while its eyes moved up across its body to change its orientation. A thick string shot out of one of its eye sockets and attached to the ceiling to keep its drop from crushing its metal legs. Alistair leapt back, his AirSoles giving him a boost. The creature landed an instant later and wasted no time scurrying forward. Ares used his MechSuit's boots to propel himself into the air, where he floated like a god over his horrible offspring.

Alistair landed on his ass on the deck and slid backward. The insectoid was nearly on him, and he slashed at it with his Whip. Sparks bounced off the metal deck as his team's beams fired at the creature. Its massive body shrugged off the blasts as if they were little more than annoyances. Alistair somersaulted backward and got to his feet before spinning left. He slashed his Whip in its fluid form, but the insectoid darted back on five of its legs while the sixth jutted forward, growing longer as it tried to impale him.

Ares floated over the top of Alistair, trying to get to his six. The creature marched forward as beams blackened its red eyes.

"USE A FUCKING PULSE!" Alistair shouted over the comm as he kicked off the deck into the air, using his soles to try to gain space between both Ares and the insectoid.

The metal creature bounded into the air as well, webbing shooting from three of its functioning eyes. Alistair's Whip took the solid form and slashed at the strings before they could touch him. He sensed Ares' Whip falling from above, and he let the AirSoles drop him. The Whip slashed through where he'd been.

He hit the deck hard, and the breath rushed out of his body. He couldn't fend them both off for much longer.

A MechPulse hit the insectoid with full force. The creature hadn't been expecting it since its spider-like brain was focused on the kill. Two of its six legs were pulverized, and its undercarriage dropped to the floor, scraping the deck as it tried to reach him.

Another pulse obliterated a third leg, and the creature dropped even closer to the deck, unable to hold up its great weight. Alistair leapt to his feet, flashed to his right, and brought his Whip down on the thing's back. Its strands sliced through metal and flesh alike, and the abomination gave a pained shriek as he cut it in half. Black blood spilled across the floor as its remaining legs collapsed and the red eyes on its back faded to black.

"Above you!" Thoreaux's voice shouted over the comm.

Alistair looked up, knowing who was coming for him. Ares flew down, rage and hate propelling him as much as his suit. His Whip was fluid and struck at Alistair's neck with abandon. Form was forgotten; all that remained was a desperate need to kill, but Alistair didn't falter. When Ares attacked in rage, he met him with calmness and spun, letting Ares' suit and forward momentum slam him into the deck.

Alistair kicked the back of the MechSuit and felt something give in his foot. His legs' strength was unlike anything he'd imagined: the metal dented, and Ares sprawled out. His Whip clattered on the deck, the white lasers retreating into the hilt as it left his hand.

Alistair pounced on his back and let his Whip extend fluidly to wrap around the MechSuit's neck. The smell of burning metal filled his nostrils as he ordered, "Yield, Titan."

The warfare around him had stopped. Only the pilots, who were synced with the ship, weren't staring at the two monstrous men.

Ares laughed. "Don't you get it yet, Alistair? Yes, I yield, but it makes no difference. You're dead. Look around you."

The Fallen Titan looked around without removing his Whip from the Titan's neck.

Brenyo's voice came over the comm. "He's right. Dreadnoughts are turning toward us. The pilots alerted the rest of the field that you're here. They're going to nuke us as soon as they can get their cannons positioned."

Relm walked over to Alistair and pointed the Mech-Pulse at the Titan's head. "I've got him, broth."

Alistair let his Whip retract some and stepped off his former protégé. "If he moves, decapitate him."

"No *problemo*," Relm responded.

Alistair walked over to where Thoreaux and Brenyo stood near the head pilot, who had her hands on the DeskPad in front of her. She was staring straight forward, her eyes full of static. She was still harmonized with the ship.

Brenyo and Thoreaux looked at him as he walked over. Something had shifted in the order of things since they'd boarded the ship. Alistair didn't pause or look at anyone else, just let his Whip unfurl in front of the pilot's face. "How long until the cannons are in position?"

The pilot didn't move. "Ten minutes at minimum."

Thoreaux's voice came over the private comm. "Use the receiver. Now. Get to the AllMother. She'll tell you what to do."

Alistair ignored him. The Whip danced in front of the pilot's face. "Relm, how's my friend doing over there?"

"Oh, he's playing nice."

Alistair nodded as he stared out the bridge's windows. "What sort of escape pods does this ship have?"

The pilot's voice was as calm as Alistair's. "Your Spider crashed into the escape bay. From what I can tell, we have one left, but it's damaged and will have to be flown manually. Ten minutes until impact."

Thoreaux's voice raged over the private comm. "Use the fucking receiver *now*."

"Can you fly it?" Alistair asked the pilot.

"Yes, sir," she replied.

Eyes turned to her then—her colleagues'. Ares laughed from the deck. "You *dripping-hell* traitor. If you fly them out of here, I'll make sure none of your kids reach old age. Do you understand me?"

Brenyo moved closer to the pilot. "You going to trust her? She could simply take us to the nearest dreadnought."

"No choice," Alistair replied. "What's your name, pilot?"

"Faitrin."

"You'll get us to an escape pod and then to the ground?" he asked.

"You won't kill me?" the pilot responded.

"That's a fair deal," Alistair said. "Deharmonize, and let's move."

The static in the pilot's eyes faded, revealing the pale blue irises of a Plutonian. She stood and walked over to Ares, leaving Alistair and the rest to stare after her. She spat on the Titan. "I prayed to the gods that I might make a difference in this mission. Now I finally can."

"You'll burn like the rest," Ares said. "And any of your family that's still on Earth? They'll burn too."

The pilot said nothing else but marched to the exit of the bridge, not pausing to see who followed.

"Alistair, what do you want me to do with this cretin?" Relm called to him.

Alistair was walking across the bridge, the rest of his company covering his six as they followed the pilot. He stopped and looked at the man he'd once thought of as a brother. "Give him another shot at glory later down the line."

Relm chuckled as he glanced at the fallen Titan. "He's nicer than me. Good luck, broth."

He fired the pulse at one-quarter power. The blast damaged Ares' shield and knocked him unconscious. Relm looked up. "That work?"

"Looks good. We gotta double-time it if we're going to make it." Alistair started jogging after the pilot, who had left the bridge.

Thoreaux came over the private comm again. "You've disobeyed direct orders."

"Not the one that counts," Alistair responded. "I haven't died."

As they left the bridge, Alistair knew without any doubt

the remaining pilots were reporting their escape. Alistair understood that their chances of survival were near zero. They'd come here to destroy a ship, and it had simply been bad luck they'd landed on the one that held Ares.

Even if they somehow made it back to Pluto, what then?

Alistair pushed the thoughts from his head as the team made their way back through the wrecked corridors. The pilot moved quickly, without looking back. Most likely, the other ships wouldn't believe the remaining pilots, thinking that Alistair had forced them to say he was escaping. The missiles would come all the same.

They reached the shredded escape bay. The Spider's webbing still held, though the pod bay door had been destroyed.

"How much time?" Alistair asked the pilot.

"Approximately two minutes until impact." After Faitrin passed her hand over a panel on the lone pod, a hatch opened and she stepped inside, once again not waiting to see if anyone joined her. The contingent stepped in after her, each strapping into one of the seats. Faitrin sat in the pilot's chair, already harmonizing with the pod. That was what she'd meant by manual, but only mutants like her could fly ships now—those who could harmonize, their brain's synapses becoming one with the machines.

"Hold on," Faitrin said, her voice as calm as it'd been when she spat on Ares.

The escape pod leapt forward and smashed into the webbing that blocked the opening. As it lurched into the cold nothingness, Faitrin integrated fully with the controls, and the ship sped into the blackness' embrace.

Alistair let his skin's hood melt into the neckline, revealing his face to the rest of the contingent. The blood under his eyes had dripped down his face, making it look like he'd wept blood. He was the only one who did that, so he couldn't see how stressed the rest of his team was. The woman with the injured leg appeared to be coping, but she would need medical attention soon.

"He's escaping," Faitrin said. Her eyes were static-gray again.

"Who?" Brenyo asked.

"Ares. I'm still connected to the other ship."

Brenyo was seething. "Did you know that would happen?" he asked her.

Faitrin sounded as if they were discussing the weather on Mercury. "No. I only know that his presence was scanned in a small pod that's moving faster than our ship. Missile impact imminent."

Alistair relaxed. In space's vacuum, explosions couldn't spread. The missiles would destroy the dreadnought and nothing else, so they were safe—for now, at least.

"Where are we heading?" Faitrin asked without turning her head.

Brenyo looked at Thoreaux. Of course he'd known the man was along for the ride. Did he know why, though? That Thoreaux's whole purpose was to keep Alistair alive?

What in the hell is happening here? Alistair wondered. *You don't send a general to help keep a private alive.*

Thoreaux spoke, still strapped into his chair. "How far can this pod travel? Does it have fourth-dimension capabilities?"

"No," Faitrin answered. "It's meant for rescue. It won't get us more than ten thousand kilometers."

Thoreaux leaned back in his chair and stared forward. Alistair knew what he was thinking: to go to Pluto meant death. He'd hoped they could use this to get the Fallen Titan out of the vicinity, but that wasn't happening.

Alistair shook his head. "No. We have to go back to Pluto."

The rest of the contingent turned to look at him, all bringing their hoods down. No one said a word, but their thoughts were apparent on their faces. Alistair should not be challenging someone so high up. It didn't matter how well he fought; he was still no one in this force.

Alistair ignored their looks. "The portal. That's our only chance."

Thoreaux was quiet, not showing the anger of the others in the contingent. He considered what Alistair had said, and after a moment, he nodded. "If I give you coordinates, can you get us there?"

"Yes," Faitrin responded. "We need to hurry, though. The Commonwealth is tracking us. They know we've escaped."

Thoreaux spat out coordinates. Alistair didn't know if they led to the portal or somewhere else, only that they were heading back to Pluto. There was no private comm channel now that their hoods were off, but he caught Thoreaux's look. The receiver still worked, and the separate pod was still following them. Even after all this, he wanted Alistair to use it.

The former Titan gave a small shake of his head.

Thoreaux looked as if he might murder him, receiver be

damned. After a moment, he turned back to the pilot. "Can you get us away from the trackers?"

"Should be able to. They've got Blazers, but they don't have me."

"Get us down there," Thoreaux commanded, "and you'll have whatever you desire, pilot."

Faitrin turned her head at that. She looked positively spooky with her gray eyes staring endlessly at Thoreaux. She raised her right eyebrow. "Careful what you promise, Subversive." She had a sly grin on her face as she returned to focusing on flying the ship.

Minutes passed in silence. Alistair leaned his head back on the chair. Whatever happened when they landed, he had to get back to his room to get Obstinate. Then they could worry about the rest. If he was going to die in nuclear fire, he'd at least die next to the closest thing he could find to a dog.

"Incoming," Faitrin said. "Hold on."

The ship jinked to the left. The chair's restraints held Alistair in, keeping him from spilling out on the deck. As soon as it went left, it rocked back to the right, then dove straight down. Alistair slammed into the seat as the speed increased.

"Broth, are you trying to fucking get us killed?!" Relm shouted from Alistair's right.

"I said, hold on," Faitrin responded in that same calm voice.

The ship was picking up speed. Alistair felt his lips peel back, his teeth showing like he was a mad jester.

"Bay's not opening," Faitrin said. "Need it opened in the next minute and a half or we're dead."

Thoreaux shouted a passcode at her. He wasn't panicking, but he understood how close they were to dying. Alistair's pulse sat at sixty-two.

"Opening," the pilot said. "Ground support is keeping the Blazers off."

The ship slowed quickly, Alistair's body jerked off the seat but was restrained by the straps. The pod finally came to rest, and the pilot's eyes returned to normal. The pod door opened to reveal a soldier who met Thoreaux on the bay floor. "We're under siege, sir."

Thoreaux walked toward him, his skin's hood still melted into the neckline. "Where is the AllMother?"

"In her bunker," the soldier responded. "It'll be a battle to get to her. The halls are clogged with Titans and Commonwealth soldiers."

"MechSuits?" Thoreaux asked.

"Yes, sir."

The contingent was following Thoreaux, but he stopped and turned. Alistair could hear explosions from behind the bay walls; screams, too. This was a massacre. "Alistair, you're with me," the leader instructed. He looked at Brenyo. "Bring the rest of the contingent to the front of the assault. Keep the Commonwealth away from the AllMother until you get more instructions from me."

"Yes, sir," Brenyo responded.

"Where's Servia?" Thoreaux asked.

"I don't know, sir."

Thoreaux turned to the pilot. "Do you know how to use a weapon?"

"I do," Faitrin responded.

"Keep honoring your planet, pilot. If we survive, I'll make it worth your while."

She nodded. "Just don't forget what you said on the ship. Whatever I desire if we survive."

Thoreaux put his fist to his chest, a Subversive salute, then walked away from the explosions. Alistair caught up with him quickly. "We've got to get the Drathe."

Thoreaux shook his head. "Not happening. We're going to the AllMother and getting instructions. Our entire endeavor was almost a complete waste."

"But it wasn't. The dreadnought was destroyed." Alistair stopped walking, forcing Thoreaux to as well. The contingent was out of earshot now, heading toward the battle's front. Alistair didn't want to challenge him again in front of his soldiers. "Listen to me. If you think we're not going to encounter enemies on the way to this AllMother, you're delusional. The Drathe will help us get to her. You've seen how massive he is. More, he's smart. Also, I'm not going anywhere without him, so either you can head to the AllMother by yourself, or we can go as three. It's up to you."

Thoreaux still showed no anger. It was as if he was studying Alistair, deciding something that had nothing to do with the current predicament, and once again, he acquiesced. "Let's go get the damned animal."

CHAPTER EIGHTEEN

"Why are you doing this?"

"Because humanity deserves better than what you've given them. I plan to show them a better way."

"One man can't rule the world."

"Let me worry about the future, Prime Minister. The past is yours."

–Final conversation between Canadian Prime Minister and the First Imperial Ascendant

They passed through the halls like ghosts. Alistair was surprised by how well Thoreaux moved. Even lacking the modifications the former Titan had, he kept up relatively well. Alistair cut through the few combatants who ended up in his path, his Whip a creature whose bloodlust couldn't be satisfied.

As they got closer to the room, Alistair began to wonder if someone had broken in and those combatants he'd cut down like wheat in a field hadn't done the same to his animal. He'd only known the creature briefly, but he felt a strong kinship with him.

When they reached the room, the door was closed. Alistair wasted no time bursting through.

Obstinate leapt into the air as Alistair brought his Whip down, ready to destroy whatever was attacking him. He pulled it back at the last second as the Drathe's paws pushed him to the floor. Alistair stared up at dagger-like teeth, thinking it was over for him unless he killed the creature.

He couldn't bring himself to do it, though, and then he felt a wet tongue licking his face.

"Gods, this is too much." Thoreaux had drawn his weapon and was pointing it at Obstinate's back. He slowly lowered the beam. "Can we get the fuck out of here? There are things to be done."

"Up, Obs. Up!" Alistair commanded as he laughed. Seeing this mutt was the best thing that had happened to him since he'd leapt out of the building back on Earth. The Drathe got off him, positively smiling at Alistair as he climbed to his feet. "Look, boy, we gotta get to this person called the AllMother. It's going to be dange—"

The Drathe lunged out of the room and trotted down the hall. Alistair stuck his head out. "What the hell?"

"Apparently," Thoreaux said, "the damn thing knows where to go since that's the way we're headed."

The Drathe stopped at the end of the hall, just before turning right. He looked back and yelped, and the two went after him. They reached the end of the hall, headed to the right, and wound through the underground lair. Obstinate led the way and Thoreaux kept following, which meant they were heading in the right direction. Alistair could tell they were winding farther down into the ice planet, though by that point, he was lost.

They turned left and stopped. Obs was standing a meter in front of them with his head lowered, growling. Alistair stood behind Thoreaux and stared at one of the biggest humans he'd ever seen. His shoulders filled the hallway, and his head was mere centimeters from the ceiling. His eyes were as red as Alistair's, though this man's body dwarfed his.

"Obs, to me," Alastair commanded. The Drathe didn't move, only kept growling.

"I knew I'd need your eyeballs to get to her." The man's voice was deep and carried as if connected to a microphone. "You're the one they call Thoreaux?"

Alistair looked the man over. The armor on his chest appeared to be Earth-made steel, and a red eye stared from the center of it. Some nearly lethal blow had carved a scar over the top of it. "What the hell is this?"

Obs took a step forward, his growls more menacing.

"Come now, Subversive. You knew you would meet me sooner or later. I watched your father die on a planet far from this one. It seems only right that I should kill his son." The god-sized man pulled a hilt from his waist that looked similar to a Whip. He pumped it once toward the floor, and a single laser shot out of the bottom. It didn't move like

Alistair's Whip did but remained solid like a staff. He thrust it toward the ceiling, and the same type of laser shot out of the top. "Bring your lackey and the Drathe, too. No reason all three of you can't die here, though I only need your eyes to get to the AllMother."

Alistair didn't understand what was happening, who this man was, or how he knew where the AllMother waited. The only thing he knew for sure was he didn't like how close Obs had gotten to this massive boulder of a man. "Obs, to *me*."

The Drathe was taking another step forward but paused, obviously hearing his owner. Thoreaux fired his beam, and the mutant moved quicker than anyone Alistair had ever seen. His weapon sliced through the air and destroyed the beam particles. Thoreaux fired again and again, hitting the trigger on the small weapon. The mutant moved as if he weren't human but a paranormal creature. He hit every beam particle that flew toward him.

The beam overheated before the mutant was struck.

"The only thing that's kept you from me is you hide well. Like an insect." The mutant wasn't even breathing hard. Obs had backed up, hugging the wall to stay out of harm's way. "Are you ready to die now? Or would you like to let me in first and watch your queen die?"

The Drathe barked, no fear in his animal voice.

"Get back," Alistair whispered.

Thoreaux obeyed the order. Alistair knew it wasn't out of cowardice or a desire to see him die. There just wasn't any other possibility of getting to the AllMother. They could retreat, but eventually, the enemies would arrive here. Or Servia would show up and this creature would kill her first, using her eyes to get in.

"Obs," Alistair said loud enough for the Drathe to hear, "stay back. You'll know if I need you. Don't interfere otherwise." The animal looked up at him, his teeth now behind his lips. The Drathe didn't like the order, but he appeared to be ready to obey.

Alistair stepped forward and let his Whip unfurl from the hilt.

"The insect sends you, a mutant. I'll never understand why you give up your own kind to play in the dirt with these creatures. The AllSeer could use you. Sure you don't want to come back with me?"

Alistair had no idea what this mutant was talking about, but his answer couldn't be misunderstood. He raked his Whip across the floor, the three laser tentacles scraping the metal. Sparks shot around him, then smoke rose to drift toward the ceiling.

"So be it," the mutant said. "You won't be the first of our kind I've put down, though I must say, you're a prime specimen."

Alistair had neither fought nor seen this type of weapon before. The hilt was wide enough for both hands, but the creature was obviously strong enough to swing it with one. Death could come from either side of it.

The monster moved forward, his shoulders almost scraping the walls as he did. Alistair thought he was big, but he felt small compared to this thing barreling toward him. The mutant took no forms, only moved forward as if he were the Grim Reaper.

Alistair went to meet him, no longer the man of his birth name. He was now the Titan Odin.

Leaning forward, the mutant sliced down with his laser, trying to cleave the Titan in half. Odin dodged the laser and slipped past the mutant, hoping to get behind him and cut through his armor, but when he turned, the mutant was facing him. They were too close to use their weapons. The mutant slammed his elbow into Odin's nose, and blood spurted from his face. He knew he had to separate himself from the massive beast. If the mutant got a grip on him, he'd rip him limb from limb.

Odin dropped onto his ass and slid down the hall as blood dripped from his face, then somersaulted and came to his feet, taking form once again.

"You're new to your body," the mutant mocked. "Not used to using it yet. Too bad you won't get the chance. You know you could have run and left me here with the insect and his queen."

Odin saw Obs behind the mutant. The Drathe wanted to jump in; it was killing him to keep obeying. The Titan's face felt like a star had exploded inside his nose, but his mind pushed that out of the forefront of his consciousness. His pulse remained at eighty, his heart beating steadily as he tried to figure out how to remain alive. This creature was unlike anything he'd seen: no form, no technique, just pure physical brilliance, better than Odin or anyone he'd seen.

The mutant lunged again, moving down the hall with no fear of what the two behind him might do. Odin caught a glimpse of Thoreaux, but his beam was still overheated. A diamond blade wouldn't matter to this hulk.

Odin waited until the last moment, wanting the mutant to commit. He lunged forward with his laser, and the Titan fell back. The weapon sliced up his suit, burning through it and the skin beneath.

He went straight like a board, his Whip taking a sword-like form. The mutant was fast and strong but too heavy, so his forward motion kept him going. Odin stabbed upward, knowing that if it didn't work, he was dead.

The Whip plunged through the chest plate and sank into the monster, and he fell on top of the Titan. The laser pole was inches from his face, the lower half still burning his flesh. He shoved up hard, burying the Whip hilt-deep in the man. The mutant stared down as blood spewed from his mouth, splashing Odin's face.

He yanked the Whip upward, wanting to cut the mutant from his chest to his neck.

The mutant coughed up more blood and looked to be trying to adjust his weapon, but his head was suddenly ripped up into the air, taking his laser with it. Obs was dragging him backward by his hair, pulling him off Odin and keeping the deadly weapon at bay. Thoreaux reached the mutant a second later, grabbing his leg and yanking.

Odin pushed himself the opposite way down the hall, clear of the danger.

Thoreaux flipped the creature over, and Obs wasted no time. He took the mutant's throat out with one huge bite.

The hallway grew still. Thoreaux breathed heavily while the Drathe stood atop the dead mutant, staring down at him and growling. Alistair became himself again, dropping his Titan persona.

"You aces?" Thoreaux asked.

Smoke rose from Alistair's SkinSuit, and the flesh beneath was badly burnt in a line that went straight up his chest. Blood ran down his body and splattered his face. He honestly couldn't be sure what was his and what was the dead mutant's. "Yeah, I guess we don't have much choice now. You're going to have to explain that fucking freak to me."

Thoreaux nodded and leaned down to offer his hand. The Whip moved away from him as he did, and Alistair turned it off. He strapped it to his tattered suit, then reached up and gripped Thoreaux. He got to his feet; Obs was there, licking the back of his hand. "Good dog."

The Drathe took Alistair's whole hand in his mouth and lightly pressed down with his teeth. It was a friendly warning, but when the animal let his hand go, it was covered in blood—the mutant's. "Glad you're on my side, Obs."

"Let's go." Thoreaux jogged down the hallway, and Alistair and Obs followed him. It only took another minute to reach the door the mutant had been talking about. He had attempted to blast and burn his way in, as well as everything else he could think of. The door was badly damaged, with weapons scars on the metal exterior.

A blue light appeared at the top of the door and moved from there to the floor. Thoreaux kept his eyes open as it ran over his face.

A voice spoke next, booming from the entire hallway as if it were an enormous speaker. "Voice confirmation."

"Ender Wiggins wore a gunslinger's hat."

A sigh came from the door as the air compression was released, then the burnt slab of machinery sank into the floor. Thoreaux went in, and the other two followed him.

"Idiot wouldn't have been able to get in if he decapitated me. Would have still been outside, raging at the door with my head in his hand."

Alistair wiped his face as he walked, only half-listening to the man. He imagined he looked like a nightmare.

The door slammed shut the moment he and the Drathe were inside.

Still wiping his face, Alistair searched the room quickly. When his eyes landed on the woman, his whole body paused. Even his hand quit trying to wipe away the horror on his face. The pain across his chest stopped mattering.

It's her, he thought. Above them, enemies were streaking through the sky to kill him. Strange man-beasts walked the halls, talking as if the Commonwealth might as well not exist, yet in Alistair's mind, none of it was important.

The woman's back was to him. She looked old, ancient even. She wasn't tall like a Plutonian but looked like someone Earthborn. Her arms were thin, her hair white and in a bun on her head. She clasped her hands in the small of her back, focusing on a holovid that Alistair couldn't have cared less about. The woman possessed a presence that sucked all the energy out of the room.

The only word to come to mind was "AllMother." It simply fit.

Servia stood from a far couch. "Gods, man, did you get him killed?" She was obviously talking about Alistair's wounds and face, but he hardly heard her.

Thoreaux ignored his colleague and stepped closer to the old woman. "What would you have us do now, Mother?"

When she spoke, her voice...

There wasn't any other way to put it. She sounded like a mother, one deeply concerned for her children, with love everlasting running through her heart. "I'd like to speak to him now."

Thoreaux's eyebrows went up. "Now?"

"I didn't stutter, did I?"

The soldier lowered his head. "No, ma'am."

The Drathe padded in front of Alistair and came to a stop just before he reached the woman. Even he felt something special about her, though he wanted to stand between the two of them.

"Obs," Alistair whispered, "heel."

The Drathe didn't move, refusing to listen to his master.

"It's okay," the AllMother said. "He's been waiting his whole life for you. The Drathe know their purpose from the moment they're born, while we spend our whole lives trying to find ours. It's only when our life has played out that we hopefully realize we accomplished it." She turned around then, a smile on her face. "I feel I might finally be looking at my purpose. It has been a long time coming, but it's a true pleasure to meet you, Alistair Kane, Fallen Titan, Odin."

Alistair slowly dropped his hand to his side and blinked, not sure what to say. Not sure what to do.

"Time is short," the old woman continued, "though I wish it wasn't. To say that finding you was an endeavor would cheapen what we did, and it would also lessen what you mean to this family. Years, Alistair. Years and lives— that was what it cost to get you here. To get us all here, including those who come to kill us now."

She stepped forward, the Drathe backpedaling with her

so as not to let her get close to Alistair without him there. Still, Obs didn't growl. The AllMother extended her hand. Alistair looked at his own, covered in blood.

"It's okay," she said. "I've never been scared of a little blood."

Alistair raised his hand to meet hers, and they shook. Her grip was firm, no fear in it.

"Why?" he asked as he pulled his hand back. "What is all this for?" The other two people in the room had fallen away for him. There was only this strange old woman.

"You will bring us peace or ruin, Alistair Kane. All of this..." She turned and spread her arms out to the holovideo showing her world under attack. "I'm going to give it to you."

Alistair heard someone gasp to his right, and his eyes narrowed. "I don't want it." He shook his head. "I don't want any of this. You're about to die, don't you see that? We're all about to die. I just wanted..." He looked down at the Drathe standing next to him.

She finished his sentence. "Your wife back. I know. You might think I'm arrogant or insane, young man, but I know you almost as well as you know yourself. I've watched almost every piece of your life. I know you want your wife back, and I know you think it hopeless now. You think I'm an old crone who didn't know what she was doing when preparing for this battle. I promise you, I've been preparing my entire life for this *war*. Now I'm giving it to you if you'll take it."

"AllMother," Thoreaux whispered harshly from across the room.

Her head whipped toward him. "Did you build this?"

Thoreaux didn't lower his eyes, but he shook his head.

"Then I'm curious why you think you have a say in who leads it? The only say you will have is if you want to serve and who you allow to serve under you. You will not have a say in who I choose to serve or lead."

Thoreaux remained silent. Alistair couldn't read what he was thinking, not from his face, at least. He thought he understood, though. This soldier couldn't believe something he loved dearly was being given to a person who had been an enemy combatant not even two months ago.

The AllMother looked at Alistair again. "I'm not saying taking over will be easy, but it's necessary. You will have to convince an army you're the right person to do it, though I've known for a long time that you are."

Alistair nodded at the holovideo behind her. "It's too late for us. The nukes are coming, and they're going to burn this planet until nothing remains. We're already dead."

"You know that's not true."

He did, too. The portal...if he could get there, they could go.

What the dripping hell am I even thinking about? I don't know the first thing about portals or where they open up to. He shook his head once again. "Those things aren't supposed to exist. I don't know the first thing about them, and no one will follow me anyway. You're mistaken in choosing me. This isn't my war to lead. I'm a soldier, or I was. I just want my wife back."

The old woman nodded in response. "Okay, then. We'll all die here if that's what you decide."

Servia came to him then. The Drathe watched her

cautiously but remained still. Alistair wasn't sure how much he understood about what was going on, though it was clear he was suspicious of every word of it. Stopping slightly behind him, she placed her hand on his shoulder. He turned his neck slightly so he could see her.

"If the AllMother says we follow you, then I pledge my loyalty to you. If you say we die here, then we die here." Her friendliness and levity were gone. There was a depth to her seriousness that belied her devotion to the old woman. "We can get off this planet. I can show you how. If we don't, though, the chance of seeing your wife again disappears. Each second we stand here talking about it, our chances get worse."

"Don't you use her. Don't twist her name to get what you want."

The woman didn't take her hand off his shoulder. "I'm simply explaining the truth of the matter to you. Whatever you choose, Thoreaux and I will go along with it, but if you choose death, your dream dies with it."

She stepped away. Alistair felt the Drathe pressing against him, leaning into his hip. He said nothing, simply stared down with his mouth closed. He didn't need to speak. The Drathe didn't want to die here but would if he was commanded to.

He would have died in that hallway with the freak, Alistair thought. He looked up then and glanced around the room. Everyone in here would die for him. Perhaps two of them didn't want to, but they would because the woman in front of him had somehow earned their undying devotion. They waited for his response, and all he could think about was his wife. The chances of seeing her again were zero if he did nothing.

That couldn't happen.

They'd stolen her. He had to get her back.

"Fine. How do we get everyone to the portal?"

CHAPTER NINETEEN

"Am I the last one you're visiting? Have you eradicated the rest of your enemies, Alexander?"

"I'm eradicating the peoples' enemies. And yes, you're the last."

"Who will you kill next?"

"Whoever else rises."

–Final conversation between the last Chinese President and the First Imperial Ascendant

Veena looked at the escape pod crossing the sky. She knew who was in it—not the target she wanted. No, the Titan she wanted had escaped, and the Blazers chasing him had been destroyed. No, this pod held the arrogant man who'd somehow lost despite having everything on his side. A ragtag group of Plutonians had taken his ship and then escaped before the missiles could destroy them.

"What would you have us do, Primus?" her pilot asked.

Veena showed no emotion. She knew what she wanted to do, but she also knew what duty commanded. The DNA scan inside the pod was positive; it was Ares. "Call the pod to us. Make sure the Titan gets the medical help he needs. I must leave the bridge to communicate with the Ascendant."

Her pilot said nothing, though she knew he was communicating with the rest of the pilots.

Veena left the bridge. She understood what was expected of her at this moment, but it still bothered her. She wanted one more confirmation from the Imperial Ascendant. She went from the bridge to her private quarters, in which a communication chamber sat. Interstellar warfare would be impossible without it, or at least real-time communication would be. The Commonwealth had conquered interstellar communication before travel, and it was the communication that had given them the idea of moving into other dimensions.

The chamber was transparent, a box that one sat inside. Centimeters were valuable in outer space, so this chamber had been custom-fitted to her quarters. She had not used it since they began this journey, and truthfully, she was a bit anxious to do so now. The Imperial Ascendant was not someone to question twice, yet history would remember this moment for eternity. As long as a human drew breath, they would know about the moment Pluto burned. She would have the order come from the most high before she did it.

Veena sat down in the chamber, and the door slid shut when it registered her presence.

"Connect me to the Ascendant," she told the AI. It was a primitive intelligence system, but that was what Veena preferred on her ships. While other captains used AIs to help them navigate and engage the enemy, she always felt her edge over them was fear, something that an AI could never feel. It was why she was the Primus. She didn't want to die. Regardless of programming, she believed a non-life-based intelligence could never understand that.

A few moments passed as the transparent box turned black. Veena could no longer see outside of it.

The Ascendant's voice filled the box like the first god's must have filled the void of space. "Yes, Primus de Ragnimus?" His firm voice had made its way from Earth in seconds, able to travel faster than the speed of light in the upper dimensions.

"We have arrived, my liege. According to pod scans, Ares was wounded when he came into contact with Alistair Kane. Kane escaped to the planet, and I wanted to..." She paused, unsure of how to ask the next question.

"You wanted to what, Primus?"

"My liege, do you give the order to use nuclear warfare against Pluto?"

Silence came back to Veena. She knew the Ascendant couldn't see her right now since the Chamber transmitted light at a slower pace. In a few minutes, he would see what she'd looked like as she asked the question.

Finally, his voice came back, colder than any wind that had ever blown across the planet she'd come to destroy.

"You have permission to engage in nuclear warfare against Pluto. Do you have a problem with that, Primus?"

"No, my liege."

"Then do it," the Ascendant snapped in reply.

The black tint cleared, allowing her to see the room again. Veena stood and stepped out. She didn't sigh. She didn't falter. This was her duty, and it served the greater cause. What happened here was beyond her understanding, but she would do her duty for the Commonwealth.

One People. One Purpose.

Alexander de Finita, the Imperial Ascendant, understood what no one else did. It was a weight he would carry until his eyes closed forever, but he could not shirk his duty. He'd given the order, and shortly reports would arrive that would tell him it was finished. That the threat was gone, and he could rest knowing the Commonwealth was safe. There would be things to deal with when this was finished, any number of things that would demand his attention.

None of it was as important as this.

His place in history would be determined by people other than him. He understood that was why the Primus had chambered him. She wanted her place in history to be documented as the one who obeyed the order, not the one who gave it. Fine. It was his mantle to carry, as it had been that of those who had come before him.

Alexander left his communication chamber and headed for the Room of Ascendants. He moved through the throne room without paying the Praetors standing guard any attention. He rose and disappeared into the room above, seeing little of the royal purple that decorated the walls. Alexander's mind was focused as it had been trained to do nearly since his birth.

An orb floated in front of him. It was a deep-space gray, with a single point of light directly in front of Alexander. The Ascendant knelt, bowing to the orb. "We will turn the planet to ashes."

The point of light shot out to become a single line that wrapped around a third of the orb. "If he escapes, the chances of the Commonwealth's survival drops greatly." As the words spilled from the orb, the line shrank and grew, almost as if a mouth was speaking. Nine voices rolled out as one.

Alexander stood up, still staring at the orb. His ancestors resided inside it, all nine Imperial Ascendants who had come before him. Their minds had been loaded into this space, creating the most complex artificial intelligence ever devised. Alexander didn't know for sure if he was talking to his father, but it was the closest he'd ever get. One day, when his body could no longer handle the pressure of this world, he would be uploaded into it as well. He would serve with the other nine, advising his own progeny on the correct moves to make to ensure the Commonwealth's survival.

"What are the chances if he escapes?" Alexander asked his ancestors. Their minds were tied to an AI that allowed for calculations that humans could not possibly run.

"The Commonwealth's survival drops to one in two," the orb answered.

Alexander remained calm and still. "He won't escape.

The dreadnoughts are surrounding the entire planet. A fire rain is about to fall on it. There won't be anything left."

The orb's light went to a single point again, pausing for a few moments before resuming its line. "The probability of a portal is high, Alexander. How long until the fire rain?"

The portal was the worst part of all of this. The probability had been high for years that the Subversives had built a portal, but it was stealthed, and the manpower that would be required to find it was too great. The Commonwealth was almost certain the Sanctum planets didn't have them, but the Edge most likely had at least one, and the probability was that it rested on Pluto, the farthest it could get and remain in the solar system. However, without burning the entire planet, they wouldn't be able to destroy it.

Alexander turned away from the orb and walked to the edge of the room. He felt anger rising in him and knew it wouldn't be helpful. An Ascendant was supposed to be calm at all times under any circumstance the universe threw at him because so much of humanity relied on their decisions. "How did you not predict this? How, with all the time and resources given to you, were you all not able to see this coming?"

"Our sight is not forever, boy," the nine voices said as one. "Do not question us until you are here. It is your job to steer from out there, and we told you in time to stop this. The Titan should never have made it off Earth, let alone to Pluto."

Alexander closed his eyes, trying to retreat into his citadel, a place the Ascendants trained their entire lives to enter. A place where they could not be harmed either physically or emotionally, where they could rule dispassionately.

He peered out from inside his citadel. As he floated above the orb and looked down at his body, he could see the entire room. His ancestors might be correct, but one in two was nothing to be angry about. Ascendants had dealt with worse odds, and if the Subversives used the portal, they would no longer even be in the Solar System. The AllSeer would still hunt the AllMother, of course, and he could use them to his advantage. Where the AllMother went, Kane would be. Yes, from within his citadel, Alexander saw how things would play out.

The Ascendant came out and opened his eyes. He did not look at the orb, however. "The fire will fall in moments. If he does escape, he'll be like dust in the wind, scattered to the far reaches of the universe. Then, we will hunt him. He won't return." He folded his hands behind his back. "I will take a fifty percent chance, my fathers."

Alexander finally turned around. The single point of light stared at him. "I won't fail you. The Titan will die, one way or another. The Commonwealth will remain strong. I only came to let you know of the fire about to engulf a Commonwealth planet. Have you considered what the fallout from that will be? What can I expect to happen here on Earth?"

The light shrank to a pinpoint, showing his ancestors' displeasure at the question. "You've taken the necessary precautions, have you not? Your communications czar is putting out the correct information?"

"He is."

"Then worry about that *if* you stop the Titan. Otherwise, it won't matter what happens here on Earth when the Imperial Ascendancy falls and anarchy, or worse, Demockracy, takes over."

CHAPTER TWENTY

"You trade your souls for the promise of riches. I only wish I could see the day when your payment comes due."

–Translation of Alejandro Ortega's last words, final Brazilian Prime Minister, moments before facing a firing squad

Four humans and single Drathe stood around the holovid.

"Their dreadnoughts are encircling the planet. Once they're in place, the fire rain comes," the old woman said.

"Do they know about the portal?" Thoreaux asked.

Alistair didn't look away from the holovid. The might of the Commonwealth was stupefying. "I don't know," he whispered. "I don't think so, but the Edge was out of the realm of my duties."

Thoreaux stepped to her side. "AllMother, you have to get to the portal now." He looked at Alistair. "How much time do we have?"

"Half an hour, maybe. The ground retaliation and air attacks slowed them some, but they're on the move now. They're figuring their invasion has failed, so they'll drop fire."

Thoreaux's face was lined with stress. He didn't care about the holovid anymore; the whole of his attention was on the old woman. "Let him get you out of here. Servia and I will start the evacuation protocols. We'll get as many people as we can to the portal. You have to go now."

Alistair finally broke away from the space scene. "I don't know how to get there. I don't even know where I am right now, let alone how to get her safely to the top."

The AllMother didn't look away, her voice serene. "I built this place. I'd know my way around it blind."

"Go, then," Thoreaux demanded. "We have to move *now* if we're going to have any chance of escape."

She turned to Alistair. "Care to accompany an old lady to her vehicle?"

Alistair couldn't help but smile. He took his Whip from its place on his hip. "I'll do my best."

Looking grave but not angry, Thoreaux stepped between the two of them. He put his hand on Alistair's arm. "Please keep her safe. She means more than you can possibly know."

"I'll do my best."

Thoreaux turned back to the old woman and kissed her on the cheek. "Hurry," he whispered.

Servia came to her as well and kissed the other side of her face. "We'll be with you soon, Mother."

The AllMother stepped past both of them. "Come on.

These two are sentimental about an old woman when they have other people to save." She looked down at his Whip. "You know how to use that weapon?"

Obs gave a bark.

The old woman glanced at the Drathe. "I like him."

"Damn it, *go*," Thoreaux nearly shouted.

Alistair turned around, but the door was solidly in his way. The AllMother stepped past him, saying nothing, and the door opened just before her toe touched it. She walked through and turned to look at Alistair. "You coming?"

Alistair shook his head. She may be motherly, but she's going to be a handful, he thought.

He stepped forward, and the Drathe quickly followed. He walked through the door and shot one glance over his shoulder. Servia and Thoreaux had already moved to the other side of the room, messing with some sort of large DataTrack system—alerting the planet to its impending doom.

The door slammed shut, leaving Alistair and Obs alone with the AllMother.

"Well, you certainly weren't playing with this young man," she said as she looked at the dead body.

Obs barked and then rushed forward, passing both of them and taking the lead.

"Does he know where we're going?" Alistair asked.

"I'd imagine so. He understands what we say, and he's been waiting for you for a long time. He's had a lot of time to wander these halls."

Alistair shook his head again.

"There's more to this universe than you can imagine,

David Beers & Michael Anderle

my son," the old woman said. "I'll do my best to show it to you, but time is short. Now protect me, Fallen Titan, or Thoreaux will have you drawn and quartered."

Alistair followed the Drathe as they moved through the corridors. A few minutes into their march, a loud siren came over the intercom. Thoreaux's voice followed shortly.

"CODE COMMONWEALTH. THIS IS NOT A DRILL. CODE COMMONWEALTH. THIS IS NOT A DRILL."

The repetition that didn't stop. Alistair didn't know where the rest of the people inside this underground labyrinth were, and he had to hope the exit protocols worked. His only responsibility was the one moving just behind him, moving surprisingly swiftly for someone so old. The Drathe continued down the halls, attacking them with a speed that Alistair couldn't match. Each time Obs got to the end of one, ready to turn into the next, he came to a stop and looked impatiently at the two following.

He didn't bark, though, as if he knew the noise might draw unwanted attention.

The AllMother put her hand on Alistair's arm and drew him to a halt. "Tell the animal to stop."

Alistair's eyes flashed to her. She wasn't looking at him but was staring down the long hall. Her eyes seemed to be somewhere distant.

"Obs, stop!" Alistair called down the empty hall.

The Drathe halted and looked over his shoulder at the humans. After a moment, he turned around and sat on his haunches.

"What is it?" Alistair asked.

The AllMother shook her head but said nothing. Above

226

them, the sirens still wailed, and Thoreaux's voice continued announcing Code Commonwealth. Eventually, the AllMother spoke. "Tell the Drathe to get behind you. You get behind me. Whatever happens next, you'll need to trust me, Alistair Kane."

She went forward without waiting for him to respond. The Drathe's furry ears perked up, and he cocked his head to the right.

"Obs, to me," Alistair commanded. The animal stood and padded past the old woman, who was walking down the hall alone. Alistair waited until the Drathe was next to him before following with his Whip unfurled, the weapon sensing his apprehension. The red lasers floated in the air next to his leg, ready to snap out and kill at a moment's notice.

The old woman stopped just before the next turn. Alistair was a few meters from her, and he watched as she closed her eyes and took a deep breath. After a moment, she let out her breath and stepped into the next hall, disappearing without looking back at Alistair. He took off, his feet barely touching the metal floor as he flew toward her.

The Drathe easily bounded ahead of him, rounding the corner a few seconds before he made it.

Both stopped a half meter behind the AllMother. She had paused too and was staring down the hallway.

Giants stood at the end of it, creatures that looked like they had been carved from planets. They were mirror images of the one Alistair had fought earlier, only now there were three.

Was it possible that they were bigger? Gods, yes, it was.

They stood in a circular room that looked like it might contain an elevator to the surface. They'd been so close to escaping, so impossibly close.

There would be no escaping death now. They could retreat, but to where? The fire would fall soon, and nothing would survive it.

"Here you are, AllMother," one of the giants called. He slammed a closed fist on the strange armor the other giant had also worn. The red eye stared out of it as if it saw everything. "The fire is about to fall, but do not fear, we won't wait for it. Come with us and make this easy for everyone. We'll let the animal and his pet live if you'd like."

Alistair moved forward, sliding past the AllMother so that he stood between her and the giants. Obs was half a second behind him. The Fallen Titan looked over his shoulder. "Go. Find Thoreaux or Servia. I'll fend them off as long as I can." He turned back to face the three. He knew they would cut him down in moments, but it might be long enough for her to turn the corner.

What are these things? he wondered, knowing he'd never get an answer.

"You're the one who killed our brother, yes?" a giant with red eyes on the left asked. "You and that Drathe?"

Alistair didn't understand how they could know, but it didn't matter. "Hug the left wall," he whispered to Obs. "I'll stay on the right. If we die, we do it together."

The Drathe growled in response and started to stalk forward, head lowered and teeth bared.

"Stop."

The AllMother's voice pierced him from behind,

bringing both human and animal to a halt. There was no possibility of not listening to her command. Alistair kept his eyes on the three at the other end of the hall even as he tilted his head over his shoulder. "You have to go now. I can't hold them off for long. They're simply too *big*."

"Get behind me, Titan," the AllMother whispered as she stepped forward. She placed her hand on Alistair's shoulder as she moved past him. Alistair followed her with his eyes, in a weird state of being mesmerized but not understanding how it was possible. She'd left him nearly immobile with a few words.

When she spoke next, it was to those in front of her. "You have traveled long to find me. Now I'm in front of you. What are you waiting for?"

Alistair's breath caught in his throat. There was a pause in the giant's movements, perhaps even fear in them.

"What do you wait for? Am I not the reason you've crossed galaxies? Weren't you each born to find me? Come get me, and let's end this farce now."

The three giant mutants each activated their pole-like lasers. However, they hesitated when it came to entering the corridor. The AllMother didn't venture forward either. If they wanted her, they'd have to come to her.

She turned her head toward Alistair. "Whatever happens, stay behind me."

"You're going to die," he pleaded. "You can't stand against them."

"How many men have told me what I cannot do?" she remarked as she returned to face the horde. "How many times must I prove you wrong?"

They came then, all three. They could only walk down the hall one at a time, hunching to make sure their heads did not scrape the ceiling. Alistair tried to step forward, but the AllMother put her arm up, her palm to him. She shook her head without looking at him.

Alistair's Whip hung useless at his side.

When the first one was a few meters away, blood flooded from his nostrils. He tried to take another step forward, as if he didn't understand what was happening to his face. His leg buckled, then his shin bent the wrong way, and his knee shattered when he hit the floor. The face of the giant behind him was already coated in the blood that was leaking from the corner of his eyes. He tried to lift his pole to throw it at the old woman since he was able to tell something was wrong, but his hand detached at the wrist, and blood spurted out across the floor.

The third giant stood, the hand holding his laser shaking. He was bleeding too; it looked like he was weeping blood. With great effort, he took a step forward, not caring what he stepped on. He hit his colleague's back, and his ankle collapsed. The weight of his body was too great for one leg to support, and he hit the floor with a loud thump.

Veena de Ragnimus looked at the screens on the bridge of her ship, which displayed the ice world beneath. They were all magnified, allowing her to see ten times closer than her eyes were capable of. The dreadnoughts were nearly in place, and the fire rain would begin within minutes.

Right now, she was looking at something she didn't think possible that had been reported to her minutes before. The Blazers had missed it while they were scoping the planet, though it hadn't been their fault. The Subversives had used stealth technology on the thing, and it wasn't until the Commonwealth's troops set foot around it that they became aware of it. The Titans had destroyed the small boxes that created the cloak, and now Veena could see it.

"What am I looking at?" she said aloud. None of her pilots turned around; they remained harmonized with the ship. Her words were addressed to one of the Titans on the planet.

"I'm not sure, Primus." The answer came back through the comm in her ear. "I've never seen anything like it."

She wasn't surprised the soldier hadn't. This was probably the first time the Titan had left Earth. Veena had never seen anything like it either, at least not in person. *It's not possible*, she thought, though she couldn't deny what she was looking at.

A parabola stared back at her, an arch two hundred and fifty times taller than the Titans standing next to it. "Can you see through it?" she asked.

"Yes, Primus."

Veena was looking at an intergalactic portal. There were rumors of them throughout the Imperial Fleet, though no one ever claimed to have seen one. The theory was, the portal worked as a black hole. It allowed items to move from one point in the universe to another by connecting two black holes, but the portal somehow kept the items or person from either being destroyed or trapped in the intense gravity.

If this was here, there had to be another—at least one—somewhere else in the universe. Otherwise, it would make no sense to have this one. And if that was true, then...

What else is out there? she wondered. She was Primus General of the Imperial First Fleet, yet she had not known this existed, not outside of rumor.

"Primus?" the Titan asked over the comm. "What would you have us do?"

Thoughts ran rapidly through her mind as she tried to figure out the best way to handle this. Her orders were to loose the fire rain, but she didn't know if the Imperial Ascendant was aware of this artifact, and if he was not, would his mind change? Was it more important to burn this world or save this scientific breakthrough? "Do you see any Subversives?"

"No, Primus," the Titan responded. "The premises are clear, though scans show that the area beneath is hollowed out with tunnels."

"Give me a minute, Titan." Veena walked to her Primus Pilot. "Can you run a scan of a kilometer circumference of the parabola and tell me what you see beneath?"

"Yes, Primus," the pilot answered. A minute passed in silence before the answer came back.

"Titan, still there?"

"Yes, Primus."

Veena's eyes narrowed. Half of the bridge's screens showed a heat map of the tunnels beneath the parabola—the *portal*. "Titan, you have a massive number of incoming enemies. They haven't yet reached what appear to be elevators, but they will be storming upward in a matter of minutes." Veena was quiet as she watched the red and yellow heat signatures moving through the tunnels. The Titans had pods that would launch them into space just before the rain of fire fell, though she knew many of them wouldn't make it out alive, but this artifact changed things drastically, and there wasn't time to contact the Ascendant.

"Primus?" the Titan asked during her pause.

"Listen to me very closely," she said over the comm. "No one is to cross beneath that arch. Do you understand? Call whatever reinforcements you need, but you are not to let a single soul pass beneath it. Die before you do. Got that?"

"Yes, Primus. Understood."

Veena ended the communication. "Hold the rain," she ordered her second in command.

She left the bridge. She couldn't destroy something like that, not without explicit instructions. The ability to travel the stars in the blink of an eye? It was a miracle, so once again, she went to contact the Imperial Ascendant.

The two men reached the elevator behind the Drathe. Linc had led them to SkinSuits since they were necessary to deal with the little-terraformed world above. Obs didn't need one since he was apparently capable of existing in multiple harsh environments. The animal had turned around and was staring at the old woman. His mouth was closed, and he whimpered as they approached.

Immediately after the last of the giants died, she had collapsed on the floor. There'd been no blood, but Alistair hadn't been able to wake her. Linc carried her now, though that was only after he'd found them trying to access an elevator they didn't have permission to use.

"It's okay, Obs," Alistair said. The Drathe didn't look over at him but kept his worry-filled eyes on the AllMother. Alistair passed his hand over the panel, but nothing happened. "Damn it. You want to get this thing running?"

Linc moved past him and scanned his hand, and the elevator's door slid inside the circular wall. Obs and Alistair stepped aside, letting Linc board with the AllMother. When they went inside, the door shut, but the elevator didn't rise.

"What are we waiting for?" Alistair asked. He had his Whip in his hand, though the lasers were a quarter of their normal size, twirling at his hip.

Linc looked at the ceiling. "I scouted the area before Thoreaux told me to find you all. Ten Titans were about fifty meters off. The portal is stealthed, but only from the sky. Anyone on the surface can see it, and they spotted it before I left. I need you to understand what's about to happen. Those Titans have destroyed the stealth boxes that keep those in the sky from seeing the portal, so the Fleet knows about it now. If they're smart, the fire rain is already falling, but I don't think it is. You've got thousands of people rushing from underneath the planet to reach that portal, and if they make it through, they're going to step out on a planet they've never seen before."

He looked at Alistair.

"That's if they make it through the portal." His eyes turned to the AllMother. "With all that said, the only person that matters, the only one that *has* to make it through, is her. Whatever it takes, Kane. Whatever you have to do, she has to get through."

Alistair nodded. "Is it on? The portal?"

As if the instrument had heard him speak, a rumble ran beneath his feet. The vibration continued upward, encircling him and the elevator and spreading to the walls beyond.

"It is now," Linc said. "Even if you die, she has to live. Don't forget that. She is the heart of us, the best, and if she goes, so does everything." He raised the unconscious woman's body toward Alistair. "Take her. Get her through. Me and the Drathe here are going to act like sheepdogs and corral everyone else."

Alistair turned the Whip off, then took the old woman in his arms. She felt like a bag of sticks, all bones—almost nothing to her. He almost couldn't believe this woman had destroyed three massive beasts minutes before. Would not have believed it if he hadn't seen it.

Linc was looking down at the Drathe. "You okay with that, pal?"

Obs turned to his master, and Alistair nodded. "Do what you can. I'm not sure what any of us can do, to be honest. If I make it through the portal, you find your way through too, understood?"

Obs gave a single bark, then stood up on all four legs and yawned. He leaned back on his haunches and stretched his front legs, then straightened. Linc bent down and patted his head. "Truth be told, I miss the bastard."

The trainer waved his palm over a panel, and the elevator started up. Alistair looked at the old woman in his arms, her eyes closed, her body limp. They were moving up, and he knew death awaited them at the top. Ten Titans and thousands of terrified people trying to cross a limited area. Yet, death had waited for him ever since Ares attempted to kill him on Earth, and he was still alive. This woman, though...she believed in him. She brought him here for some inexplicable reason. And the people that followed *her*? She was a goddess to them, bigger than life, bigger than humanity—a deity.

They kept entrusting her to him.

She had entrusted them to him.

The elevator stopped, and the door opened. They stood on the planet's surface about two klicks away from the portal. There were ten Titans surrounding the thing. Alistair's new eyes could see in detail what they were doing, and as he watched, one raised their arm to point at him. The lines were drawn.

Alistair tilted his head up. A dreadnought sat high above him, floating over the area. The fire rain was still inside the terrible warships, but Alistair knew their time was nearly up. Perhaps it was over already. The moment the nuke dropped, none of this would exist anymore.

"We're not going to be able to cross." Alistair's eyes spotted the mines planted fifty meters out from the Titans. They'd spent the past few minutes creating a net of death that would kill anyone who didn't know exactly how to traverse it. "Or rather, we will, but no one else. And we'll only be able to cross so long as the Titans don't kill us, which isn't going to happen."

"There isn't time to talk about this." Linc raised his hand and pointed past the portal. Alistair saw what he meant. Dots of light were appearing across the landscape as elevators rose and disgorged their cargo—people the Commonwealth called Subversives, who Alistair now had to protect. The lights winked out as the lifts dropped back into the earth to grab more people. Hundreds of them went up and down, more than Alistair had ever thought possible.

"We have to go," Linc said. "You have to kill the Titans." He looked up. "And do it before *that* kills us all." He took off without another word, moving like a ghost in Pluto's blackness.

Obs looked up at Alistair.

"Go on. Don't fucking die," he told the Drathe.

Obs barked and took off after the trainer.

Alistair stood with an old woman in his arms, once again having no idea how he was going to survive this, let alone keep her alive.

He started walking toward the portal. He knew only one way to fight, and it was to go directly through the middle. You killed until you were killed. It had served him well thus far, so he would die practicing the same brute warfare tactic he'd used his whole life.

When he was two hundred meters from the Titans, he stopped and knelt. He laid the AllMother at his feet and looked up. Eight of the Titans were on his side, all of their Whips floating lazily at their hips. Beyond those eight stood two facing the opposite direction, and beyond them were thousands of those Alistair was supposed to save, with more flowing from below the ground every second.

Alistair looked at the sky and saw a ship falling, another success by the Spiders. It was the second dreadnought he'd seen fall. Soldiers had died in them, though—his troops, the ones this old woman wanted him to lead.

He stood up, alone on a cold, strange world. Eight men in MechSuits faced him, and for what felt like the hundredth time that day, Alistair Kane went toward his death.

CHAPTER TWENTY-ONE

"To those who say the pen is mightier than the sword, I say look at history. The pen may lead to action, but that action is always the letting of blood. Indeed, blood is the only thing that has changed humanity."

–Aurelius de Finita, two days after being crowned Imperial Ascendant of Earth

Thoreaux reached the planet's surface and immediately looked up. He, and Servia at his side, knew death would come from above. Sure enough, Thoreaux saw the instrument would end his brief life: a ship with cannons facing Pluto, blue light circling the massive holes that would spew brilliant pain on everyone around him and those still trying to reach the surface.

Servia saw it first. "Look." She stepped off the elevator and pointed into the distance.

People were flooding around Thoreaux, all pressing toward the portal. Beneath his feet, the ground hummed with the energy such a creation took to go live. Indeed, to run it too long would break the entire planet apart, so it was on an automatic shutoff loop that would power it down if the danger grew too great.

As Thoreaux looked on, his heart sank. These people, *his* people, would never make it to the portal. Death waited in front of them as surely as it did above. "We have to get to the front," he told Servia. He pulled his beam from his side and took off running. Servia bolted after him, both of them turning their SkinSuits' hoods transparent so people would recognize them and get out of the way.

They pushed forward, but the crowd was thick. Thoreaux looked ahead and saw one of the Titans pull a MechPulse off his back. "No," he whispered as he tried to get through the crowd. He didn't consider how quickly he would be mowed down if he got to the front, only that he had to try to stop this. Thoughts of Alistair and the AllMother consumed him—anything beyond killing the enemies in front were whispers in a hurricane.

The pulse in the Titan's hands fired, and it blew a hole in the crowd fifty people back, destroying limbs, heads, spines, and anything else in its way. The Titan pumped the reload and blasted again, and more Plutonians fell to the ground.

"Gods," Thoreaux whispered before screaming, "MOVE!" He raised his beam and started firing. Those around him didn't know whether to flood forward or run backward. He pushed through them, throwing people out of his way as the second Titan pulled his pulse off his back and fired.

More dropped dead. Servia grabbed Thoreaux's arm, forcing him to stop pushing onward. "Wait."

His head whipped to his side, unable to believe she was trying to slow them down. Servia wasn't looking at him, though. Her mouth was open, and her eyes were wide. Thoreaux followed her stare, then he paused, too.

Beyond the MechSuits stood their fighter. On the other side of the portal, wearing only a SkinSuit, Whip in hand, he faced down eight Titans.

There's no way, Thoreaux thought almost absently. *He's as good as dead.*

It wasn't until he saw the AllMother behind him that his body broke free of his mind's awe. "She's there, Servia. She's behind him. We have to get to her."

He started forward again as people fled the opposite way. He didn't understand why she was lying on the ground. Was she dead? He had too many questions, and there were no answers, only the need to get to her.

A pulse blast killed fifty people to his left and then his right, somehow not hitting him or Servia.

Thoreaux felt a hand on his arm, and he turned to throw off whoever was trying to hold him back but stopped before tossing Servia into the air. She was shaking her head and pointing forward with her other hand. He looked and once again found himself stunned.

The two Titans facing his side of the portal had turned too because what was happening on the other side was akin to magic. Only gods could accomplish what Thoreaux now witnessed.

He'd never seen anyone move like the Fallen Titan. His Whip was his wand; a sorcerer had come to Pluto. The first

Titan launched himself into the air, his MechSuit propelling him at a rate far faster than normal humans could travel. The sorcerer walked forward as if he didn't see the massive metal form coming at him from the air. Moments before the attacker collided with Alistair, surely to break him limb from limb, the former Titan spun. He didn't even look up, simply turned three hundred and sixty degrees.

The Titan appeared to keep falling through the air, though he was no longer targeting Alistair. When he hit the ground, his top half fell away from his bottom half. The man was in two pieces instead of one.

Kane hadn't appeared to see the man coming, but he lay dead while Odin marched forward.

Two more Titans took off from the portal. Thoreaux still didn't move, caught up in the magical scene playing out before him. He watched as the Titans dodged something he couldn't see on the ground, most likely mines. They skipped forward, one in a yellow MechSuit, the other in dark green.

This is his end, Thoreaux thought. No one could take on two suited Titans at once. Thoreaux had seen them in person and only barely made it out alive, more luck than anything else.

As people rushed around him, trying to escape what they thought a death trap, Thoreaux had a moment to wonder if he knew the men who approached him.

One came from either side. The one on the left held a pink Whip, the other a yellow, and both shone brightly in the ice desert.

"Gods help him," Servia whispered next to Thoreaux.

"They scatter like roaches."

"Is this who you left us for, Odin?"

Alistair's head was slightly lowered, allowing him to see the Titans on either side of him. "Leave now, and I'll let you live. Head back up to your ships, and no more of you need to die here today." There were nine left, and the two facing the AllMother's children had stopped laying waste to his people for the moment. They'd recognized his red Whip, and they all wanted to be the man who cut down Odin.

"Don't think you're so grand as to stop *us*," Aphrodite said from his left. "The one laying in pieces back there was fresh out of the Academy. He had more ambition than brains, poor thing."

Alistair's Whip lengthened, extending from the hilt until it nearly scraped the ground. "I'm tired of talking. Let's see if the gods exist."

They fell on him like rabid wolves.

If Thoreaux had ever wondered if there was a difference between him and these warriors, his questions ceased in the next few moments.

The two Titans flashed across the ice, and Thoreaux held his breath. Pink Whip slashed high as Yellow went low, trying to cut Alistair into thirds and prevent him from jumping high or dropping. Instead, Kane dove forward, passing between the two Whips. He placed a hand on the ground and used it to spring back to his feet and face the Titans again.

They didn't slow, using forms that Thoreaux didn't recognize. They spread out again, trained to track and kill a single enemy while barely exposing themselves. Alistair retreated, his back toward the mines and the other Titans, who were slowly encircling him.

Pink Whip slashed at him, extending his arm to give his partner on the other side a chance. For someone other than Alistair, the move might have worked, but his response time was too quick. Pink's arm and Whip detached from the rest of his body and his scream echoed across the ice, freezing Thoreaux's blood and causing the rushing crowd to slow.

Those who had been passing Thoreaux and Servia turned.

"He's doing it," she whispered, her voice the only thing he could hear besides the dying Titan's screams. She was right. This was why there had been no evacuation. This was why the AllMother had forced them to fight.

So that they could bear witness.

Eight left, but Kane moved quicker than the gods themselves. His Whip slammed down, and when the Titan reacted, Kane crouched and spun, cutting him off at the knees.

Servia pointed again. "There. It's Linc."

Linc and the damned Drathe were streaking across the ice on Thoreaux's side of the portal. The Drathe was running ahead but stopping every twenty meters or so. It took Linc a moment to catch up, but the Drathe waited in silence as if he knew he didn't want the Titans' attention turned to them. As he sped across the landscape, Linc fired what looked to be a mine disabler at the ground. The moment he did, the Drathe took off again.

"Gods, we might do it," Thoreaux whispered.

The Titans were converging on Alistair, but two more had already been dispatched, their heads rolling across the frozen ground.

Five left. Two fired their pulses at the same time. Alistair barely survived by leaping into the air. The ground beneath him was pulverized. He backpedaled as he hit the ground, and the other three with Whips raced after him. His arm and body moved like a whirlwind, dodging, feinting, blocking, and above all, *killing*.

In the end, there was nothing the Titans could do.

They fell to his Whip the way the warriors of old had fallen to the blade.

He stood in the darkness, the lasers of his Whip illuminating his blood-streaked figure. Thoreaux didn't know what to say or do. He'd never seen anything like this, and as he stared forward, he realized those around him were doing the same. The fear and panic had subsided, and everyone had witnessed...

"She was right," Servia said. "She was completely right."

Thoreaux had no words. It was only when Alistair turned to retrieve the AllMother that Thoreaux snapped out of his trance, and his head jerked to the sky again. The blue cannons were brighter than before. The fire was coming.

"TO THE PORTAL!" he screamed. "EVERYONE CROSS THROUGH THE PORTAL!"

CHAPTER TWENTY-TWO

"Largely, the Commonwealth has no more enemies. However, the Academy ensures that the best of us are ready for war. It ensures that our strongest will never lose because we are always vigilant."

–Marcus de Reespen, Current Primus Academy Director

"What were your orders?"

Veena had never heard a voice sound so cold. It was as if the person speaking had been thawed after a thousand-year freeze.

"My liege, there can be no doubt about what I'm looking at. It's a portal, a stargate that can change our entire universe." She couldn't believe what she was hearing from the other side. This was a theoretical piece of technology brought to life. "I've sent you holovids of it. I—"

"*What were your orders?*" the Ascendant snarled.

"Kill the Titan. Use nuclear warfare if necessary."

"And has it become necessary?"

"Yes, my liege."

The ensuing silence seemed to fill eternity. As Veena sat in the black chamber, she thought it would go on forever.

Finally, the Ascendant spoke. "If the Titan escapes, if *Alistair Kane* escapes, it is on your shoulders, Veena de Ragnimus. You will be held accountable."

Veena opened her mouth to speak, but the chamber was already turning transparent. The Ascendant was gone. Veena touched the comm on her ear, allowing her pilot to hear her. "Fire at will. I repeat, fire at will."

Alistair held the old woman in his arms. He hadn't chambered his Whip, but it floated near the hilt and avoided the AllMother. The dead lay around him: people he'd known for years, people he'd trained to be the killers they were. Even in their SUITs they hadn't been enough, and he was the only one still alive. Still able to kill.

He scanned the land in front of him. The AllMother's children were surging toward the portal now, or a lot of them were. Some lay weeping near their dead, begging them to get up, to rise and finish the journey. Others squirmed on the ground as their insides leaked onto the tundra, slowly freezing to death.

The injuries Alistair had sustained beneath the ground were far from his mind now. He couldn't see Obs, though he heard the Drathe barking in the distance, most likely trying to push people toward the portal. A blast went off to Alistair's right, a triggered mine. Fifty people were vaporized.

He decided what he had to do. His allegiance was now to the woman in his arms and the Drathe who was still trying to save people. He felt that Obs' connection to him was deeper than his to the animal, or at least *different*. The Drathe would come before it was too late, or at least attempt to, so right now, Alistair had to get the old woman to safety. He wished he'd asked more questions about the fucking arch that stood in front of him, like whether he could cross back once he went through. If he couldn't, going through now wasn't an option.

And not knowing meant it wasn't an option.

But he couldn't just drop the AllMother through without knowing what would happen on the other side.

"Gods, what have I gotten myself into?"

He started running, giving the mines on this side of the portal a wide berth. Some of the people were already passing under the arch. Alistair watched as they rushed under it, trusting that something would be on the other side. As Alistair ran, he couldn't tell one way from the other. They stepped under the arch and their bodies froze, then slowly faded to black before disappearing.

More and more hit the arch, but there were thousands still left.

Alistair felt the cannons above them open before he saw or heard them. Warm air rushed down, heating up his suit in a matter of seconds. His soles were carrying him quickly to the portal's other side, but he skidded to a stop and looked up. Two cannons, each a tenth of a kilometer across, looked down on the planet. Blue fire rested in a ring around them, and inside, white heat blazed.

Out of hell came demons.

Alistair ran again. He should go toward the portal; he knew that with every fabric of his being. To stay here would not only kill the AllMother and him but also the reason he'd done all this: seeing his wife, yet he wouldn't leave the Drathe. The creature that had already shown he would die for *him*.

He crossed the outside plane of the arch and saw Servia. Thoreaux wasn't with her, but he couldn't consider that now. She was his only chance of getting both the AllMother and the Drathe to safety. He launched himself in the low gravity, smacking down on the tundra before leaping into the air again. He crossed the distance quickly, landing in front of Servia like one of the superheroes he'd read about as a kid.

Someone hung onto her shoulder, and the two of them were struggling forward step by step.

She glanced at him, the hood of her suit transparent. "You always going to make entrances like that?" She trudged forward, her eyes focused on the arch. "She's alive, I can see that, but how is she?"

They were a hundred meters from the portal, and the heat from above was increasing. There was enough atmosphere for the nukes to explode before hitting the planet, and the flame and wind from above would push the resulting explosions down, forcing them across the land instead of back toward the assaulting ship. Alistair was absently shuffling forward with Servia, not paying attention to her question. He was looking at all the people trying to make it under the arch. "Why the hell didn't we evacuate first? Why are all these people still here? We're not going to make it."

Servia shook her head. "You'll see soon enough. Keep walking. It's our only chance."

Alistair shook his head. "I have to get Obs. I can't leave him here. Where's Thoreaux? One of you has to carry her."

The old woman was a sack of feathers to Alistair, but he understood Servia couldn't carry both the AllMother and the wounded person already hobbling with her.

"The Drathe can die." Servia's voice was cruel. "The AllMother cannot. Get her through that portal, or I swear on all the gods both ancient and future, I will kill you myself." She didn't look at him as she spoke. Her face was grimly determined.

Alistair saw fire from the corner of his eye, far in the distance on the planet's horizon. The fire blazed down first, and through it a globe fell, twirling as it got white-hot. Alistair couldn't pull his eyes away, and he watched as it disappeared into the landscape. The fire and wind from above obliterated the after-effects for a moment, but then he saw them.

The mushroom cloud that should have bloomed into the air was rushing toward them, moving at a speed faster than that of sound.

"Gods," Servia whispered, still putting one foot in front of the other. The heat was increasing. The oncoming radiation cloud wouldn't matter in a few moments because another warhead would drop on them. "Faster. We have to move faster."

Alistair scanned the horizon, looking for the Drathe, and he saw him two hundred meters away. He and Linc were still pushing people toward the arch. Linc had someone over his shoulder; Alistair couldn't tell how close they were to death. He didn't see Thoreaux anywhere near them, but it was clear neither was paying attention to the sky. They were single-minded in their quest to get people to the arch.

Alistair glanced at Servia a few feet ahead of him. He had no choice. Linc and Obs needed him, and so did the AllMother. He had doubted he would make it through this since the moment Ares told him about his death warrant, yet...

He was still here. Still alive.

"Servia."

She turned her head to look at him.

"I don't see Thoreaux anywhere. You have to find him. I'm going to Obs and Linc. I'll see you on the other side." He glanced down at the old woman. "We both will."

He didn't wait to hear her response. He threw the AllMother over his shoulder like a sack and sprinted toward the Drathe.

The heat increased, as did the winds from the detonation as the radiation came for them all.

The Drathe barked the moment he saw Alistair, still twenty meters away. His attention left his herding task, and he focused on his master. Linc, who, like Alistair, was carrying someone, looked up. The former Titan simply pointed at the horizon. Linc followed his finger before meeting his eyes. He gave a single nod and took off toward the portal.

Obs rushed toward Alistair. The Titan went first, leaping as he had to get here, but now rushing toward the portal. Obs could have zipped ahead of him but didn't; he stayed within five meters of him at all times.

Alistair lost track of Linc, Servia, or Thoreaux—anyone except the AllMother and Obstinate. They flew past the dead and dying and those without their ability to move as quickly. There wasn't anything he could do, not if he wanted to save the woman he carried. Perhaps he would be judged a coward after this. He didn't know, but he didn't slow down because the AllMother mattered more than him, more than those he passed, more than anyone in this whole sordid affair.

He was fifty meters from the portal when the flames and wind started from above. The fire didn't engulf them all at once but came down like tongues of death, licking the ground and the people around him. He watched as it touched down on his suit. "GO!" he shouted at the Drathe. "GO!"

Ahead of him, he saw figures hitting the portal, freezing, and then fading to black. Obs could make it. If he just moved like his body was made to do, he could get through to whatever lay beyond. The Drathe didn't speed up one notch, though, only barked angrily at his slow master and nipped at his heels.

Alistair wanted to curse him but couldn't waste the breath. Instead, he closed his eyes, gritted his teeth, and put every bit of strength he had into crossing the distance. He felt the suit beginning to burn and knew it was happening to the AllMother's as well, but the Portal would soon be nothing more than flaming rubble if not ash, as would every other human on this planet.

The heat was unbearable. He felt his flesh burning, falling off his bones. "*GO, OBS!*" he screamed once more, then everything went dark for Alistair Kane.

CHAPTER TWENTY-THREE

*"The problem with Demockracies was that they thought
life was precious. If the universe has shown us anything,
it's that it doesn't value life. Indeed, it may actively hate
life."*

–Alexander de Finita, Current Imperial Ascendant

Veena looked at the world beneath her. She'd commanded
the bridge's screens to show her a 10X magnification.

Another human had felt this sort of destruction before,
and she repeated what he had said centuries ago. "Now I
am become Death, the destroyer of worlds."

"Sorry, Primus, what did you say?"

Veena shook her head. "Nothing." The world beneath
her was burning on its own, the dreadnoughts having
stopped their flaming attacks. The warheads had been
strategically dropped across the planet, and now the little
atmosphere that had been terraformed allowed the fire to
burn. There was nothing left. She saw not a single human

standing, and the portal had collapsed into ash ten minutes before. All that was left on this world were flames, and all that would exist forevermore would be ash. There would be no recolonization, not by Subversives or the Commonwealth. Pluto was now dead, and only ghosts would live here.

"Primus, the Ascendant is asking for you in your chamber."

She swallowed and continued staring at the ghosts of thousands. "Let him know I'm on my way."

A moment later, Veena left the bridge. She knew the question that would be asked of her, but not what answer she could give. Nothing the Ascendant would want to hear, at least. As she made her way to her quarters, she tried not to consider what that would mean for her. It was a tough thing to push out of her mind, but after what she'd just done, what didn't she deserve? She didn't know if she'd killed Alistair Kane, and if not, punishment was surely coming, but did the reason matter as long as punishment was doled out? Veena thought not. She'd killed a world to get a single man, and perhaps no punishment would ever be enough for such an act.

She entered her quarters and then the chamber for the third time in what felt like very short hours. It went black, and she knew she was connected with the Ascendant, though he said nothing for a minute or so.

When he did speak, his voice was firm. "Did anyone make it through the portal, Primus?"

Veena took in a deep breath and let it out quietly. "Yes, my liege. Some did make it through." She'd been able to watch the final showdown, at first able to recognize former

Titan both from his SkinSuit and the way he moved, but after he'd laid waste to the other Titans, she'd lost track of him. There were simply too many people.

"I'm going to assume it is not possible for you to use DNA tracing on the ashes to tell me if the Titan survived."

It wasn't posed as a question, but Veena answered it anyway. "Yes, my liege. That is correct."

"I want the recordings of the rain sent immediately. How long will the fires burn?"

"The recordings are in transport now. You should have them momentarily...We used a forced accelerant, so it will burn for the next year. Nothing will survive it. The ice may fully melt before the flames die."

Veena listened in the silence of the chamber, understanding that the Ascendant would have an AI comb the portal recordings billions of times per second, layering every possible movement of the man with the red Whip until he knew for sure if Kane had died.

"Bring your fleet home. I expect Ares' healing to be finished by the time you arrive. Both of you will meet me the moment you step foot off your ship."

The chamber grew transparent immediately. They would know shortly if the fallen Titan had survived, but regardless, Veena knew her life would never be the same.

In another part of the ship, a person with a different mindset waited.

"Show me again," he said to the AI that controlled the room. He lay on his back, staring at the ceiling. He felt no pain, not now at least. The pain had been there before getting in here though, gods, yes. The little miscreant who had used a MechPulse on him might have turned the blaster on low, but it had still shattered the upper third of Ares' body. His skull had been cracked, his collarbone almost obliterated. Three vertebrae in his neck had snapped, paralyzing him.

He still didn't know who had dragged him to that pod. Ares had decided that when he rose from this table, he would ensure that the person who'd saved him and their family for four generations need never worry about credits again.

As machines moved silently over his body, Ares watched his former master dismantle him. He observed how the man moved as if he knew what was going to happen before it did. Ares' MechSuit could barely keep up with the man. Whatever those modifiers had done to him, it had made him more than human.

"Can you confirm Alistair Kane's death?" he asked the AI, watching the video play for the hundredth time. Ares' voice would trigger the AI to answer since he had the necessary clearances for that information.

"No, sir, I cannot."

He had been saddened at the thought of Alistair Kane leaving the universe. That had changed, though, as he lay there unable to move, an invalid.

Good, Ares thought. *I hope you survived. It'll make the glory that much greater.*

CHAPTER TWENTY-FOUR

"The worlds outside our Solar System? Let them flourish.
Those creatures can barely be called human anymore.
They will never challenge our supremacy."

−Marcus de Finita, Third Imperial Ascendant

Alistair heard noises around him. His eyes were still closed, and he didn't recognize the sounds—something clanging, metal on metal, and a gruff voice that didn't speak the Ascendant's Common, nor was it the Low spoken in the gutters. Alistair had never heard the language before, so he kept his eyes closed, hoping that whoever spoke wouldn't know he had awakened.

He scanned his body, his memory telling him everything it could. He remembered the flames reaching down from above and the nuclear warhead preparing to drop. He remembered the Drathe nipping his ass to make him move faster, and then everything had gone dark.

There were no more memories to be had, not of him, the AllMother, or Obstinate.

The burns were there on his body. He felt them across his face, down both arms, and a streak down his back. The pain was dull, though, not what it should have been, given the fire that had blasted him.

I made it through the portal, he thought as the strange language continued. A single person was speaking, and there didn't seem to be any response—just the person's continual drone.

Okay, he told himself. *I made it through, and mostly in one piece. They're using some kind of medicine on me, or else I'd be in real pain right now. But for what reason?*

He stretched his senses to hear something else— anything else—but the world outside of wherever he lay was closed to him.

The person inside the room gave no indication that he knew Alistair was awake, at least not from his breathing or speaking patterns. In the end, what choice did he have? Eventually, he would have to open his eyes.

He slowly let the light in without moving any other part of his body. His breathing remained the same as he took in the world around him. The room was carved into the rock, and it had not been done with an eye for beauty. Pale light came from two corners, though the corners were rounded. The room might have been four meters tall, the ceiling barely high enough for Alistair not to scrape his head, though some of the rocks hanging down would if he wasn't careful.

His eyes fell on the man, who was short in stature but thick. He wasn't wearing a shirt, and his skin was as pale as alabaster. Muscles covered his back, and he held a hammer in his right hand. That identified the clanging sound; he brought it down over and over on something in front of him, but Alistair couldn't see what.

His braided ponytail stretched down the middle of his back. Sweat dripped down his sculpted muscles. How long had he been hammering and talking to himself? He showed no signs of slowing.

Alistair wanted to be standing when this strong though short man finally saw him. He glanced down at his body and saw patches on both arms, and they marched up his chest toward his neck as well. Yet there wasn't much pain, so there was something coursing through his veins.

He thought he could stand, so he tried to move his feet off the table quietly.

Stars appeared in his vision, and he felt like he was about to black out. He lost control over the rest of his body and fell on the floor.

He groaned, trying to keep from closing his eyes as he writhed. The short man glanced over his shoulder and saw Alistair, and he went back to his droning and hammering. His face didn't change.

"Please," Alistair groaned. "Help. Medicine."

The man appeared not to hear him, just kept hammering steadily and talking incessantly in that unknown language. After a few moments, he raised his left hand to his mouth and gave a whistle that nearly split Alistair's head in two.

It carried on until Alistair thought he might break down and cry, but the man finally quit. The former Titan's ears rang, but the pain in his body was slowly fading. He let himself relax on the cold stone floor, lying on his back and not even thinking about moving again. He didn't care what the ponytailed man did as long as there was no more whistling and he could just lie here and let the pain fade.

He heard the footfalls in the distance. His heart wanted to soar, but he wouldn't let it. What he heard wasn't possible.

The footfalls grew louder, echoing off the rock outside the room.

Then the huge Drathe stood in the entryway. Obs didn't look at the ponytailed man, nor did he look at Obs. The two ignored each other. Alistair smiled at the huge animal. "Easy, boy. Easy." He didn't know whether he'd been in danger—whether the man was a threat or not—but right now, it didn't matter. Obs wouldn't let anything happen to him.

The Drathe padded over and gently licked Alistair's neck where there was no dressing. "Easy, boy. Be easy. I'm hurting here."

Obs gave him one more lick, then sat down on his haunches and stared at his master. Alistair nodded at the man with the hammer. "You know who he is, buddy? He's not much for talking, but he brought you to me, so he can't be all bad."

Obs stood up, gave a bark, and bounded out of the room, leaving Alistair alone again. He sighed, wishing he understood the Drathe as well as Obs understood him. "Hey," he said to the ponytailed man. "Do you understand me? Where am I?"

The man just kept hammering, his shoulder looking like a piece of rock from the wall.

Alistair heard two sets of footfalls next, and he was able to distinguish Obs' from a human's. So he wasn't the only person who had made it into this lair, though it sounded like the other person was much more mobile than he was.

Obs bounded into the room again, a little too fast this time. He had to skid to a stop, or he would have landed on Alistair.

"Damn it, ya mutt," Alistair cursed as the Drathe stared down at him. He gave a defiant bark before turning to the door.

Servia stepped into the room. She wore a very simple brown robe that looked like it was made out of the same material as the ponytailed man's pants. Her hands were in small pockets at her hips, and her eyes widened when she saw him lying on the floor.

"It looked more comfortable," Alistair explained.

Servia burst out laughing, bending over and putting her hands to her face. It took her long moments to get herself under control, but when she finally stood up, tears were streaming down her cheeks. "What in the hell happened in here?" she said through a smile, looking at the man with the hammer.

He finally turned around. He had a heavy brown beard that fell to the middle of his chest, and the front half of him was just as muscular as the back. He finally lowered the hammer. Sweat dripped down his body, but he showed no signs of exhaustion.

He said something in that strange language, guttural words that Alistair couldn't begin to make out.

"Take it easy on him, Brunus. It's his first time beyond the Milky Way."

The Milky Way? Alistair wondered. The Milky Way contained a hundred billion stars and was a hundred thousand light-years across. No human had ever gone from one end to the other. What madness was this woman talking about?

The ponytailed man said something, but Alistair continued to stare at her.

Servia stepped across the room, then squatted in front of him. Her skin was twice as tan as that of the man with the hammer, even for someone who lived on Pluto. "It's going to hurt to move for a while. The Terram have technology that doesn't exist in our solar system. That's what the pain is right now. There are nanobytes healing your body, and when you move, it pisses them off."

The ponytailed man mumbled something sounding like, "Nick-nuck-nuck-nick," then turned back around and started hammering again.

"There's a new name going around for you, Phaethon." Servia grinned. "I may not be able to call you that anymore."

"I don't really care. How the hell do I get off this floor?" Alistair asked.

Servia ignored his question. "They're calling you Prometheus, the Bringer of Light. I fear I might lose my tongue if I call you the other 'P' word."

Alistair closed his eyes. "Why? How many did we lose, Servia? Did Thoreaux make it? What about the AllMother?"

Servia nodded, still smiling. "They're both alive. Thoreaux got hurt trying to get to you or to the AllMother. Some poor bastard dragged him through the portal, and now he's healing like you." She looked at the floor that surrounded him. "Well, not exactly like you. He's been able to remain in his bed."

Alistair glanced at the elevated rock he'd been lying on. "For people who have such advanced technology, they should look into the meaning of the word 'bed.'"

Servia looked over her shoulder and spoke that guttural language. After a second, the man turned back around. "We're gonna have to get you back up there, and it's going to hurt. Try not to bitch too much."

"I'm fine here," Alistair responded. He was desperate not to move again. "Seriously, what's the difference?"

The man walked over, shaking his head in disgust.

"Servia," Alistair said quickly, "I'll lay here. It's fine. It's—"

The pain came once again, and the only thing half as loud as it was Servia's giggles.

CHAPTER TWENTY-FIVE

"Why are we in charge?"

"Because we are the strongest and the boldest."
"Will I be in charge one day?"

"As long as you are the strongest and the boldest, yes."

−Conversation between an Imperial Ascendant and his firstborn

The Imperial Ascendant, Alexander de Finita, stood with his back to the door. The room was gravely silent until the door opened and two people entered.

He had just left his fathers, and their words had stung more than lashes from a Whip.

The Commonwealth was at risk, and the two now standing behind him had helped make it that way. In the end, Alexander knew that he had failed, but the failure wasn't limited to him. It spread like a disease.

Things had to be done, and Alexander did not have much time to figure out the best path. They had burned a planet and sacrificed countless lives but had not achieved their goal. The AI had tracked Kane's movements and reported him killing a contingent of Titans before escaping through the portal.

There was no time for self-flagellation, only time to act. To hold the Commonwealth together. Only Alexander could see the threads moving through the brick foundation, the decay that would split society to its core.

He would hold it together, and so would those beneath him. If they couldn't or wouldn't, he would kill them rather than let their decay spread.

Despite the issues running through his mind, Alexander knew he could not refuse to sit on his throne today. Perhaps no one in humanity's entire history understood better than he that challenges, even Solar-System-threatening ones, did not excuse someone from ruling.

If anything, it chained him to his throne.

He slowly walked the four steps that would put him above everyone else in the room and ascended, then turned and sat down before leaning into the backrest.

The double doors to the room remained open. When Alexander spoke, his voice carried to everyone, including his Praetorians. "Leave us."

Those two words had only one meaning and initiated a protocol Alexander had never before broken. His father had only done it once in his entire reign.

The Praetorians paused for the slightest of moments, then walked to the open doors, sticking to the sides of the circular room.

No one said a word as the room emptied of everyone except the two Primuses and the Imperial Ascendant. For perhaps the first time in his entire life, Alexander could legitimately be threatened. The double doors finally closed, and the two in front of him went to one knee. Their heads remained bowed, neither of them glancing up to look their Ascendant in the eye.

Alexander's voice filled the room. "We have failed. That means I have failed, but it also means you two failed. Ares, Primus of Titans, where did you rank in your Academy class?"

With his eyes still lowered, Ares answered, "First, my liege."

"And you, Veena? What was your rank?"

"First, my liege."

Alexander nodded and stroked his hairless jaw. "Do either of you know how many people advance from the Academy each year?"

"Ten thousand," Veena answered.

"And do you know how many we send? From all the worlds of the Commonwealth, how many humans enter?"

"One hundred thousand," she responded. Ares remained silent, his head still bowed.

"That's right. We purposely only graduate ten percent of those deemed worthy to enter the Academy. Out of all the worlds the Commonwealth controls, a minuscule percentage even test in, and from there, we weed out all but those of the highest caliber. You both advanced as the Rex of your class. I am sure I need not ask, but I will all the same. Do you know where the term 'Rex' comes from?"

Ares nodded. "The dead language Latin. It means 'king.'"

"Yes." Alexander nodded in silence for a few seconds. "You were each deemed the king of every human born in the same year as you. The brightest minds for generations have calculated that people like you...that *you* will continue to make the Commonwealth strong and allow us to maintain our unrivaled peace. And yet, here the three of us are, having failed the Commonwealth. Having let a single man move from one end of our solar system to the other, then step outside our galaxy."

Alexander pursed his lips for a second.

"Ares, you of the Whip, with all your skill and strength. Your raw genius. You let this man beat you into submission, then return to the very planet he'd just rocketed away from. For the second time, you let this man escape. You are twenty-six years old, he forty. I do not care if he was modified. Your breeding, your *heritage*, should ensure that *no one* bests you, yet he did. Twice."

The Titan said nothing, and Alexander turned his attention to Veena.

"Veena de Ragnimus. You are perhaps the greatest interstellar commander the Commonwealth has ever seen. You control the First Fleet and answer only to me, the Imperial Ascendant. Your ability to maneuver fleets and see multiple moves into the future has let you surpass everyone, not only in your age cohort but in all age cohorts.

"The orders you were given weren't complex. They were not hazy in their direction. You were to kill Alistair Kane by any means necessary. Ground assault first, then nuclear warfare if needed, yet when it was time to use fire, you asked me to confirm an order I'd already given. But that wasn't the worst of your transgressions, was it?"

Alexander shook his head in disgust.

"No, because when you saw the portal, you came back to ask again. You've read about portals—stargates—in your Academy books. You thought them to be mere possibilities, so you go to your fucking *chamber* and ask me *again* about my orders. *You* let him escape. *You* let that planet of nothings have a leader trained by the Commonwealth. *You* failed your fellow men."

The Ascendant stopped speaking and stared. Silence weighed heavily on the room.

"I must ask myself, Veena, if you are a fool or simply think you are greater than your Imperial Ascendant. It is hard to believe you a fool, given your accomplishments, so, Veena, let me put the question to you. Do you think you're smarter than I am? Are you greater than me? Is your knowledge vaster?"

The Primus' voice betrayed no emotion. "No, my liege. Such thoughts have never entered my mind."

Was she weak? Was that the issue with her, and all these people who had promoted this woman missed it? That truth would be discovered soon enough.

"You read about the theoretical possibilities for a portal but thought them impossible," the Ascendant mused. "Perhaps you were trying to help the Commonwealth, or perhaps you're stupid. Either way, never question me again. *Never* question an order I give you."

"Yes, my liege," the Primus answered with her head lowered.

Alexander let out a heavy sigh. "My choices here are

limited. I can replace you both with the Capo, or I can trust that you have learned your lessons. That this will not happen again. I do not want answers from either of you, so say nothing."

In truth, the Ascendant had decided what must be done, but he wanted to let them fear the possibility of removal and what that would mean for them.

"I have known of portals since I was a boy, Veena," he finally said as he leaned his head back against his throne. "Not theory, but of their existence. At the same time the Commonwealth discovered de Finita-189, we also figured out the black hole problem that plagued instantaneous travel. Portals have been around for nearly a thousand years, though we did not know about the one on Pluto. You told me something I was aware of when I was seven years old, and you let Kane escape."

Veena and Ares looked up, unable to hide their shock.

"This is why we are alone now," the Ascendant continued. "Why my Praetorian Guard left us. What you just heard? Very few in the Commonwealth have that knowledge. If either of you ever mentions it without prior approval from my mouth, you will forfeit your life." He stared at both for a long moment after that, letting it sink in. "Now, I'll continue this little explanation, for what happens next presupposes you both know exactly what is happening."

Alexander was lying. Neither of these two would ever know the whole story, but he would tell them enough.

"Get off your knees," he commanded, then watched both Primuses rise to their feet. "Your failures are forgiven, but the Commonwealth will not forget them. Do not fail me again."

Both subjects answered at the same time. "Yes, my liege."

"When the portals were first created…" He shook his head, pausing as he thought about how to explain it. "Perhaps it was a mistake of the first Imperial Ascendant. He trusted more people than he should have with the knowledge, and innumerable people left through them. He thought the Commonwealth could control portal travel, but he soon found out—too late, I might add—that it was impossible."

Alexander waved his hand, dismissing the whole business.

"I could speak forever about this failure, but it matters not. You think only our solar system is populated? Much more of the universe than you can imagine is inhabited by humanity or offshoots of our DNA. It has been a thousand years since the portals were first used, and even though the Commonwealth has outlawed their usage within our small piece of this universe, others outside use them regularly. They do not come here for they fear our might, but beyond the Milky Way? It is a primitive state of animalistic and brutal warfare. What the Commonwealth has saved humanity from *inside* our solar system."

He studied their faces for a moment. These were two of the greatest that humanity had to offer, and they'd just been told everything they understood about the universe was a lie. They didn't crumble, but had they, Alexander would have had them killed the moment they left the throne room. Only the strongest would survive what came next.

"Come. It is time I showed you some things." Alexander stood and went to the edge of the room. The window descended into the floor, then the floor extended out past the building, creating a ramp. The wind blew harshly outside, but only for a moment since fields went up on either side of the ramp, blocking the wind this high up.

A personal taxi dropped down from above and stopped just at the edge of the ramp, then its door opened. Alexander walked across the ramp and entered the ship, then sat in the very back. It could comfortably hold five people.

The Primuses sat in seats near the front, and the ship took off as the building returned to its normal state. Alexander was silent in the back, staring out the window as the ship moved through Earth's greatest city.

Buildings stretched up past the clouds into an atmosphere that had once been far too thin for humanity to live in. The skies were quiet and peaceful. Poverty? Crime? Those were things most people had only heard of. To live in squalor under the Commonwealth's rule, one had to actively try. That was what the Ascendants had given to humanity and what the Subversives wanted to take away.

It was only a twenty-minute flight and the ship's AI navigated perfectly, connecting to all the other ships and keeping chance collisions at a zero-percent probability. The Commonwealth had given this to people. The Subversives wanted to deny it all.

The ship stopped near the Earth's surface. Alexander

led Ares and Veena into a nondescript building, using a StealthCapsule to keep anyone from seeing them from street level or above. Once inside the building, they moved through various security checkpoints, heading down level after level. No one was inside, but without passing the tests the building set before the Ascendant, they all would have been annihilated quickly.

The building was a death trap for anyone who was not supposed to be in it. If someone did somehow gain access and move deep under the ground? The building would self-destruct.

What was at the bottom had to be protected at all costs.

The Primuses remained silent as the three descended. Alexander could feel their growing apprehension and their curiosity as well, the emotions palpable.

Finally, they reached the lowest level. Alexander extended his hand into a small hole in the wall, where a needle pricked his finger and instantaneously analyzed his DNA. A previously unseen door to their right opened, and the three walked through.

"Here," Alexander said as everyone examined the artifacts in front of him, "is where humanity tried to play God."

Alistair looked at the old woman, desperately wishing he had done more back in the hallway. He should have been the one to step up to those three beasts and not let her do... whatever she'd done.

Three weeks had passed since they'd arrived on this

strange planet. Alistair had healed. Thoreaux had healed. The AllMother was still unconscious. Alistair didn't begin to understand the technology these strange versions of humans were using on her, but it didn't appear to be working.

Alistair sat in her room, Obs lying at his feet. The two of them were alone. Alistair had come by himself each day for the past week and stared at her. He said nothing, simply watched. He thought of his wife Luna and how impossible his goal of getting back to her now seemed. He thought of what had been put before him, the responsibilities laid at his feet.

He didn't understand this group, and now he, a warrior, was supposed to lead it? To be a general. Some kind of false Imperial Ascendant.

He had made no decrees, no moves at all yet. He'd healed and remained silent, trying to think his way out of this. So far, he had failed.

And still the AllMother did not awaken.

There were no doors inside the cavernous lair, so when Thoreaux stepped to the entryway, only his footfalls announced him.

Alistair turned. The tall man who'd been so standoffish, so clinical in his study of Alistair, had changed. It was hard to name the signs, except to say that he appeared to be starting to...believe? It was the only word that fit, even if Alistair didn't share that belief.

The one that said he was a prophet of sorts, meant to save these people, now in Diaspora.

"Do you want to be alone with her?" Alistair asked, scooting to the edge of the chair.

Thoreaux shook his head. "Wanted to talk to you if it's possible."

"I'd like that. There's a lot I need to understand." He stood up, and Obs immediately followed suit. "You got somewhere we can talk?"

Thoreaux nodded and led the way. The Plutonian clearly didn't fit this new world. He was too tall, his limbs too gangly. Alistair had been fully awake for a week, and he only knew what these short, muscular people called themselves: *Terram*. Nothing else.

He wasn't sure if they were purposefully keeping him in the dark or if there'd been too much else going on to tell him anything. He'd decided to wait until someone came for him. They were calling him Prometheus, the Fire Bringer, but he just felt like a survivor.

They reached a small cavern Alistair hadn't seen before. It was carved into the rock, just like everything else in this lair was—the hallways, the rooms, everything. There were carved rock benches on either side of the room. Thoreaux went to the far side, and Alistair sat closest to the entryway. Obs studied the seat for a moment and decided to remain on the floor.

"Are you ready to answer my questions?" Alistair asked.

Thoreaux nodded and stared at the ground. "Yes. I'm sorry it's taken so long. Besides our injuries, there have been...delicate things we've had to deal with. The Terram weren't exactly happy to see us, nor are they happy to have us here. They know who *we* are, but you?" He sighed, still not looking up. "It's thrown a lot of things into commotion, but yes, I'm ready." Finally, his eyes met Alistair's. "Where would you like to start?"

"What's wrong with her?"

Thoreaux looked out of the room as if trying to find the AllMother. "Mostly I think it's her age, though that's not what you're getting at. She's the first and last of her kind, but to do what she did on Pluto? She just isn't strong enough anymore. She shouldn't have done that."

It was like Thoreaux was talking to himself, having forgotten the question that had been asked.

"Thoreaux, you're not making much sense," Alistair whispered.

"Sorry." He sighed and turned his attention back to Alistair. "You've been modified, right? There are a lot of humans like you, those with physical additions that make you different from me. Different from everyone except those created like you."

Alistair nodded. He didn't want to believe what he already knew to be true. It was too frightening, what he'd seen in that hallway, if it was what he now thought.

Thoreaux saw his understanding. "She was modified too. Like I said, she was the first and last to be done."

Alexander and the Primuses stood in front of two glass containers. Each rested on top of a circular black platform.

Each held a body, floating in some sort of liquid. A female was in the left, a male in the right, both naked. The bodies looked young, and their eyes were open, staring endlessly forward except that their eyes held no pupils or irises. They were totally white.

The woman's hair floated above her head. The man's

head was shaved down to the skull. Each looked like perfect human specimens. The man was heavy with muscle, his shoulders broad enough to brush the glass around him. His legs were tree trunks made of human flesh. The woman possessed a beauty and femininity that were hard to put in words, but they radiated from the glass container all the same.

"What is this?" Ares asked as he stepped up to the male's container. His head tilted so he could see the man's eyes. Veena moved toward the woman's side, and Alexander remained behind both in the middle.

"My ancestor," the Ascendant said, "was a man of fantastic ambition. He believed he could change the course of human history by changing humanity. He thought there should be a master race, but not for the same reasons other humans had in the past. He didn't want to use this master race to kill others but to lead them. To guide them. What you're looking at here are his first two offspring, brother and sister."

Veena whispered, "Are they…are they alive?"

Alexander nodded. "In a way, they are. They don't think like you and I do. They don't know we're in here, but they are preserved. Their cells continue to live and replicate. Sustenance is given through the liquid they are suspended in."

"Why?" she asked, unable to stop looking at the woman.

"The first Ascendant couldn't stand the thought of losing his children, so he created clones of them. If something went wrong with his test, he still wanted to have his kids, but his ambition wouldn't let him use anything other than his blood as the test subjects. These two are the clones. Their lives outside of these tanks was brief and frightening."

Alexander slowly circled the glass enclosures.

"The son, who should have been the next Imperial Ascendant, was modified in ways that you've heard about. His physical body was changed, more than what you're familiar with. They said there was almost no physical test his body could not pass. He was to be one side of the coin that would pay humanity's way to the next level of evolution."

Alexander reached the woman's tank.

"She was to be the other side of the coin. Her mind... even now it's hard to describe. While others have been modified physically, *she* was the only one modified mentally. Telekinesis, telepathy—radical abilities humanity thought were fiction. My ancestor made them possible, and it should have been glorious. These two should have shepherded us into a different age, one where humans surpassed the inherent limitations of their minds and bodies."

He stopped walking, having completed the circle.

"Unfortunately, it all went bad. Never again would it be tried in the same way. The fledgling government made up reasons why mutants couldn't be made or used and exiled them. It was all nonsense, devised to keep the Ascendant's failure from becoming widely known." Alexander nodded at the male. "He went mad. He should have been the greatest Imperial Ascendant to ever exist, but his mind couldn't handle the power his body gave him. The Ascendant decided he had to put his son down, but before he could, the boy escaped first Earth, then the Solar System."

Alexander turned his attention to the woman.

"She was a mistake for a different reason. She did not go mad, but the Ascendant realized no one should have that much power. She could not be controlled, not by her father or anyone else. What can you do to a person who can unlock any cage they're thrown into?"

The Imperial Ascendant sighed and looked down at the floor. "There are rumors that *he* still lives."

Ares finally pulled his eyes away from the male's container. "How would that even be possible, my liege? He would be a thousand years old." Ares absently pointed at the tank. "Even these two aren't actually *alive*, and they're kept suspended in this liquid."

Alexander chuckled before speaking. "It must be nice knowing everything, yes, Ares?" He paused for a moment. "How he lives, I know not. I have theories, but they aren't important right now. Veena, did you hear reports of strange mutants on Pluto?"

"Yes, my liege."

"I read them too. Those are *his* people. The Commonwealth uses mutants from time to time, but they're scaled down. They're manageable, and their minds aren't broken. When *he* left the solar system, he began creating what he considered to be a master race. They live somewhere in the black pool of the universe far away from us, but he swore he'd return and enslave humanity. The rumors are he lives, and his kind call him the AllSeer. Whether or not *he* is still alive doesn't matter. His dream lives on, which was proven on Pluto."

Ares asked, "Why were they there?"

"The AllSeer wants to possess his sister first. When she is dead or under his control, he'll come for us."

Veena's eyes widened, and Ares' mouth opened.

The Ascendant nodded. "The AllMother is his sister."

Alistair leaned his head against the rock wall and looked at the craggy ceiling. "What you're telling me isn't possible. No one can live for a thousand years."

"Think about it, Pro." Thoreaux had taken to calling him a shortened version of Prometheus, whether or not he was aware of it. "Mutants already live longer than naturals. Everyone knows that. The average lifespan for someone like you is a hundred and twenty years. Me? Ninety." Thoreaux pointed out of the room. "Her, though? Her brother? They were the first mutants, built differently than you or anyone else. Their modifier was an Overlord of the craft unlike any heard of before."

Thoreaux shrugged.

"I could be wrong, but what you saw in that hallway, I've seen before, and I've never seen anyone else with that capability. I only know what she told me, and I know what I believe."

Still staring at the ceiling, almost unable to believe what he'd heard but unable to deny it either, Alistair asked, "The mutants I saw in the hall? The one I managed to kill and the ones she destroyed? They were her brother's offspring?"

Thoreaux shook his head. "I'm not sure if they were offspring or creations. I don't know how he does what he does or if he's as fragile as she is now. They call him the AllSeer, and they call themselves the Myrmidons, after the warriors who fought for Achilles. Their symbol is that red eye, for their leader sees all. They've been after her since they both escaped the Commonwealth."

Alistair raised his head and lifted his eyebrows. "A thousand years?"

"Close to it, at least. She hasn't always been on Pluto, obviously, but somehow they knew the attack was coming, so they arrived as well. Whether they used interdimensional travel or something else, who knows? The point is, they're still coming for her. Even now, the AllSeer is moving toward this planet. He will stop at nothing to possess or kill her, I don't know which." He waved his hand at Alistair. "Don't ask me why, either. I don't know what that psychopath's plans are, only that we are fighting a two-front war, escaping the Myrmidons and battling the Commonwealth."

Thoreaux leaned forward. "I need to ask you a question, Pro. Will the Commonwealth keep coming for you, or will they let Pluto's burn be enough? I know what she would say, but I need to know what you think."

"Why?" Alistair asked. "Why does it matter what I think?"

Servia's voice came from the entryway. "Because it mattered to her, and now it matters to us. She put you in charge, Prometheus the Fire Bringer, and now we follow you. She let thousands of us die on Pluto so that the ones who survived would spread your legend. Even now, it grows." Her voice was sweet and her smile radiant, but Alistair wasn't fooled. Her words were serious.

He looked down at Obs, who had glanced at Servia and laid his head between his paws again. "They'll know I lived. Their AI will scan videos of the entire planet, sequencing every single person down there. If they'll burn a planet, then they'll keep coming. I don't know where we are or how they'll get here, but logically, I don't see why they'd stop if they know I'm alive."

Servia looked at Thoreaux. "Do you want to show him?"

He stood and responded, "Yeah, it's time."

Alistair's eyes narrowed. "Show me what?"

"Come with us, Pro," Servia said as she exited the room.

Obs ears perked up, and he looked at his master.

Alistair stood, and the Drathe followed. He padded over first, checking out the hallway before Alistair had taken his first step. "Where are we going?"

"Just come on," Servia said. "You and all your questions. They're never-ending."

Thoreaux walked past Alistair. "He's worse than the AllMother."

The four went into the hall and continued through winding corridors carved out of the rock. Alistair hadn't ventured out much farther than his room and the AllMother's, so he had no idea where he was traveling.

After about five minutes, they stopped in front of an entryway about six people wide. Alistair was a meter or so too far away to see what was beyond it.

Thoreaux turned to him. "Tell the Drathe not to freak out."

Obs cocked his head as Alistair raised his eyebrows.

"The Commonwealth cannot afford to leave Alistair Kane alive," the Imperial Ascendant said. "The AllMother and the AllSeer are merely variables in this affair, ones we must account for but not the most important factors. The AllSeer will still hunt his sister, as he has his entire life. The Myrmidons will be worthy opponents for your Titans, Ares, but we must succeed regardless."

Ares raised an eyebrow. "We're going after Alistair?"

Alexander nodded. "You both are. While the Commonwealth officially denies portals exist, we have a network capable of being used. Right now, we're doing our best to find out where Kane landed, then you two will be going to capture or kill him. Veena, the Commonwealth has fleets outside this solar system. You will be in charge of them. Ares, you are to choose the best Titans available to you."

The Ascendant met their eyes.

"You will capture or kill this man, or you will not return to Earth. This is the most important mission of your lives, and failure will not be accepted. Do you both understand?"

The Primuses dropped to their knees and bowed their heads. They knew this was their chance to redeem themselves in the eyes of their Ascendant. "Yes, my liege," each said.

Alexander looked down at them. "You'll be traveling with Hel."

His subjects raised their heads, hesitancy making its way across their faces.

"I thought she was retired?" Ares asked. That was the most polite way to phrase what had happened to Hel.

"I have told her about the importance of this mission, and she has agreed that her duty to the Commonwealth supersedes her retirement. You will be meeting with her tomorrow morning just before you leave through the portal."

Alistair followed Thoreaux and Servia, Obs trotting at his side, eyes peeled for any possible danger. He couldn't see beyond the two in front of him, but the noise was growing louder up ahead.

When they passed through the entry, Thoreaux and Servia split to the left and right, leaving Alistair standing at the edge of a rock ledge. Beneath him, thousands of blue-eyed Plutonians milling around, living in a tent city. Alistair stared at them, seeing some were still injured or missing limbs or eyes. Others were healthy, though, and all seemed to be going on about their days in this new world. None of them looked up at Alistair or the small group that had arrived.

"These are the people you saved," Thoreaux told him.

"These are the people you will lead back to Earth, my liege." Servia knelt at Alistair's side and bowed her head.

Thoreaux stepped toward the edge. His voice rang out in the cavern below them. "Children of the AllMother, standing before you is the one you call Prometheus, the harbinger of freedom. The Fire Bringer." Thoreaux turned to Alistair. "My liege, I present your people."

He took a knee on the other side and bowed his head.

Alistair stared down into the cavern, and everyone gazed back at him. Thousands and thousands of eyes.

The chanting started.

"Pro-me-the-us! Pro-me-the-us! Pro-me-the-us!"

The chant spread until it echoed off the rock walls and ceiling. The people beneath, wounded or not, screamed with their fists pumping in the air.

Prometheus' generals knelt at his feet.

His people. His army.

We're coming, Luna, he thought. *We're coming for you.*

CHAPTER TWENTY-SIX

"If war comes to the Commonwealth, it is not their military we should fear, but their hearts. Weapons only march as far as their warriors are willing to carry them."

–Aurelius de Finita, First Imperial Ascendant

Alexander could have called the Primuses to him again, but he wanted to meet them in their own territories. He didn't want them to expect him, and he wanted to meet them one on one. No Praetorians, just him.

He went to Ares in the late hours of the night or earliest hours of the morning.

Ares answered the door to his quarters in a red robe. His eyes went wide as he saw the Ascendant, and with a word, he sent a naked woman scrambling into one of the far bedrooms.

Alexander watched her go but said nothing, then entered the room and sat down on the couch opposite the one the naked woman had been on.

Ares followed him, color returning to his face after the shock.

"I won't stay long," the Ascendant said. "I see that you have company. I don't blame you, given how long it might be before you have such company again. Have a seat."

Ares did as he was told.

"I need to know," Alexander continued, "that you can kill this man if you see him again. Do you hold any kind of allegiance toward him any longer?"

The youthful Titan shook his head, an emotion close to anger taking his face over. "No, my liege."

Alexander studied him for a moment. "You will kill him? You give me your word?"

"Yes, my liege."

"Good. The fate of mankind rests on you doing just that."

He left the Titan to his lustful conquest then, wanting to talk to Veena before the morning came and they traveled to planets far distant from this one.

There were no lustful conquests in her room. She was awake and sitting by herself, staring at a holovid with no sound on.

She didn't bother turning it off when the Ascendant entered, nor did she look surprised like Ares had.

"My liege," she said and opened the door wider. "Would you like to come in?"

Alexander said nothing. He walked inside, his eyes narrowing at the holovid showing a world burning. He didn't sit down as he had with Ares but stood just outside the holovid, watching it. "Does it still bother you?"

"Only half of them made it through," Veena answered as

she stood next to him. "Half burned. I'm bothered both by our cruelty and my hesitancy to be that cruel, but I know what is needed, and I will do it when the time comes if that is why you're here, my liege."

"Humanity's evolution is no different than any other species'. To maintain order, cruelty is sometimes needed," Alexander said. "When we are cruel to keep our pack orderly, we are creating a world for our children that they need not fear. Since the Commonwealth's creation, war has ended. Murder, rape, and all other violent crimes are nearly non-existent. What we do now, we do for the future of that."

He nodded at the holovid.

"If you love your people, if you love the Common-wealth, then the next time you're faced with such cruelty, you won't think about those who want to destroy us, but your future children and grandchildren." Alexander turned to Veena. "Do you understand?"

"I do, my liege. I will remember my duty."

"Good. One people. One purpose."

With that, the Ascendant left. There was one more person to visit, the one neither Ares nor Veena had asked about tonight. Hel.

Her name incited fear as much because of her deeds as the mystery that surrounded her. Alexander had sent her into retirement over a decade ago. Her cruelty... She was a monster, and Alexander knew monsters should not be set on the population. No, monsters were kept hidden until they were needed. Only when another monster rose should yours be released.

And such a monster had arisen, one that all the mathematical formulas were indicating would be a grave problem.

So Alexander took a ship an hour outside of the city to where he had summoned her.

She sat alone in a skyscraper, the building having been emptied for her. The ship took Alexander to the very top floor, where the walls opened at his arrival.

"*Salve*, my liege." She had a drink in her hand, something clear with an olive in the bottom. The sun was a few hours from coming up, but she was wide awake.

"*Salve*, Hel vi Thraxus. How are you this evening?" the Ascendant asked as the walls closed behind him. He moved into the room. The couch where she sat was in a slight depression below the rest of the room.

She lifted a drink sitting on the table next to her. "I'm well, Your Highness. Would you like a drink?"

Alexander descended the steps. "How about I take yours and you have that one?"

Hel laughed loudly. "Would I poison my Imperial Ascendant? Am I such a base creature?"

"All the same, I believe it would be better for my health."

"As you wish, my liege." She took a sip from her glass before handing it to him.

Alexander swirled the liquid and sniffed it. Vodka. Strong. He took a sip, more hoping that the demon hadn't decided to kill him than trusting it. Perhaps the antidote to the poison was swimming in her veins.

He felt no immediate effects and took a seat on the opposite couch.

"Am I your last visit or your first tonight, my liege?" Hel asked.

"You're my last."

She smiled and took a sip of the new drink. Her lips were pure seduction, and Alexander wondered if Ares would be able to resist her powers. She would eat him like a black widow if given the chance. She would eat Alexander if she could; indeed, he thought she would eat the entire world, just because.

"To what do I owe this honor? It has been a long time since the Imperial Ascendant graced me with his presence. Ten years, almost to the day. Do you remember our last visit, my liege?"

So she did hold onto anger. Alexander had known that would be the case; he would have been a fool to think anything else. "I need you to understand the parameters of your mission, and I need you to hear them from me."

Again, the demon smiled her sultry smile. "Did your little ball tell you that the Titan's escape was bad for the Commonwealth? Did the ghosts that haunt you say something must be done at all costs? I figured that was the case when you decided to burn an entire planet to ash."

She was too smart, and Alexander knew it. If it wasn't for her specific talents, he would have killed her all those years ago.

Hel took another sip. "I heard your propaganda messages, and I've seen the polling. Seems like most of the Commonwealth believes your little reasons. One People. One Purpose. All of that beauty." A longer sip this time, then she set the glass down on the table. Out of everyone in the Commonwealth, she was perhaps the only one who had no fear of the Ascendant, but then, Hel possessed no fear of anyone. "Soon we leave this solar system, my liege, so tell me what you came here for so that I may finish my drink in peace."

"Of all the warriors in my stable, I hate you the most, Hel. Do you realize that's a dangerous position to be in?"

She shrugged. "Perhaps I will die and save you the trouble of killing me. You can try your hand at it now if you'd like. It may look like you're alone, but I doubt that to be the case. The Ascendant is never truly vulnerable." She waved away her words with a fluttering hand. "What is it you've come for?"

Alexander discarded his drink. "The two I'm sending with you are young. The woman is...weak. Perhaps it is a sign of the Commonwealth's decay, that our best are so easily beaten. Either way, I do not trust them to finish the job. That is why I've brought you out of your *retirement*—because I need someone who can accomplish this mission. If either of them weakens, I want you to kill them. If one of them does not obey my every command or yours, I want you to kill them. Whatever happens, all that matters is that you get the Fallen Titan. I'd prefer you bring him to me, but if you cannot, kill him. Do you understand?"

The seductress smiled again, a demon wrapped in human skin. "Yes, my liege. I understand perfectly."

Alexander stood up. "I'll tell you the same as I told the other two. If you fail, die. Do not let him escape and think there will be space here for you."

She took a drink, pausing for a second as she swallowed the alcohol. "And the Myrmidons? I'm sure I'll see them here and there. The AllMother?"

"Kill them all. None of them matter. The only one you

need concern yourself with is Alistair Kane. Bring him to me, Demon, and I may give you your freedom at last."

The woman put her glass down. The seduction disappeared from her face. "Do not play with me, Ascendant. If I bring this Titan back to you, I shall have my freedom? You'll remove this Particle from my neck?"

Alexander nodded.

Hel smiled. "Those ghosts must be telling you very bad things are around the corner. Worry no more, Imperial Ascendant. You will have your Titan."

THE WRITTEN HISTORY OF THE GREAT INSURRECTION

Perhaps the lines were drawn long before I was born, the side of the Commonwealth and the side of those who wanted freedom. I do not know, and I don't concern myself with fate.

I know that the line is drawn now, though.

I doubted him in the beginning. But what I've seen... The AllMother was right.

I bowed to Alistair Kane—Prometheus the Light Bringer. Other than the AllMother, he is the only human I've dropped to my knees for. I know now he will be the last man I bow to.

My future is tied to his. *Our* future is tied to his.

Mankind's future, as far as I can see it, is tied to his.

Let the Myrmidons come. Let the Commonwealth come.

The Great Insurrection now has its Warlord.

For my long-time readers, they know that I write a lot of my own life into my books. The year in which these books were written (a large part of the Great Insurrection) was the hardest of my life. During that time my father and my brother passed away, leaving me with no core family left. I don't say that for sympathy—I've probably had more than enough of that over the past year—but to show a bit of the mindset I was in when creating this universe.

Alistair had his family ripped from him, and he was pulled from the only home he knew.

The odd thing is, I didn't realize I was mimicking my own life until I sat down to write this author note. I thought I was just creating a new story, a new universe.

I suppose it's both.

I think Alistair is partly who I want to be. Maybe he's partly who we all want to be. To have everything taken from you and continue to push on. To be on your knees time and time again, forcing yourself to rise. It is—at least in my mind—someone to aspire to.

People often ask me who my favorite character is, out of all the ones I've written. I think it may be Alistair.

His story has a long way to go yet. I hope he continues to rise.

Thank you, Michael, for helping me create this universe. Thank you, readers, for reading.

Rise on.
-db,
Atlanta, GA, 2021

AUTHOR NOTES - MICHAEL ANDERLE

WRITTEN FEBRUARY 9, 2021

Thank you for not only reading through the story, but back here to our author notes as well!

Who Am I?

I wrote my first book *Death Becomes Her* (*The Kurtherian Gambit*) in September/October of 2015 and released it November 2, 2015. I wrote and released the next two books that same month and had three released by the end of November 2015.

So, just at five years ago.

Since then, I've written, collaborated, concepted, and/or created hundreds more in all sorts of genres.

My most successful genre is still my first, Paranormal Sci-Fi, followed quickly by Urban Fantasy. I have multiple pen names I produce under.

Some because I can be a bit crude in my humor at times or raw in my cynicism (Michael Todd). I have one I share with Martha Carr (Judith Berens), and another (not disclosed) that we use as a marketing test pen name.

In general, I just love to tell stories, and with success comes the opportunity to mix two things I love in my life.

Business and stories.

I've wanted to be an entrepreneur since I was a teenager. I was a very *unsuccessful* entrepreneur (I tried many times) until my publishing company LMBPN signed one author in 2015.

Me.

I was the president of the company, and I was the first author published. Funny how it worked out that way.

It was late 2016 before we had additional authors join me for publishing. Now we have a few dozen authors, a few hundred audiobooks by LMBPN published, a few hundred more licensed by six audio companies, and about a thousand titles in our company.

It's been a busy five years.

SUPERBOWL AND SLEEP

Right now, on an overcast Tuesday morning, I'm suffering from too many up-lates over the Superbowl weekend and fairly lousy sleep patterns.

I would say it was because I'm getting old, but that really isn't true in this case. While I don't have a personal problem fingering "old" as a possible cause, it's more truthful to admit I haven't been able to deal with lack of sleep since I was in my teens.

So, I was either old for my age or always suffering from TLSD (Too Little Sleep Disease), often caused by an onset of "must finish this book right away," which turned into "Holy @@#%! It's 3 A.M.!"

I suppose I can blame authors. Now that I am one,

blame me for your problems. *I think there is just way too much blame being thrown around.*

People should be adults and admit when they made bad life decisions (like staying up too late to finish a book), but we keep all the blame to ourselves.

And the author who wrote the book that kept you up.

I see I'm not getting anywhere here. While I am being honest, I must admit I love to know when any of our stories cause you, the reader, to lose sleep. It's one badge of a story well told.

When I'm older, I'm going to go through the reviews of the books and find the reader comments of those who couldn't go to sleep until they finished the story...

And smile.

Ad Aeternitatem,

Michael Anderle

Nemesis

She's coming and no one can stop her...

An alien Queen, Morena, was removed from power and forced into exile. Doomed to roam space forever, with no hope of return.

Until a random party brings a man named Michael to her crashed ship. For the first time in millennia, Morena sees her salvation. First, in Michael ... and then Earth. The perfect place to repopulate her species. And those already here? **They can bow or die.**

As Morena begins her conquest, can Michael warn the world before it's too late? Can anyone stop the most powerful force the world has ever seen?

Earth's final Nemesis has arrived.

Don't miss this pulse-pounding science fiction series! If you love thought provoking thrill-rides, grab this book today!

The Singularity

One thousand years in the future, humans no longer rule...

In the early twenty-first century, humanity marveled at its greatest creation: Artificial Intelligence. They never foresaw the consequences of such a creation, though...

Now, in a world where humans must meet specifications to continue living, a man named Caesar emerges. Different, both in thought and talent, Caesar somehow slipped through the genetic net meant to catch those like him.

Eyes are falling on Caesar now, though, and he can no longer hide. The Artificial Intelligence wants him dead, but others want him to lead their revolution…

Can one man stand against humanity's greatest creation? A don't-miss epic science fiction novel that pits one man fighting for the future of all people!

Red Rain

What would you do if you couldn't stop killing?

John Hilt lives The American Dream. His corner office looks out on Dallas's beautiful skyline. His amazing wife and children love him. His father and sister adore him. John has it all.

Except every few years, when Harry shows back up. Harry wants John to kill people. Harry wants to watch the world burn.

Murderous thoughts take hold of John, and as flames ignite across his life, the sky doesn't send cool rain water, but blood to feed their hunger.

If you love taut, psychological thrillers, grab Red Rain today and prepare to sleep with the lights on!

The Devil's Dream

He'll raise the dead, at all costs...

Perhaps the smartest man to ever live, Matthew Brand changed the world by twenty-five years old. In his mid-thirties, he still shaped the world as he wanted, until cops gunned down his son on the street.

Brand's life changed then. He forgot about bettering Earth and started trying to resurrect his son.

Eventually, Brand's mind overpowered even death's mysteries; he discovered how to bring back the dead--he only needed living bodies to make his son's life possible again. Why not use the bodies of those who killed his son? In the largest manhunt the FBI's ever experienced, how do they stop a man who can calculate all the odds and stack them in his favor?

CONNECT WITH THE AUTHORS

Connect with David and sign up for his email list here:

Email list
http://www.davidbeersauthor.com/mailing-list

Website
http://www.davidbeersfiction.com/

Social Media:

https://www.facebook.com/davidbeersauthor

Email List: http://lmbpn.com/email/

Connect with Michael and sign up for his email list here:

Website: http://lmbpn.com

Email List: http://lmbpn.com/email/

Social Media:

https://www.facebook.com/LMBPNPublishing

https://twitter.com/MichaelAnderle

https://www.instagram.com/lmbpn_publishing/

https://www.bookbub.com/authors/michael-anderle